KINDLING FOR
THE *Heart*

KAREN LEGASY

BELLA
B O O K S
2018

Bella Books, Inc.
P.O. Box 10543
Tallahassee, FL 32302

Printed in the United States of America on acid-free paper.

First Bella Books Edition 2018

Editor: Lauren Humphries-Brooks
Cover Photo: Taken by Pamela Laidler of Ottawa, Ontario. Photo taken near Timmins, Ontario.
Cover Designer: Judith Fellows

ISBN: 978-1-59493-606-7

Other Bella Books by Karen Legasy

My Forever Hero

Acknowledgments

I've always loved the north, and being out in nature. It's in my blood and I wanted to write a story about two women confronted with the challenges of the vast Ontario landscape. Thank you so much to Bella Books for giving me the opportunity to bring *Kindling for the Heart* to you.

Lauren Humphries-Brooks, a heartfelt thank you for your dedication and hard work as my talented editor who once again helped me bring out my best with this story.

Of course Pam, my partner in life, I couldn't do this without you. Your continuous support when I get lost in my writing, and then providing me with insightful comments after reading various drafts is very much appreciated and loved.

This book is for you, the readers who ultimately make all of this possible. Thank you for reading.

About the Author

This is Karen's second romance with Bella Books. Karen Legasy (pronounced legacy) lives in Ottawa, Ontario, Canada with her life partner, Pam. They have one adult daughter, Lisa. Having grown up in Timmins, Ontario in a loving family of six, Karen enjoys the outdoors and spending time in nature. She has always loved to write. Karen has co-authored two field guides for identifying forest plants while working for the Ontario government. Karen loves blue skies, chuckles, and all things chocolate.

Dedication

To Pam, you are the kindling for my heart.

CHAPTER ONE

Samantha White teetered in the fresh snow on the seemingly frozen lake in front of her cottage, alone and about to sink into her favorite childhood swimming hole. It was the first week of January and the temperature was well below zero. The lake should've been frozen solid by now, but the abnormally mild start to winter hampered its progress.

Sam had only taken a few steps from the dock when the ice beneath her feet started to crack and water began seeping up through her aluminum-framed snowshoes. Her foothold finally crumbled in the slush and she dropped into the frigid water.

"Oh shit. Somebody help me! Please!" Clawing at the ice, feet and legs thrashing in the water, she struggled to stop herself from going under. "I've fallen through the ice. Help!"

Her shouts went unanswered. It was a Friday morning and no one else was on the deserted lake, other cottages closed for the winter. Sam's mitted fists dug into the slush, her feet flailing in the open water as she tried to heave herself up onto the fragile surface. Her legs were heavy, winter footwear and snowshoes dragging her down as her wet skin stung from the glacial water. She kicked off her boots, braced her hands on the ice, and in one desperate thrust, pulled her legs up out of the water, then rolled away from the hole.

"Shit. Fuck." Blinding light reflected against the sparkling landscape left by the first big snowstorm of the year. Her eyes hurt, sunglasses lost in the scuffle. She lay on her back, thankful for the thick wool socks as her feet dropped into the snow like cement blocks. Shore wasn't far, and the sun beamed warm rays against her red cheeks as she breathed hard in relief.

Sam turned over to try to crawl to safety then realized she could barely move. Her wet snowsuit pants were heavy and stiffening in the frigid air. The sun would be setting soon—she desperately needed help to get back to the cottage. Warm tears crystalized on her eyelashes.

"Help! Is anyone out there?" Sam shouted into the stillness as her teeth began to chatter from the cold. The reality of her predicament renewed whimpers of dread. Was this how it was all going to end for her? Freezing to death because of a stupid mistake? Is that what she deserved?

Then, through the silence, she heard a dog bark.

Josephine Lavigne stopped to study Mollie. Her golden retriever had suddenly come to a standstill, sniffing into the wind before barking wildly. The only tracks in the snow were hers and Mollie's, but something was obviously amiss.

"What is it, Mollie?" She lowered her hood and removed her toque to listen. Except for a few chattering gray jays, all was quiet. They were close to a small community of cottages closed for the season, but she'd been walking for the last hour and was far from any roads that would have been kept cleared.

Then Mollie was off, barreling through the snow as though on a mission to find some buried bone or hidden treasure. Josephine followed as close as she could, trying to listen for what Mollie must be hearing. Nothing.

"Hello! Is anyone around?" Jo called.

"Help me." A distant voice echoed through the trees. "Please."

"Where are you?" Jo shouted back, surprised at the reply of a woman in distress.

"I'm on the lake." The yells were barely audible in the quiet forest. "I've fallen through the ice."

Jo's heart began to race. She knew the ice was still too thin to walk out on. "I'm heading your way. Hang on." She motioned to her agitated dog. "Come on, Mollie. Let's go."

There was no clear trail, and Jo had to maneuver her snowshoes through thick bush and over fallen trees to find the quickest path. She was an expert navigator in the boreal forest, but her legs and hips ached as she hustled through the deep snow toward the lake. Mollie was used to accompanying Jo and found her own pathway through the fluffy powder.

It was a small lake, spring fed, and Josephine knew it well. Fifteen cottages lined the shore; she had once considered buying one. When Jo reached the shoreline, a red jacket stood out against the snow. It was near one of the cottages on the other side of the lake. She saw movement.

"I can see you," Jo called out, trying to catch her breath. "Stay still and I'll make my way along the shore."

"I will," the woman yelled back. "All I can see is the sky."

"Are you hurt anywhere?" Jo squinted to get a better look at the woman in distress, but the sun obscured her view. "Should I call for help?"

"I'll be okay if I can get back to solid ground."

"I'll be there in a minute. Hang tight." Jo raced along the edge of the forest, Mollie close at her side. She knew it would have to be a snowmobile or helicopter rescue, if one was needed, because the road into the cottages hadn't been plowed after the recent snowstorm. There wasn't time anyway for saving someone right now on this deserted lake. Jo was her only hope.

Samantha's feet were numb and her toes all but frozen. At least she'd worn heavy snow pants and a down parka, but she was starting to shiver. Uncontrollably. Smoke from the cottage chimney teased her nostrils as she envisioned the warm crackling fire within the pine walls. She shifted her shoulders and slush stung her neck. The ice was giving way again.

"Oh shit," she said. "I'm sinking. Hurry."

"Just hold on." Crunching snow and heavy breathing were getting louder. "I'm coming!"

"There's nothing to grip!" Sam flailed her arms, fruitlessly searching for something to grab onto as she began to slide into the water. "I'm falling in!"

The woman was close now, the ruffling of her movements giving Sam hope.

"Stay, Mollie." Who the hell was Mollie? Sam heard barks and panting. Ah, the dog. "Grab my hands."

Sam began hyperventilating as she struggled to reach out, the weight of her soaked snow pants pulling her into the water. "I can't." The ice crumbled more. "Help me! Please!" Her arms thrashed through the air, unable to reach anything.

"Let me try something else. I'm going to crawl out to you."

"No, you'll fall in too." Sam heard the swish of something being flung toward her.

"Just wait." There was another crunching of snow. "I've thrown my snowshoes onto the ice. I'll use them for support as I crawl toward you." Sam felt a tug at the hood on her parka. "I've got you. Reach back and grab my arms."

Sam reached backward over her head and clamped onto arms. "I've got you."

"You're pulling me in!" Sam felt the woman wriggling and started to let go. "No, keep holding on. Come, Mollie. Help me."

The barking dog got closer, and then began to growl as though tugging at a toy. "That's it Mollie. Pull on my snow pants. Pull."

"I think this is working." Sam shifted her hips as she slid out of the water and along the snow. "Pull, Mollie! Whoever you are."

"She's my golden retriever. Your savior."

"Who the hell are you then, besides my guardian angel?"

"I'm Josephine. You can call me Jo. What's your name?"

"Sam. Samantha White."

"Try to help me more, Sam." Her voice was comforting, encouraging. "I know you can do it. Keep moving your hips and ease back toward me. That's it. We're almost there."

The hard wooden boards digging into Sam's shoulders gave her a sense of security, despite the pain. Arms jammed under her shoulders and then hoisted her up onto the snow-covered dock, where she rested for a moment, breathing. Alive.

Then Sam rolled around and clung to the woman who'd just saved her life. "Thank you." She buried her face into a strong shoulder and kissed the fabric of a navy parka.

"We need to get you inside." The woman began pulling away and stood. Sam watched her grab snowshoes from the ice then stand, dangling them at her side. A goddess dressed for the cold, fluffy white fur surrounding red cheeks buried in the navy hood, strands of blond hair sticking out onto her forehead. Blue eyes twinkled in a ray of the fading sun. A snow queen had just rescued her.

"Good girl, Mollie." Jo bent over and hugged her dog, its tail sweeping snow on the dock. Her attention went back to Sam, the blue eyes piercing. "Can you stand?"

"I think so, but I'll need some help. My pants are starting to freeze."

Jo's gaze followed the trail to the cottage then settled on the smoke coming out of the chimney. "How long have you been on the ice?"

"Not long at all." Sam struggled to get up, the rigid legs on her pants restricting her movements.

"Let's get these off." Sam felt hands reaching up inside her jacket, undoing her heavy pants, and then yanking them down. Her jeans beneath were damp, but not yet frozen. "See if you can stand now." Sam grabbed onto Jo's arms again and managed to stand.

She let out a deep breath, giddy with relief. "Thank you, Jo. I can't wait to put another log on that fire."

Jo held onto Sam as they made their way up to the cottage. "We might have to spend the night. I don't imagine your road has been plowed out, and it's a long walk back to my truck. I'd rather not do it in the dark. I hope you have an extra bed."

"Nope." Sam hobbled toward the cottage, feet numb in her wet socks. "You'll have to sleep in mine. With me."

CHAPTER TWO

A warm fire was still crackling in the woodstove when Jo maneuvered Sam into the cabin's pine-paneled interior. Daylight was beginning to fade, so Jo clicked on the kitchen light to brighten up the small room that smelt of smoke. Mollie plopped next to the fire while Jo helped Sam to the nearest chair and began to undress her.

"I think this is a first," Sam said through chattering teeth. "We've known each other less than thirty minutes and you're already taking my clothes off."

"Very funny." A sudden awkwardness descended. Jo's gaydar had never been all that great and the last thing she was looking for now was another partner. That is, if Sam was a lesbian too.

Jo looked up. The woman was indeed attractive, with her piercing brown eyes, short, disheveled hair, and dimples that expanded with every smile.

"How old are you?" Sam asked.

"Forty-two."

"Wow, I thought you were younger." Sam hugged herself and shivered as Jo helped her out of her wet jeans. "You have a great body for an older woman."

"Are you always this direct?"

"Why waste time? I'm thirty-seven, in case you're interested."

"Well, I'm not." Jo grabbed an old quilt draped over a rocking chair next to the woodstove. "Let's get you wrapped in something warm. I'll hold up this blanket while you strip out of your underwear."

"Aren't you going to help?" Sam smirked.

"No." Jo fought off the urge to walk out on this preposterous situation. She looked over at Mollie relaxing by the fire while Sam finished undressing.

Sam took hold of the thick blanket and wrapped herself in it. "Thanks. It feels good to be out of those wet things."

"I'm wet too." Jo's cheeks burned at her bad choice of words.

Sam held out the edge of her quilt. "Well, why don't you strip then, and we could keep each other nice and toasty under here."

Jo folded her arms across her chest, trying to control her anger. "You're unbelievable. You don't even know me and have no right to be making those kinds of remarks. Keep it up and I'll walk through the bush in the dark to get back to my truck if I have to."

"I'm sorry." Sam lowered her head, cheeks reddening. "You're right. I don't know you. You just saved my life and I guess I'm still in shock."

"That doesn't give you the right to make assumptions about me."

"I know." Sam dropped into the rocking chair, her dimples deflated. "I'm sorry for being so crude. I have no right to be like that. Please accept my apology."

Jo shrugged and sat on the floor next to Mollie. She began to massage her dog's floppy ears, taking comfort in the soft skin and fur. Her clothes were still damp, but she was damned if she'd try to get out of them now. She should have been almost home by this time.

"Can we start over?" Sam fidgeted in her chair. "I promise to be good from now on. Besides, I'm getting hungry. We should eat. I made a pot of chili this morning—it's been warming all afternoon. I hope you like chili."

So that's what was cooking. The garlic aroma had been teasing her taste buds ever since they got inside. "I'm vegetarian." Jo kept her focus on Mollie.

"Good. It's vegetarian chili." Sam's chair squeaked against the floor as she rocked.

"You're a vegetarian?"

The dimples broadened "No, not at all. I'm a carnivore, but I prefer vegetarian chili."

"What can I give Mollie? She's used to dog food. She needs a water dish too."

"Grab some bowls out of the cupboard." Sam motioned to one with the door slightly ajar.

"I wouldn't want to use your dishes for my dog." Jo caught a faint whiff of varnish as she pulled open the door to three small shelves of mismatched dishes.

"I don't have anything else," Sam said. "Besides, she's special in this cottage. Get water from the tap and grab a steak or two out of the fridge to feed her. She can sleep in my bed, too, if she wants. You can put her between us if you like."

She actually expected them to sleep together? Jo took one of the bowls and gave Mollie a drink then looked in the crowded fridge. A big carton of orange juice almost fell out as she tried to find something for Mollie. "Is anyone else staying here with you?"

"Nope. Just me. I'll be here for a while, so thought I'd stock up." Sam's chair kept up a steady rock.

"I see." Jo took out a plate of cooked chicken breast covered in cellophane and held it up. "Okay if I give this to Mollie?"

"For sure. Give her whatever." Sam stood, her chair continuing to rock without her as she clutched the quilt. "I think you should get out of your wet clothes too. You're shivering. I have extra sweats and shirts in my room that should fit. I'll get them."

Jo followed Sam into the tiny bedroom that smelled sweetly of damp pine. It had a queen bed in the middle, a small chest of drawers against the wall, and hooks full of clothes behind the door. A window looked out over the lake, light fading with the setting sun.

Sam handed Jo an armful of clothes. "You can have a hot shower before changing. My grandfather had a well and septic system installed years ago, so it's not really like roughing it."

"That would be nice," Jo said, "but I think you should go first. You're still full of goose bumps."

"All right. Please make yourself comfortable. Eat whatever you want and relax by the fire. I won't be long."

Jo left the dry clothes on the bed and sat by the woodstove while Sam went into the bathroom. She realized she'd better call her mother to let her know she wouldn't be home tonight. They didn't live together, but since Jo often worked alone in the bush, her mother insisted she check in at the start and end of each day she was out by herself. She pulled out her cell phone— three bars. It was usually harder to get a good signal this far out.

Her mother picked up on the second ring, TV blaring in the background.

"Hi, Mom."

"Jo! I'm glad you're home. It's supposed to snow again tonight, and I was beginning to worry about you getting stuck in the bush."

"I'm not at my place. I'm staying in a cottage at Button Lake."

"Button Lake." Her mother gasped and the television suddenly silenced. "Nobody stays there in the winter. What happened? Did you get stuck and have to break into a cottage?"

"No." Jo sighed. "It's a long story. I had to help a woman at one of the cottages. There wasn't time to get back to my truck before dark and she offered to let me stay."

"She's out there by herself? Who is she?"

"Her name is Samantha White, and she's at one of the cabins on the south side of the lake." Jo looked at the small Arborite table beside the kitchen counter. "She said it was her grandfather's."

She glanced toward the bathroom door, the taps turning on. "It has running water and everything. It's really cozy on the inside with pine walls and ceilings." Jo scanned her surroundings, a few framed bird prints hanging by the woodstove—probably pages from an old calendar.

"I know that cottage," her mother said. "The owner's name was Roy. I heard his granddaughter is a *lesbian*."

"Mom, you say it like there's something wrong with her. Don't forget that I'm a lesbian too."

"I knew it." Sam stood outside the bathroom door, a large towel wrapped around her.

Jo cringed. "I have to go. I'll call you later."

"Be careful, dear. You don't know this woman."

Jo put the phone down, cheeks burning. "I thought you were in the shower."

"I almost was, then remembered the chili needs a stir." Sam smiled. "Do you still live with your mother?"

"Of course not." Jo's jaw tightened as she moved toward Mollie. "I needed to let someone know where I am." She knelt on the rug and reached for the soothing fur. Mollie's back was hot from the fire.

A spoon clanked against the pot as Sam stirred the chili. "So you live by yourself?"

"No." Jo turned away, hoping Sam would just go back in the bathroom.

"Well, who do you live with, then?" Sam hovered in the doorframe.

"That's none of your business." She lived with Mollie, which was enough. She didn't want to talk about her love life, or lack thereof, with anyone, let alone this strange woman.

"I'm trying to make conversation, that's all." Sam retreated into the bathroom, the door closing. Water splashed as the shower turned on.

Jo sat by the fire and contemplated walking to her truck in the fading light instead of spending the night sleeping here with Sam. Her clothes were wet, though, and it wouldn't be safe. She was stranded for the night.

CHAPTER THREE

The bathroom door eased open and a refreshed woman emerged from the mist. Jo had lingered in the shower, and Sam was pleased to see her looking much more relaxed after a long soak.

"It smells so good in here." Jo's nostrils flared, her stomach growling loud enough for Sam to hear. "Oops. Sorry." She patted herself.

Sam lay sprawled on the floor beside Mollie and the fire, petting the tail-thumping golden retriever. "You have a beautiful dog. How long have you had her?"

Jo knelt beside Mollie and stroked her. "It's already been three years. She's a good friend. The best, actually."

"I can see that." Sam tried not to stare at Jo's feathery blond hair, the tips still wet from the bath. "She's so gentle and well-behaved."

"Golden retrievers make good pets and are great companions. She's very smart too."

"It was unbelievable how she helped you on the dock. You must have trained her well."

"I had to. She's often my only partner when I'm working in the bush. We rely on each other."

"And when you're not working in the bush? Who's your partner then?"

"I think it's time to eat." Jo stood and shuffled to the kitchen stove. She stirred the chili, sniffing a steaming spoonful. "Mmmm. I can't wait."

As they worked in silence to get things ready for dinner, Sam contemplated Jo's reluctance to discuss anything personal. She sensed sadness in Jo, the way she ignored the question about having a partner. Had someone broken her heart?

It took less than five minutes to set the small dining table, including lit candles and full wineglasses that gave a romantic aura to the comfortable cottage in the middle of the bush. Mollie stayed next to the fire while Jo and Sam ate.

Jo dipped a piece of bread into her bowl. "This is really good. I love chili with bran and lots of vegetables. You're a good cook."

"Thanks." Sam smiled.

"I don't picture you as the type of person who likes to cook." Jo sipped her red wine. Her cheeks were beginning to flush an attractive shade of pink.

Sam nibbled at her bun. "My talents are better outside the kitchen, but I do have a few favorite recipes I can manage to whip up." She looked up and caught Jo's gaze. "Do you like to cook?"

"Sometimes, especially in winter. It always helps warm me up when I eat a good hot meal on a cold day."

"Like today?" Sam sure felt like Jo was warming up, the way she seemed to be enjoying dinner. Heck, so was she. She was certain she was blushing.

Jo cleaned the bottom of her bowl with the last of her bun. "Yep. This was really good. Thanks."

"What kind of food do you like to make?"

Jo played with her paper napkin, straightening out the wrinkles and folding it into little squares. "Just about anything vegetarian. I especially like Asian and East Indian dishes."

"So do I." So they shared similar tastes in food. That was a plus.

Sam listened to the fire crackling and Mollie's soft snoring from her place by the stove. It seemed surreal, as though their meeting was meant to be.

Jo got up and began to clear the table, a perfect guest. She carried their bowls to the kitchen sink and filled it with soap and water. She found the small dish drainer in the cupboard beneath the sink, putting it on the counter as though a familiar routine.

Sam got up to help, taking the rest of the chili out of the pot and putting it into a bowl for the fridge. There was barely enough room for the two of them to work together in the small kitchen as she constantly hit against the table edge in her effort to give Jo some room.

Sam was impressed with the way Jo took control. Her confidence, her bravery out on the lake this afternoon was outstanding. And now here she was again, taking lead on the simple task of initiating cleanup after supper. She seemed so self-assured, so in control.

"Who else do you cook for, besides yourself?" Sam asked. She was going to find out if this woman was single, dammit.

Jo buried her hands in the suds. "I often make extra for my mother."

"Does she live near you?" She picked up a dishtowel and dried a few utensils.

"Not really, but it's all relative, I guess. Timmins isn't that big, so it doesn't take long to run back and forth between our places."

Sam reached for the bowl, dripping and still warm from the water as she began to dry it. She felt like they were on a first date—a good one at that. "What's your place like?"

"I live on a five-acre property." Jo started washing a wineglass as the blackened window above the sink covered in steam. "It's on the outskirts of town."

"Wow. But don't you find it lonely living in the country by yourself?" Sam liked living in a city, even though she was enjoying being out in the bush right now.

"Not at all." Jo glanced toward the stove where Mollie lay on her side, legs stretched out and eyes closed. "I have Mollie to keep me company, and my life's too busy to get lonely."

Sam tilted her head. She was so glad this confident and attractive woman had come to her rescue. "What keeps you so busy?"

"My work. That's my life these days, and I love what I do, so it's a good fit."

"Were you working today?"

"Of course." Jo tackled the big pot from the chili, water splashing as she scrubbed at the bottom. "I noticed you have a lot of food in your fridge. How long are you here for?"

"For at least the next month."

"Okay." Jo rinsed the pot and handed it to Sam to dry. "And then what?"

"I'll go back to my place in Toronto." She didn't want to think about that for now. Her life back there was so pathetic, given her recent breakup and history of superficial relationships with younger women. Now, as she chatted with this self-assured woman, Sam felt herself warming to the prospect of getting to know someone so much more mature than what she was used to. It was even a bit intimidating.

"When did you bring all of your stuff here?" Jo finished with the dishes and went over to wipe down the table. She was clean too—another mark in her favor.

"I drove it in on Wednesday, before all the snow." Sam put the pot away and hung her towel to dry. "I thought the plows would have been here by now."

"They don't keep this road plowed in winter," Jo said. "Didn't you know that?"

"Wait, what? You've got to be kidding. I can't stay out here all winter."

"Well, your car will have to unless you pay someone to plow it out." Jo folded her arms and leaned against the counter in front of the sink.

"It's not a car. It's a four-wheel drive SUV. I thought it would be good for northern roads and that's why I bought it. Shit. What am I going to do now?"

All of her plans, out the window. She had planned to go into town every few days, do some shopping, stock up on groceries. Maybe even have a coffee in a place that vaguely resembled civilization. Now…

Jo was looking down at her cell phone. "We're getting more snow tonight. I can put you in contact with a grader operator if you want. It probably won't happen for a few days, though, because everyone will be busy opening up hauling roads. Even my truck will most likely be snowed in for a day or two."

Sam squeezed her fidgeting hands together in an effort to calm down. "How did you drive your truck out here today?"

"I took one of the logging roads on the other side of the lake." Jo clicked off the light over the sink and headed toward the woodstove.

"I could use the logging road to get in and out of my cottage, then?" Sam followed as Jo sat down on the braided rug beside Mollie.

Jo shook her head, patting the dog's side. "I doubt it, unless you're good with a compass and want to hike for over an hour each way through thick bush. Wow, I can't believe how hot she is."

"What if I have a compass?" Her grandfather's was on the bookshelf, beside his binoculars. Surely one of the books would teach her how to use it.

"I don't imagine you have a block heater and even if you did, there'd be no place to plug your vehicle in." Jo folded her knees under her arms. "When the temperature drops out here, you'll never be able to start it without a block heater."

Sam plopped into the rocking chair. "I'm really fucked, then. I thought I could stay out here for the month and go into town every few days. I have no intentions of becoming a hermit. I need Internet access and there's none here except for my phone. Which doesn't always get the best signal."

Jo shrugged her shoulders. "I guess you'll have to go back to Toronto, then."

"Nope. Not happening." She would find a solution. She had to. Going back after everything was just…nope. Not now.

"Then you'll have to find a place to rent in town, because you can't stay out here unless you want to buy your own grader."

"Maybe I'll get a snowmobile," Sam said.

"My suggestion would be to rent a room in town and buy a pair of snowshoes so you could hike in on the weekends. What are you doing out here by yourself, anyway?"

"I needed to get out of town."

"So you're hiding out." Jo rested her chin on her knees, looking almost like a kid, gazing up with those big blue eyes. "You're not running from the law, are you?"

"No." Sam sighed. "It's…complicated."

CHAPTER FOUR

Jo watched as Sam abruptly shoved a few more birch logs into the woodstove.

"Why did you need to get out of town?" Jo asked, somehow afraid of the answer. "To come all the way up here and hide in the bush seems a bit drastic. Toronto's a big city, with lots of places to tuck yourself away."

Sam jabbed at the fire with the brass poker. "I needed some space. A change of scenery is good too."

"Well you certainly got that. Stranded in the middle of the bush in deep snow." Jo suppressed a smile. It was a bit amusing to see this cocky woman struggling because of poor planning.

Sam shut the stove door and brushed woodchips and small pieces of bark off her knees as she stood. "I'd rather be stuck in deep snow than deep shit."

"Sounds pretty bad." Jo smirked, smoke from the opened stove door dissipating around the toasty cottage. "Should I be worried, spending the night out here alone with you?"

"It depends." Sam chuckled as she sat back down in the rocking chair. "If you're afraid of getting your heart broken, then yes."

Jo's fingers dug into Mollie's skin as Sam rocked back and forth. It figured. Another heartbreaker. Dammit to hell. The last type of woman she wanted to be trapped with in a cozy cottage in the middle of the bush. Especially one that was so attractive. Jo determined to protect herself even more, refusing to be charmed by someone who seemed so unfazed by it all. "You're running away after breaking someone's heart?"

Sam began fidgeting with the string on her sweatshirt. "Sort of, if you could call it love, but I didn't mean for her to become so needy. It was suffocating; I couldn't take it. Especially since I didn't feel the same sense of commitment."

Jo shifted, no longer amused with the situation. "How long were you together?"

"About six months. She was shocked when I said I wanted out. I wish lesbians didn't have to take sex so seriously all the time."

"And you don't?"

"No. Just because I want to have sex with someone doesn't mean I'm in love and want to spend the rest of my life with her. Can't people just have sex for fun anymore?"

Jo leaned back and held on to Mollie's tail like a life support. "Not everyone feels the same. At least you didn't wait for twenty years."

Sam stopped rocking and looked at Jo with sympathetic eyes. "Is that your story? Is that why you're single?"

"You make it sound like there's something wrong with being single." The last thing she needed, or wanted, was sympathy.

"I know it can be lonely." Sam paused, her sparkling brown eyes locking onto Jo's and causing a zing. "Hey, we're stranded out here and could help each other out with the loneliness. I do find you very attractive."

Jo startled Mollie as she jumped to her feet. "I'm not the least bit lonely or interested in having sex with you."

Sam laughed. "There's no need to panic. Just thought I'd put it out there. I don't do that for everyone, but we're stuck in the middle of the bush with a warm fire, lots of wine, and a raging storm outside. And you're not only beautiful, but you saved my life."

Jo stood by the door, trying to see through the frost on the window. So now she was *special*. Great. When she turned on the outside light, a laser show of whirling snow confirmed she was definitely staying for the night.

"Fuck." She hit the door. "I'm stuck here."

"I'm sorry. I shouldn't have been so bold."

Jo crossed her arms and glanced at Mollie, who had a definite look of expectation. "Time for outside?"

Mollie jumped at the door, her tail wagging with eagerness for a walk. Jo put on her parka and boots as fast as she could. "We'll be back." She yanked her wool toque down over her ears and opened the door wide enough to let in a gust of cold air. Then slammed it shut with a bang as she stepped into the blizzard outside.

Sam stayed by the fire, disheartened by the chill of the wind and sudden departure of her guest. Maybe she needed another glass of wine or, better yet, a hot drink to warm her insides. She was cold and numb. Not only from the stormy winter weather outside, but also from the tempest she'd unleashed on herself by suggesting sex. And then there were the events of the afternoon. She could have died if it weren't for Jo.

Sam liked Jo; there was no doubt about that. She was surprised at how quickly she'd become attracted. She'd never felt sparks like that before. Perhaps it was a sign. Could Jo be her hero and savior in more ways than one?

She took a breath. She needed to slow down, get to know this woman better. There would be no more mention of sex. Sam wanted to talk the night away instead, to find out more about Jo and her real passions in life. She got up to make some hot chocolate.

Biting snow hit Jo's cheeks as she stood outside the door. Even Mollie didn't wander far; she probably could have been let out on her own, but Jo needed an escape. The nerve of that woman! Another heartbreaker was all she needed now that hers was finally put back together.

Dammit, it had been a long time since she'd thought about sex. The taps had been turned off a while ago, but here she was, standing outside in a freezing blizzard and feeling things starting to flow again. What would it hurt if she gave in to Sam? They were both single, consenting adults stuck in the middle of the bush during a raging blizzard in a cozy cottage with a warm fire and inviting bed. If Sam asked again, Jo was certain she'd say yes.

Jo felt herself warming with the decision. It had been over three years since she'd last had sex, and Sam was certainly attractive, even though Jo had pretended not to notice. Who was she kidding? Of course those dimples caught her attention right away. And then taking off her clothes…Sam's comments had taken her by surprise and almost offended her. Now here she was, wanting to retreat from this blizzard and get naked with Sam. She called to Mollie, a skip in her step as she headed in.

"Hurry up and get inside, Mollie." Jo pulled off her toque and ruffled her hair. The flames were roaring in the woodstove and Jo wondered if they'd make out right there, on the braided rug in front of the fire. "It's freezing outside."

"I'm making us some hot chocolate." Sam was at the kitchen counter; her back turned to the room. "I'm hoping it'll help to warm us up."

"Sounds good." Jo removed her heavy clothing and followed Mollie back to the fire, warming her hands near the flames. "I hope you have some marshmallows too."

"Of course." Sam smiled, jiggling the bag.

"It's cozy in here. You would have never survived the night out on the ice."

"Thank God you came along." Sam placed two steaming cups of hot chocolate on the floor and knelt beside Mollie.

Jo picked up a cup and blew at the steam. "Mollie's the one you need to thank. She heard you calling before I ever did. This looks good, by the way. Thanks."

"Careful you don't burn your tongue."

"And if I do?" Jo tried to meet Sam's gaze, but Sam quickly dipped her head and sipped her hot chocolate. Strange...

"Why don't we get to know each other? What does a forester do?"

"Um...a lot of planning." What was going on?

Sam avoided her gaze, turning to Mollie instead and playing with her ears. "Do you work for the government?"

Jo yawned, hoping Sam would get the hint she just wanted to get on with things. "Sometimes."

"And at other times?" Sam looked sincerely interested, and completely innocent. Was this the same woman she'd just stormed out on?

"It depends." Jo took off her sweatshirt, stretching her arms, and placed it on the rug beside Mollie. She wished Sam would get the hint and just seduce her, because there was no way she'd do it.

Sam looked away, staring at the woodstove as her fingers played with a loose stitch on the braided rug. "Depends on what?"

Jo straightened. "The need for forestry consulting services."

"So you're a consultant? Running your own business?"

"Yes."

"This sounds impressive. I'd like to hear more about what you do."

Jo ate the marshmallow floating in her mug; almost relieved they weren't going to have sex after all. "I provide forest planning advice because I've always loved the bush. There's just something about being out in nature, and I feel blessed to have a job that often takes me there. It's sometimes like a magical place being out in the forest, except maybe for the bugs, and I always feel good when I'm there. Breathing the fresh air, experiencing the changing seasons, helping trees grow again after stands have been cut or burned, all the animals it sustains, the wildflowers, there's just so much to enjoy and I love it. I couldn't imagine doing anything else." She yawned. It was difficult to put into words. The sensations of just being outside, alone, nothing to worry about, except the moment.

Sam shifted closer to the fire as the wind howled outside. "So, do you have a business partner?"

"Yes. Mollie. She's the only partner I need."

Sam grinned as she massaged Mollie's back. "I see that. I've always admired people who can work by themselves."

"I work for myself, but that doesn't mean I work by myself. I've done a lot of work with forestry companies, landowners, cottage associations, and whoever else might need forestry expertise."

"Sounds impressive." Sam glanced up as Jo covered another yawn. "It looks like you're ready for bed."

Jo grabbed her sweatshirt and stood. "I am. It's been a long day."

"For sure. Go ahead. Choose whatever side of the bed you want. I'm going to stay up for a while longer and keep the fire stoked. I'll try not to wake you when I come to sleep."

"Okay, thanks." Jo bent over and patted Mollie's head. "I'm going to bed now. You can stay here by the fire."

Mollie's tail wagged against the floor. She let out a little yelp. Sam laughed. "It looks like she understands you."

"Sometimes I think she understands me more than any other person ever has. Right now, though, I believe she loves the heat. And the back massage." Jo shuffled toward the bedroom. "Good night."

Sam sat by the fire until long after Jo had gone to bed. Howling wind pounding on the door and blowing snow ticking against the windows added to her stress of thinking about next steps. The morning would bring more deep snow. What was she going to do?

She wouldn't allow herself to return to her home in Toronto just yet. She had been so looking forward to spending time in the bush, at her cottage, in the middle of winter, to hibernate while her heart healed. Hers wasn't broken, but it was lonely and just needed to mend from yet another failed relationship.

Jo saved her from falling through the ice. It had been reckless, stepping off the dock without checking the conditions. And to be rescued by someone like Jo was almost unbelievable. The way she'd lit up when talking about her work was amazing. Her eyes sparkled; Sam could see the passion. It almost made her want to get a job in the bush.

The mere thought of this beautiful blonde cuddled up in her bed brought on chills. Just the thrill of being close to Jo as they slept would be enough. She needed a friend right now more than a lover.

By the time Sam slipped between the flannel sheets, Jo's breathing was steady. She was fast asleep. Sam closed her eyes and let out a sigh as slumber took over.

CHAPTER FIVE

Daylight crept behind Jo's eyelids as Mollie's usual morning panting and whimpering roused her out of a deep sleep. She arched her shoulders and twisted her back, groaning with an elongated stretch that awakened her senses.

"Okay, girl, I'll get up in a minute." Jo rolled over, shifting her legs for one last bit of rest until her foot hit another person. Her eyes popped open to the unfamiliar bedroom and realization she was in someone else's bed.

"Good morning." Sam stretched, raising her arms above her head. "The air is a bit cold in here, so you'll need a heavy sweater until the fire gets going. You can borrow one of mine if you like."

"Thanks." Jo rolled over and sprang out of bed. The wooden floor was cold against her bare feet. "Sorry for the kick. I didn't mean to wake you."

"No worries." Sam threw back the covers and pulled a heavy fleece jacket over her red flannel pajamas. "I was already awake. I'll get the fire and coffee going while you look after yourself and let Mollie out."

"Thanks again."

Jo shivered and quickly pulled on her clothes. It was awkward, like a morning after. That they refrained from sex didn't make it any less awkward. "I hope having me in your bed wasn't too uncomfortable."

"Not at all." Sam winked as she left the room to light the fire.

Jo hurried to finish dressing and stepped outside just as Sam was putting the coffee on. She made her way up the cottage driveway to the road, trudging through the fresh snow. A lot had fallen overnight, so she knew her truck would be buried too. The temperature had dropped with the arrival of a clear blue sky; it was going to be a frigid day. She would have to make the trek out to her vehicle so she could at least start it and let the engine run for a bit to avoid it totally freezing up. She hoped to drive it out by tomorrow afternoon, once the road was plowed.

As she walked back from the road, she dialed her mother to let her know she'd be stuck there for at least one more day. She let on as though she just wanted to get back home, but the thought of another night at the cottage with Sam was kind of appealing. She was starting to like Sam, probably even more so because they kept things platonic last night.

"How did you survive the night?" Concern in her mother's voice. "Were you warm enough?"

"It was fine," Jo said. "The place is very cozy, and Sam was a good host, but I'll be happy to get home."

"Is Samantha from around here?" Jo heard the clicking of her mother's knitting needles, imagining the phone now on speaker and in her lap.

"No. She's from Toronto, just visiting the cottage."

"What about food? Did you have enough to eat?"

"Plenty. Sam had a big pot of chili on the stove and I had more than enough."

"That's good." Her mother's living room wall clock chimed for the half hour. "What about Mollie? I can't imagine you would have fed her chili too."

Jo shifted the phone in her big mitt. Mollie was bounding through the snow, jamming her head under it, then stopping to listen and sniff.

"No of course not, Mom. Mollie had chicken for dinner."

"Oh, that's nice." The clicking of the needles stopped. "Where did you sleep? Isn't there only one bedroom in the cottage?"

"Come on, Mollie!" Jo started to head back to the cottage. "I slept with Sam in her bed." She braced for her mother's response.

"Oh, Josephine. Please don't get hooked up with someone from Toronto. Your life is here, in Timmins."

"Mom, just because I slept with her doesn't mean we had sex." Jo appreciated her mother's concern, but hated having to explain herself. Especially when it involved her sex life. "There was only one bed, big enough for the two of us, and neither of us wanted to sleep on an uncomfortable couch." They didn't even sit on the faded forest green couch against the living room wall last night.

"I'm glad you clarified. What about Mollie?" Her tone raised a pitch, indicating the inquisition about Jo's sex life was over. "How's she doing?"

"She loves it here." Jo smiled as Mollie bounced through the fluffy snow, her snout covered in white from chasing rabbit tracks and following scents. "She was the center of attention by the fire last night and didn't even come to bed with me."

Her mother's knitting needles resumed clicking. "What about today? I don't imagine the roads will get plowed that soon. Do you have enough food to last another night in the bush?"

"Sam has a fridge bursting with food. She was planning to stay out here for a month until I told her the road doesn't get plowed over winter."

"She didn't know that?" Her mother's tongue clicked. "What's she going to do?"

Jo wondered that herself. "I don't know. Go back to Toronto, I guess. That is, if she can ever get her vehicle plowed out."

"What does she do in Toronto that she can take off work like that?"

"I don't know." Jo brushed a mitt across Sam's buried SUV, uncovering shiny black paint.

"Didn't you ask her? How do you know she isn't running from the law or something? You'd better be careful."

"Mom, I'll be fine. I have to let you go because my hand is cold and I'm sure my battery is freezing up."

"Keep in touch and pet Mollie for me."

"I will. Bye, Mom."

Jo studied the interior of the late model Lexus SUV as she brushed snow from its windows. Nothing had been left in the vehicle, and it was as pristine as it must have been on the dealer's lot, with the exception of dirty salt stains on the driver's mat and a chocolate bar wrapper on the passenger side floor. It had hardly been driven.

Sam stuck her head out the cabin door. "Coffee's ready!" she called.

"Time to go inside, Mollie." Jo moved toward the door, admiring the log siding that made the small building look more like a bush camp than a cottage. Smoke billowed from the chimney and the smell of melting butter wafted out the door as she stepped inside.

"It's frigging cold out there," Sam said. She was flipping pancakes on the electric grill. "You must be frozen. I hope you like pancakes. I've got maple syrup and blueberries."

"Mmmm. I sure do." Jo rubbed her hands together, coming to stand beside Sam. "What can I help with?"

"Pour yourself a coffee and sit down. I want to provide a proper breakfast for you and Mollie. I'll cook up some bacon and eggs for her, if that's okay."

"That would be nice. She'll be good with just the eggs." Jo plopped into the rocking chair by the woodstove and sipped her coffee. "I have some food for her in the truck. I'll head out to get it right after breakfast."

Sam took a dozen eggs out of the fridge. "Isn't it too cold for a long walk just yet?"

"Nah. Us northerners are used to it. You just have to know how to dress and where to walk."

Jo rocked in the chair, admiring Sam as she worked at the stove. Her short brown hair was neatly spiked, and a heavy navy woolen sweater graced her slender figure. "I'd love to come on the walk with you."

"And how do you plan to do that, especially with your snowshoes and boots frozen in the lake by now?"

Sam sighed. "Thanks for reminding me. It's a good thing I brought an extra pair of boots with me. I should be okay for a walk."

"Not without snowshoes, you won't." Jo rocked, careful not to squish Mollie's tail as she lay by the chair.

"I know, but there's another pair in the shed I can use." Sam began to dish up, a few eggs frying on the grill for Mollie. "They're my grandfather's, so they're ancient, but they work well in deep snow. Ready to eat?"

Jo moved to the table and examined the maple syrup, expecting an imitation. "Wow, the real stuff. I'm impressed."

Sam turned off the grill, leaving Mollie's eggs to cool while they ate. "Of course," she said, sitting down. "I wouldn't have it any other way."

"You'd better have a good breakfast if you want to walk with me this morning. You'll be pressed to keep up, especially since there's no clear trail." Jo poured syrup on her pancake. It was perfect, cooked to a golden brown.

"That sounds like a challenge." Sam's eyes glistened. "I'm always ready for a test of my abilities."

"Like yesterday, on the lake?"

Sam dropped her eyes. "Touché. I guess we should eat up."

"Yes, we'll need our energy because it'll be a long, cold walk." Jo smiled into her food as she realized that she was really looking forward to Sam coming along.

CHAPTER SIX

Sam's nostrils constricted from the frosty winter air. They had been walking for nearly an hour, focusing on finding the easiest path through the thick conifers, and barely spoke. It had given her time to think as she followed the trail set by Jo.

Sam knew she couldn't go back to Toronto. Yet. She also couldn't stay at the cottage if the roads weren't plowed. So what was she going to do?

Sam watched Jo slip through the trees as she expertly navigated their route. The soft way she spoke to Mollie, her strong strides through the snow, her attentiveness to making the path easier for Sam, and the way her blue eyes glittered through frozen eyelashes warmed the frigid day... There was something alluring about Jo. Sam liked the fact that Jo seemed to take comfort in the landscape, and enjoyed being outdoors despite the cold. It made her feel good to watch Jo carve a path through the bush, the aura of Jo's own natural beauty glowing amongst the trees as she led the way. Sam hadn't felt this good in a long time, if ever.

Sam stopped to catch her breath. "Are we almost there?"

"Yes." Jo motioned toward the road with a mittened hand. "It's just behind the snowbank. We can sit in the cab while the truck warms up and share the coffee I packed in my thermos this morning."

"Warm coffee in the middle of the frozen bush sounds perfect right about now." Sam glanced at Jo's hands. "Your mitts are beautiful. Where did you—"

"Excuse me?" Jo interrupted. "What the hell? Can't you show me a little more respect?"

Sam flushed. "Umm…what?"

"Oh, come on. You just told me my tits were beautiful."

Sam laughed. "Mitts. Your mitts are beautiful. Not your tits."

"Oh." Jo pulled off her hood and stared at her mitts, giving a cute little frown.

"What are they made of?"

"Moose hide. Lined with rabbit fur."

"I love the beadwork." Sam moved a bit closer and admired the intricate floral patterns, wishing for her own pair instead of the plain black leather ones she wore. "Where did you get them?"

Jo held her hands out in front to display the traditional handmade and beautifully decorated tan mitts. "I bought them years ago from a Cree woman who had a booth set up at one of our summer markets. They're so warm and I love them. They're like a piece of art. I wear them with honor."

"I can see that."

"Sorry I misunderstood." Jo shrugged and grinned, her cheeks slightly redder than when they'd stopped.

"Don't worry about it. I'm not surprised you didn't hear right, given my behavior last night."

Sam watched as Jo headed toward the road, wondering how she could have heard tits instead of mitts. Just what was going through that beautiful mind as she walked in silence?

Jo pointed into the distance. "I can see the truck now."

"You can?" Sam rushed to keep up with Jo's hastened pace. "All I can see is snow."

"That's because it's totally covered from the blizzard last night." A ridge of snow marked the snowbank along the road. Jo was the first to cross over it and navigate down to the road. She was brushing snow from her vehicle by the time Sam caught up. "Once I get it cleared off we can sit inside for a rest."

Sam ran a mitt along the hood to brush it clear. "It's a lot higher than my vehicle and the perfect opposite color to my black one. How nice. Is it new?"

"I bought it last fall." Jo climbed into the snow-filled back of the truck and opened a large toolbox at the rear of the cab. "Here you go." She handed Sam a long-handled snow broom and took a plastic shovel for herself. "I'll clear around the exhaust before I start it."

It didn't take them long to clear snow away from the truck and retreat inside the cab. Mollie bounded into the backseat and shook herself off, scattering snow around the cab.

"Wow, it's roomy in here. I love it." Sam watched Jo remove a mitt. Her neatly manicured fingers were a soft pink as she started the truck.

"Thanks." Jo revved the engine.

"I wish we could go for a ride somewhere," Sam said as the cabin began to warm up.

"I'd like to drive home right now. It's too bad the roads haven't been plowed."

"Couldn't you go anyway, considering this is four-wheel drive?"

"It's a truck, not a snowmobile," Jo said. "Besides, I couldn't just leave you here to make your way back to the cottage on your own."

"What about tomorrow, when the roads are plowed and you can get out?" Sam's voice cracked. She suddenly felt very alone. "I can't be snowed in at the cottage all winter."

"I know." Jo sighed. "You can come stay at my place, if you want."

"Really? Are you sure?"

"Yes, until you figure things out." Jo glanced at her watch and turned the heater fan down a notch. "I'll only let the truck run for another five minutes then we can start heading back. Let's have coffee. I also brought us each a protein bar."

"Super." Sam reached over the console and touched Jo's arm, squeezing the thick parka sleeve. "Thank you. I'm so lucky you came along yesterday, and I promise not to become a burden."

"Oh, I'll be putting you to work." Jo smiled as she opened her thermos and poured a cup of steaming coffee for Sam. "What do you do for a living back in Toronto anyway?"

"I'm a lawyer," Sam said.

"Perfect." Jo smiled. "I can start you working first thing Monday morning to review some legal clauses for me."

"Okay, but I'm a criminal lawyer. I can certainly help if you're in trouble with the law."

Jo chuckled. "How ironic. My mother wondered if you were running from the law and hiding out up here."

"Too funny. I am very much a law-abiding citizen…but have been known to associate with criminals after they've been charged." Sam bit into her protein bar and smirked as she chewed. Time to change the subject. She didn't want to think about work right now. "I'm really enjoying being out here with you."

"Good, because it's going to be a long cold walk back to the cottage." Jo kneeled on her seat, leaning over the console to access her pack behind. "I'll get Mollie a drink and snack then we can head out."

Sam leaned against her door, watching Jo as her shoulders straddled between their two seats. "Don't forget to bring her food back with us."

"Of course not." Jo glanced over, and Sam was caught staring. Their gazes locked for a moment until Jo turned away. Sam took a deep breath.

"We should get going." Jo turned around, sat back in her seat, and packed up her thermos. Sam wondered if Jo had felt it too—the sizzling spark when their gazes met.

The walk back through the bush was much easier and faster across the broken trail. Sam followed behind Jo, admiring her ability to lead, the way she took care to hold branches if it looked like they would snap back and smack Sam. It wasn't as if she didn't deserve a slap across the face after all her suggestions the night before.

"We made good time," Jo said as they stood at the cottage door, removing their snowshoes.

"Just in time for lunch too. I hope you don't mind leftover chili."

"I've been looking forward to it for the last half hour." Jo leaned her snowshoes against the cabin wall, then looked at Sam's SUV. "We can shovel your vehicle out after lunch."

"Like it's going to go anywhere."

"Maybe not tomorrow, but we'll figure something out. Come on Mollie. Let's go inside."

They quietly ate their lunch then relaxed around the crackling fire in the woodstove.

"Are you sure it's okay for me to stay at your place while I figure things out?" Sam sat in the rocking chair, sipping a cup of herbal tea while Jo reclined on the floor next to Mollie.

"I wouldn't have offered if it wasn't okay," Jo said, fondling Mollie's fur.

"You told me you don't live alone. So, um, who else do you live with?"

"Mollie." Jo snuggled up against her golden retriever.

Sam laughed. "What a lucky dog."

"Mollie's been a big help over the last three years."

"What happened?" Sam slid off the chair and crawled beside them, kneeling near Mollie's tail.

Jo paused. "My ex, Jan, dumped me for someone else. I thought she loved me as much as I loved her. I don't think I'll ever be able to trust anyone like that again."

"I'm so sorry." Sam reached out to touch Jo's arm, but Jo pulled away.

"Don't be. I have a good life now. I enjoy living by myself."

"That's good, I guess. I don't like being on my own."

"I find that hard to believe. Didn't you just dump someone and plan to spend the winter here by yourself?"

"If you put it like that, I guess you're right." Sam felt like she'd just been put into the same category as Jo's ex and it saddened her. "It's just that I've never been able to find anyone I want to spend the rest of my life with. No matter how hard I try."

"Yeah, well, I think you should stop looking, because it's not possible. I invested twenty years into a relationship I believed would last as long as the two of us were alive. What a joke that was." Jo got to her feet, but didn't move. She just stood there, looking angry and indecisive.

"Twenty years. Wow. That must have hurt." Sam stood and put a hand on Jo's stiffened arm.

Jo jerked her arm free. "I don't need your sympathy. Considering you're running away from breaking someone else's heart, maybe you should focus on your own love life."

"My love life was a lot more pathetic when I was trapped in an unfulfilling relationship. I really tried, but I couldn't commit to someone I didn't love. I'd hand over my heart in an instant if I met the right person."

"There's no such thing." Jo's tone was harsh, and she shook her head vigorously in disagreement.

"So you're going to let someone else determine your destiny?" Sam said. "Broken hearts do mend, you know."

"Don't you think I know?" Jo's voice raised. "It's taken me three long, painful years to put mine back together. I won't ever let anyone break it again." Her eyes glistened with unshed tears.

"Look, it's still damaged goods if you won't open it up to someone else." Sam tried to keep her voice calm. "That's the one thing I've learned over the years. Broken hearts have a way of fixing themselves. My lovers have always moved on to someone else. You should give it a try and…"

"Fuck you." Jo ripped her parka off the hook and stomped into her boots. "Come on Mollie. Let's go shovel some snow." She slammed the door shut, barely missing Mollie's tail as the two of them scurried outside.

CHAPTER SEVEN

Jo was enraged. She yanked her parka open, and her heavy breath painted the air with frost as she hurled snow over her shoulder. "Who the hell does she think she is, eh, Mollie? Imagine telling me to move on."

Mollie bounced in the snow, giving little playful yelps as she darted in and out of Jo's way. Her snout was covered in snow and her jowls flapped each time Jo pretended to jump at her.

Jo had called one of the grader operators to see if she could get her truck plowed out today, but was told there was no way it would happen until tomorrow morning at the earliest. Stranded for another night, she vowed to stay outside for as long as possible. The wind howled, but the sun shone as Jo kept digging through the snow.

The hurt from Jan's betrayal still stung, and Jo believed she'd never get over it. They'd been happy for more than nineteen years, were even planning a romantic trip to the Caribbean to celebrate their twentieth anniversary. Their flights and rooms had already been booked. Jo was looking forward to escaping the winter for a few weeks of warm weather to relax with her longtime partner.

The weeks leading up to the trip had been busy, and she'd barely noticed that Jan was going out more frequently on her own. Then one night, Jan just didn't come home at all. She'd left a note saying she'd met someone.

Jo was devastated. She loved Jan. She'd believed they'd spend the rest of their lives together. Jan was family, someone she trusted with her life, and celebrating twenty years together was proof. When Jan took the tickets and her new lover to the resort instead, Jo thought she was going to die. She'd never let that happen again. Never. Jo had extinguished all the fire in her heart for the sake of sanity. She'd eventually adapted to a contented life with Mollie, the perfect companion.

Jo paused to catch her breath, feeling a slight chill as the wind grabbed the opening in her jacket and snuck a hug of frigid air. She shook, holding her arms over chest while trying to tighten the zipper. Once bundled up tight, she resumed her manic shoveling through the snow, clearing the way past Sam's truck and halfway down the long driveway to the road. She was determined to stay out for as long as possible.

Sam watched the mini blizzard unfold outside her small kitchen window. Powdery snow whirled through the air as Jo tackled the drifts. She was like a machine, a snow blower ripping through the white mounds. Sam was afraid to go anywhere near her.

She could see Jo had already cleared the path to the woodshed, and Sam needed more kindling for the next morning's fire. Her boots had been warming by the woodstove and were toasty when she slid her feet into them. She grabbed her jacket and opened the door. Mollie came barreling toward her, barking.

"Hey, pooch." Sam held out her hands and was nearly knocked over when the dog jumped against her legs. "Whoa. You really want to play." Sam laughed, chasing Mollie, setting the dog in a frenzied run around the cleared area by the woodshed.

"Okay, I need to get some kindling because it's frigging cold out here. I'm not freezing my butt off for you, Mollie, even though you're so damn cute." Sam hurried through the woodshed door and grabbed a small ax. A few dry cedar logs leaned up against the woodpile, ready to be made into kindling to help start the fire. Mollie came inside and brushed against Sam's legs while she worked at chopping off strips of wood with the ax. She wanted Jo to be comfortable, warm in the morning, and cozy by a crackling fire.

Sam thought of Jo as she shaved off strips of wood. Cedar kindling always seemed so pure, the way it easily chipped off the block and felt so smooth in her hands. Cedar was always the best for starting a fire, even when the wood was a bit damp, and would be sure to set anything ablaze.

"Careful, girl." Sam shifted, treating Mollie as though she were a small child watching with interest, and continued to work. "We need some more kindling for the stove. Kindling to start a warm fire tomorrow morning. Cedar's the best to get flames going. I want Jo to thaw by the fire, maybe even create a spark in her heart. At least be open to the possibility." Sam sniffed a piece of fresh kindling. "It smells so good and…"

"Mollie!" The dog jerked around and rushed out the door in response to Jo's call. "Stay out here with me."

Sam watched from inside the woodshed as Jo continued shoveling. The frenzy was slowing, but her determination to stay away seemed unwavering.

Jo was getting tired and a bit cold, but couldn't bring herself to go inside just yet. Heart palpitating and lungs heaving, she watched Sam carry an armful of kindling into the cottage.

The woman was driving her crazy. The way she played with Mollie, and carried the kindling into the cottage, cradling it in her arms as though it was somehow sacred. Jo pictured Sam chipping away at the cedar block with Mollie at her side, forming the sweet-smelling kindling to start a crackling fire. The way she smiled, showing off those dimples, and felt so warm and comforting in bed the night before… Jo huffed. How could this woman be turning her on? Dammit. She didn't want to be attracted to Sam, and the last thing she needed was to dwell on the fact that they could have had sex last night.

It was getting dark by the time Jo leaned her shovel against the cottage and stepped inside, her shoulders stiff and back sore. Sam was kneeling in front of the woodstove, adding logs and stoking the fire. Her face glowed from the flames.

Jo watched as she casually brushed a hand through her hair, as though she was still by herself. Sam seemed to be a casual type of person, especially since she'd suggested a roll in the sack the day before. Jo was sure those dimples and long eyelashes could entice any number of women into her bed.

She turned away and focused on the aroma of cedar, roasting chicken, and wood smoke as she slipped out of her boots. Mollie scratched at the door, so she let her in. The dog burst into the cottage and rushed up to Sam, as though they'd known each other for years.

"Hey, girl." Sam wrapped an arm around Mollie. "Ooh, your fur is cold. Got to get you warmed up."

"It's really cold out there now," Jo said as she edged closer to the woodstove, wanting a hug too. "My feet are frozen."

"It's no wonder, the way you stayed outside shoveling like that." Sam stood up, brushing wood chips and bits of ash off the knees of her gray sweatpants. "Why don't you go for a hot shower to warm up while I finish dinner?"

"Thanks. I think I will." Jo rubbed a hand along Mollie's back then gathered her borrowed clothes from the foot of the bed and headed into the small bathroom, her hands shaking as she closed herself in. She began to strip out of her damp clothes, goose bumps galore as she thought of Sam at the woodshed. It was as though Mollie sensed something good about Sam, always eager to play with her.

Jo's legs were wobbly as she stepped into the shower stall, the warm water so soothing against her aching body. She washed, and then allowed herself a minute to luxuriate under the warm water before turning it off. Tensions seemed to ease away, and she felt refreshed at the end of it all.

She quickly dried off and stepped into Sam's navy sweatpants, shivering as the cool air touched her skin. Her nakedness in Sam's sweats somehow felt inappropriate and her goose bumps grew, but there was no way she'd ask to borrow a pair of underwear.

Sam was standing at the kitchen sink when Jo opened the bathroom door. The tap was running as she washed a few dishes, her backside swaying as though dancing to an imaginary beat. Jo smiled, hesitating in the doorway, wondering what it would be like to approach Sam and whisper into her ear. Dare she even go there and suggest that roll in the sack after all? Why not? It had been a long time since she'd had sex, and she could keep it casual with Sam. It would have to be that way. No kissing. That would be her boundary.

The timer on the oven blared, breaking the trance. The oven door squeaked open and the metal rack scraped as Sam pulled it out. She removed the roasting pan and put it on top of the stove, peeking inside the cover before dropping it back with a clang. She threw her potholders into the sink then slammed the oven the door shut. "Fuck."

"What's wrong?" Jo approached. "Is it burnt?"

Sam sighed and rubbed her eyes. "Sorry, I thought you were still in the shower. I forgot all about you being vegetarian. And here I hoped making a nice chicken dinner would help with the mood around here. Is my judgment ever off today."

"I don't mind if you eat chicken." Jo lifted the lids of the other two pots, potatoes and carrots. "The vegetables will be fine for me."

Sam went to the fridge and searched inside. "I have some marble mozzarella you could have with them. Do you eat cheese?" She held up an unopened block of mozzarella. "I sure hope so, because I wouldn't want you any more cheesed off at me."

Jo chuckled at the bad pun, but her heart was pounding away as she moved closer to Sam. This was her opportunity. "I've been thinking about things," she said, almost whispering. "A lot." Sam's eyes widened. "If you're still up for casual sex, I'm game."

Jo held her breath as Sam's face relaxed, her dimples expanding. "Are you sure?"

"Yes." Jo took Sam's hand, led her to the bedroom, and pulled the blankets back. She wanted to be in control, create her own boundaries. She closed the door to keep Mollie out, then pushed Sam back onto the bed before crawling on top. "No kissing on the lips, okay?"

"Whatever you say." Sam rolled them onto their sides, pulling Jo into a soft, but firm embrace.

Jo clutched even harder, burying her head deeper into Sam's shoulder and wrapping a leg around her thigh. It felt so good to be close to another woman, to feel Sam's heart beating against hers, to know they were going to have sex. Her breathing became short and fast, her body suddenly hot as her hands tore at Sam. The soft skin, familiar curves, and scent of sex—it had been so long. Too long, and nothing else mattered except following her lust.

Jo's breath caught as Sam's warm hand slipped under her shirt and gently caressed her hardened nipples before lifting it up for a view.

"Your breasts are indeed beautiful." Sam's tongue tickled each one as Jo moaned with pleasure.

"I want to feel yours." Jo slid hands up Sam's sweater and cupped firm breasts, erect nipples tickling her palms. "They're so soft, like my mitts."

Sam leaned back, gasping as she smiled. "I have another place for you to touch that's even softer."

"I just want to fuck you." Jo couldn't let this mean anything. "Only this once."

Jo felt Sam's fingers slip into her pants, searching until they both gasped with contact. "You're so wet." Sam's eyes were closed, concentrating on her rhythm as she rubbed. "I'm going to take you now."

"Oh yes." Jo squirmed in pleasure. Her fingers found their own way into Sam's moist center, the soft skin swallowing them up.

Touching another woman like that was so exhilarating, something she craved. Her fingers in the wet heat of arousal and giving pleasure—it was sex for the sake of sex. It had to be that way. Jo determined to keep her focus on the moment, blocking out all emotions other than the physical pleasure of touching and being touched. Sam's body swayed in tune with hers, their mutual need for release clawing to the brink of eruption.

Sam came first, her moan shrill and short, and with a convulsion that shook the bed. "Holy fuck, you're amazing."

Jo just wanted her own release. "Show me what you can do." Jo felt Sam's fingers bringing her to the verge. She was almost there, come on. Jo stopped breathing and thoughts of kissing Sam brought on a wave that started with a whimper and ended with a squeal as she crested.

"Wow." Sam's breathing was still uneven as Jo rolled away. "That was amazing."

"Thank you." Jo got off the bed, avoiding Sam's eyes as she straightened her clothes. She wanted to cling to Sam like lovers do in the afterglow of fulfilling sex, but knew she was at risk of falling for a drifter like Sam. Jo couldn't betray herself and let that happen. "I think I'll wash up for dinner now." She rushed from the room and into the bathroom, clicking the lock as soon as she closed the door.

Jo stared into the mirror above the sink, her eyes avoiding their reflection. She felt sick to her stomach. The vulnerability of her heart was still so raw. Sex with Sam could not happen again.

CHAPTER EIGHT

Dinner conversation was stilted as Jo picked at her plate of vegetables and cheese. Sam barely touched her food as well, struggling to think of things to say in the awkward silences. She kept her comments focused on Mollie, but even that strategy didn't help. In the end, she gave up and they finished their meal then cleaned the dishes without speaking.

Afterward, Jo retreated to a cold corner of the living room by herself while Sam and Mollie sprawled on the rug in front of the fire. It was going to be a frigid night, and Sam kept piling logs into the woodstove.

Her small batch of kindling was ready to ignite the morning fire, and she stared at it while rubbing Mollie's ears. If only there was kindling for the heart. She was sure Jo must have had a roaring fire in her heart before her ex put it out. Sam wanted to start it again. Her own heart was smoldering, ready to ignite, and she didn't know what to do about it.

"Mollie, time to go outside before bed." Jo slipped into her parka while the excited dog rushed to the door.

"Mind if I join you?" Sam sat up, hoping for an opportunity to ease the tension.

"Whatever you wish." Jo disappeared outside with Mollie, letting in a cold breeze before pulling the door shut.

Sam hit a fist against the kitchen counter just as Jo's cell phone started to ring. She grabbed it and rushed to the door, pushing it open and holding the phone out. "Jo, someone's calling you."

"Let it ring." Jo paced by the woodshed, kicking at chunks of snow while Mollie sniffed around Sam's vehicle. "They can leave a message."

"Okay." Sam stepped back inside and dropped the phone on the table. A chill ran through her. What if Jo left without her in the morning? She couldn't stay at the cottage, buried in snow and stranded on her own. Pride prevented her from returning to Toronto so soon after walking out on Trish. She plopped on the floor in front of the woodstove, and opened its glass door to stoke the fire inside.

She'd gotten what she'd asked for—sex with Jo, a quick thrill. And it had been thrilling. More thrilling than any sex she'd had in a long time, if ever. As Sam stared at the dancing orange and blue flames, the realization came to her. She'd just had one of the best orgasms in her life without so much as sharing a kiss.

The cottage door burst open then slammed shut with a gust of air. Mollie's nails ticked across the floor before her head nudged underneath Sam's arm.

"Ooh, you're cold." Sam rubbed the frosty fur as Mollie lay down, tail flapping against the rug. "It's nice and warm here by the fire. There's lots of room for you too, Jo."

"Thanks, but I have to return a call." Jo headed to the bedroom, staring at her phone as though it held some secret message.

Jo closed the bedroom door and dialed her mother. She answered on the first ring. "I was starting to worry. Where were you?"

"Outside with Mollie. I can't wait to get out of here." Jo climbed into the bed and pulled the heavy duvet up to her shoulders.

"Why? What's wrong?"

"Nothing. I have lots of work to do." Like protecting herself against heartbreak.

"Josephine, I can hear it in your voice." Her tongue snapped. "What's going on?"

"Mom, wouldn't you be upset too if you were snowed in at some stranger's cottage and had to share a bed with her for a second night?" Especially after what had just happened. Sam would be expecting it to happen again, and she couldn't let it.

"I hope she's at least nice. What's she going to do?"

"She's coming in with me." Jo kept her voice calm, though her heart thumped at the thought.

"Where's she going to stay?" Her mother was chewing gum, reminding Jo of juicy fruit.

"I told her she could crash at my place for now. I don't imagine it'll be for long."

"Let's hope not, because I'm sensing you don't really care for the girl."

"She's a woman, Mom."

"It sounds like you're coming down with a cold. How are you feeling dear?"

"I'm fine," Jo lied. She should have just left things alone, not tempt fate and risk getting hurt again. "I'm worried about all the snow. It's going to be a long enough day tomorrow without having to plow when I get home."

"I spoke to Anna this afternoon and she said Robbie can plow your driveway."

"That would be great. I'll give Robert a call."

"I'm making a pot of butternut squash soup tonight." Her mother's chair squeaked with the sound of her standing up. "It should be done by now. I'll bring some over tomorrow and leave it in your fridge so you and your guest can have some for dinner."

"Thanks, Mom. Her name's Sam."

"Samantha. Of course, that's it. I've been wracking my brain all day trying to remember her name."

Jo heard a scratching at the door and got off the bed to let Mollie in the room. "I should let you go so I can call Robert."

"Okay. I'll see you tomorrow." Her mother hung up.

Jo buried her face in Mollie's fur and groaned, as the dog's tail whacked against the wall. What had she just done? She ran a hand across the bed. Sam was a fantastic lover, even though they hadn't kissed and the sex was quick. She'd known exactly where to touch Jo. She also broke hearts, and Jo had to protect hers. Any more sex would be off limits.

Jo dialed her sister's place. "Hey."

"I hear you're snowed in with a woman," Anna said. "What luck. I hope she's single and sexy."

"She's both, but I'm not interested." It had to be that way. "Mollie likes her, though."

"That's a good sign," Anna said. "Animals have a way of sensing good people. You should follow Mollie's lead and have some fun."

"I'm not looking for fun. I'm looking for your son to see if he'll plow my driveway."

Anna's microwave beeped in the background. "He's already over at your place. He offered before I even asked."

"What a great guy. Tell Robert I'll pay him."

"He's not expecting anything." Anna's microwave door clicked open, muffled sounds as she lifted something out. "I'm so glad he didn't take after his father. What's she like?"

"Who?" She didn't want to talk about Sam.

"The woman you're stranded with, of course." Anna's movements stopped, and Jo knew she was going to fire away. "She must be a bitch if you're not interested after all this time on your own."

"You're a fine one to talk. How many years have you been divorced now? I seem to think it's somewhere around ten and you're still single."

"I've put my kids first."

"Anna, Robert's twenty-four and Sarah's twenty-two." Jo shook her head, fingers sieving fur on Mollie's back. "They're not children anymore. You were already married with two kids at that age."

"They're still babies," Anna insisted. "What time will you be home tomorrow?"

"I don't know. It all depends when they get the road plowed. I'll find out in the morning."

"Okay, well, enjoy your night and don't be afraid to have some fun. Besides, the temperature is falling off the scale tonight and you'll probably want to cuddle with someone to keep warm."

"Good night, Anna." Jo ended the call. Sam certainly could keep her warm, but Jo was terrified. She couldn't let lust override common sense. She had protected her heart well; she wouldn't risk having it broken again.

Jo forced herself to leave the safety of the bedroom, Mollie following.

"I was beginning to think you'd gone to bed already." Sam was sitting in front of the fire and stoking the flames with an old brass-handled poker. Mollie bounded to her side and lay down near the stove. "I have some marshmallows here. Why don't we roast some?"

"No, thanks." Jo went into the bathroom and leaned against the wooden door as she closed it behind her. It was going to be a long night. She knew she was behaving badly. Sam had done nothing wrong. Actually, she did everything right. Oh so right.

She really needed to apologize to Sam, but there'd be no hug and kiss to make up. Maybe she'd accept a marshmallow, but that was it.

Jo left the bathroom and sat on the floor beside Mollie, petting her back. "I think I might take you up your offer of a marshmallow. I owe you an apology."

"For what?" Sam opened the bag of marshmallows.

"I've been acting like a bitch and it has nothing to do with you. I'm sorry."

Sam flashed her warm brown eyes and smiled. "I'm sorry for getting you stuck out here with me. How do you like your marshmallows?"

"Just out of the package, actually." Jo reached for the bag and took one. "I never liked the burnt flavor and the sticky mess they can make if they drip." She stuffed it into her mouth and forced a grin.

"What an appropriate description of our situation, don't you think?" Sam took two and shoved them between her lips, ballooning her cheeks.

"How so?" Jo was relaxing.

"It's like we're cooked marshmallows." Sam covered her full mouth as she spoke. "You've been burnt by your ex and I'm in a sticky mess with mine."

Jo raised her eyebrows.

Sam took a breath and swallowed. "Look, I could really use a friend right now. Can we at least be that?"

Jo reached for another marshmallow, avoiding Sam's eyes. "Yes, but there'll be no kissing to make up."

"For sure." Sam touched Jo's arm. "Thank you."

"For what?"

"For being here for me. And for offering me a place to stay tomorrow."

"Tomorrow. Yeah. It's going to be a busy day and you should think about what you want to pack out with us. It may be a while before you can get your road plowed. I'm heading off to bed. Come on, Mollie."

CHAPTER NINE

Sam stayed sitting alone next to the fire, feeding logs into the stove and wondering about her future. Being rescued by Jo had been one of the best things to happen to her in a long time, if ever. She had the sense the woman could do so much more than just pull her off crumbling ice. Her destiny, she was sure, was now somehow linked to Jo. Sam's stomach churned with excitement that kept her awake long into the night, until she finally fell asleep on the floor in front of the fire.

It was midafternoon the next day before Jo got confirmation her truck had been plowed out. They would have to hurry on their walk through the bush to make it to the road before dark. Sam packed only the essentials, as they'd have to carry everything.

She had already turned off the water system. The plan was to return once the cottage road was plowed to get the rest of her stuff. Jo even offered to help, their friendship budding after shared marshmallows and a night of sleeping apart.

"The fire's almost out." Sam closed up the woodstove and took one last look around. The kitchen counter was clean, the table bare and the quilt draped over the back of the rocking chair by the woodstove. "I think we have everything for now."

"Good," Jo said. "Let's get going. The wind is starting to pick up and I want to make it to the truck before we get any more snow."

They meandered through the trees without speaking. Jo kept the lead on their trail that had been blazed the day before. Mollie skipped along, darting on and off the packed path as though chasing some imaginary prey, while Sam struggled to keep up.

The weight of Sam's pack was slowing her down, even though she only took a change of clothes and a few food items that would go bad if not eaten soon. If it wasn't for her excitement and anticipation about going to Jo's place, she would have been downright depressed. She liked to be in control and wanted to impress Jo, but instead felt like a loser as she trudged at the rear.

"We're almost there." Jo stopped and turned around, waiting for Sam to catch up. "How are you doing? You look tired."

"I'm a city girl." Sam panted as she reached Jo's side.

"I can see that. You look like you're going to collapse. Why don't you catch your breath for a minute while I go ahead and start the truck? I'll come back while it's warming up and carry your pack the rest of the way."

"I think if it was me...I'd just want to...get the hell out of here." She forced a smile, struggling to control her heavy breathing. "You will come back, won't you?"

Jo grinned. "I don't dump women and leave them stranded in the middle of the bush."

"It's a good thing we're opposites then."

Jo held her eyes for a minute, a tease in her grin. "For you, yes." She turned to Mollie. "Come here and stay with Sam while I go to the truck." She pointed to a spot near Sam's feet and the dog rushed up and sat down.

Sam took off a mitt to greet Mollie. "I can't believe how she listens to you. I think I'm falling in love with your dog."

Jo swung around. "Don't you dare break her heart."

"That's impossible." Sam chuckled, but Jo's reaction stung. "She's totally dedicated to you. Despite what you may think about me, I'm not into home wrecking. I only date single women."

"I'm glad my sister Anna's not a lesbian then, because she's been single longer than me. I wouldn't want her to get hurt." Jo started walking away.

"What makes you think she'd even be interested in me if she was a lesbian?" Sam called out, her tease ignored as Jo stomped toward the road.

It didn't take long for the soothing sound of the truck to echo through the trees. Thank God. Sam couldn't wait to get out of the cold and into the cozy cab. "Let's hurry up, Mollie."

Sam followed Mollie, scrambling through the thick spruce stand with her big pack to make sure she didn't get left behind. Not that it was a possibility, but still. She didn't want to keep Jo waiting.

"Whew." Sam jumped down from the snowbank and stopped at the opened rear driver's-side door of the truck. Mollie was already perched on the seat inside, her tongue hanging out as she panted.

"Afraid I was going to leave without you, eh?" Jo's tease followed with a smile. "You can put your backpack on the seat beside Mollie. Your snowshoes can go in the box with mine."

Sam put her snowshoes with Jo's then climbed into the passenger seat and gave a relieved sigh as she buckled herself in. Jo was at the wheel, putting the truck into drive and turning them around with a three-point turn between the snowbanks. Once they got on their way, the ride was smooth and quiet.

"Thank you again," Sam said, gently patting Jo's leg. "I'm so glad to have you as a friend." She eased her hand back.

"We won't get home until after dark," Jo said, shifting in her seat. "It'll take us about an hour and a half of driving to get there, so I hope you're not hungry."

"I'm fine." Sam smiled as she studied the white road ahead. It looked more like a tunnel between the thick spruce trees and high snowbanks. Maybe, just maybe, there was a light at the end of this tunnel, and for once in her life she'd find something more than the superficial relationships she was used to. Sam wanted to get to know Jo more than she'd ever longed to get close to another woman, even if it was just as friends. "I look forward to the ride."

Daylight soon faded into dusk then darkness as they drove along to soft music from Sarah McLachlan. By the time Jo turned into her long driveway, she was surprised to realize how much she was beginning to really like Sam as a person. She was looking forward to having the woman as a guest on her turf.

Sam was intelligent—that much was obvious from the start—and she had a keen legal mind. During the drive home, they had discussed work. Sam had listened attentively as Jo explained her issues with some nearby cottagers who opposed the cutting of a small stand of old growth white pine. Sam agreed to review some of Jo's legal files, even if they had nothing to do with criminal activities. A lawyer's mind was what Jo needed. She'd put Sam's beautiful brown eyes to work on something more productive than trying to seduce her again.

"Wow, I love your place." Sam studied Jo's house as it glowed under the lights. It was a modern bungalow on its own, a country property just outside of town, surrounded by fields and bush. "How long have you lived here?"

"It'll be eight years this summer." Jo parked in front of the door with relief at finally being home. "We'll get our stuff inside first and then I'll put the truck away. My mother said she'd drop off some soup for us."

"How nice. I wish my mother would have done stuff like that for me."

Jo paused, her hand on the truck door as Sam slowly pulled on her hat. "Didn't she?"

"No." Sam shook her head, the darkened cab hiding her facial expression. "My mother was never around much and when she was, we usually argued." Sam's eyes glistened in the reflection of the porch light. "After she died, I realized that we'd never really bonded the way a mother and daughter should."

Jo put a hand on Sam's arm. "I'm sorry. How did she die?"

"A car accident. She was drunk and either fell asleep at the wheel or drove into the transport on purpose. We'll never know."

"Oh my God, Sam. When did this happen?"

"Last summer. That's how I ended up with the cottage." Sam paused, wiping a tear on her cheek. "It's probably why I'm so screwed up too."

"Everyone's messed up in one way or another. I'm so sorry." Jo didn't know what else to say so she leaned over and hugged Sam, then opened her door. "Let's go inside and have some soup."

"Eucalyptus." Sam sniffed as they huddled on the big mat in the front entry, taking off their boots and coats. "I love that smell. What a nice fragrance to welcome guests." She inhaled again, and admired the high ceilings and orange walls brightening up the entry. "What's that other aroma? It's sweet too."

"Open the closet to hang up your coat and you'll see," Jo said.

Sam pulled open a white folding door, the cedar-lined closet revealing the scent. "I'm scared of closets because I spent a lot of time in one when I was younger." Sam chuckled.

"I find it hard to believe you'd have been closeted," Jo said as she grabbed a hanger. "I didn't think anyone from a big city would have to live in a closet, especially you."

Sam removed her parka. "My mother hated gays. I do love the cedar paneling in this one, though, and could imagine myself curled up inside it."

"Thanks," Jo said. "Why do you think she was like that?"

"Who knows, maybe she was a lesbian herself. I didn't know my dad and I never remember her dating anyone. She was a teacher in the Catholic school system. It was probably more acceptable for her to love the bottle instead of another woman."

"Have *you* ever really loved another woman?"

Sam glared at her. "Is that why you put nice-smelling cedar in your closet? So you could crawl into it and hide from big bad lesbians like me?"

Jo's cheeks reddened. "I deserved that. I'm sorry for being so crass. It's been a long day and I'm tired. Let's eat."

"Yes, but first if you could point me to your bathroom, that would be great."

"Of course." Jo led Sam to the hallway and motioned to the washroom. "It's just down the hall. I'll give you a tour once we settle in. In the meantime, come back into the kitchen when you're done, and we can have some soup."

"Sounds good." Sam rushed down the hall, eager to have a minute by herself.

She closed the bathroom door and leaned against it. Her emotions were too raw. All those years growing up and knowing she was a lesbian. Living in fear that her mother would somehow find out. She never did tell her mother.

It had been a while since she'd talked about her mother and was surprised at how easily she confided in Jo. This was definitely turning into a friendship she wanted to nurture.

CHAPTER TEN

"This is so good." Sam smacked her lips, pushing away her now empty bowl of butternut squash soup. "You'll definitely have to thank your mother for me."

"You can thank her yourself tomorrow. She's going to drop by in the morning. As soon as you're done, I'll give you a quick tour and show you to your room." Jo was already clearing the table, anxious to organize herself for the next day. Her mind was humming with her workload and how she could get Sam to help.

"I'm ready now." Sam put her bowl into the dishwasher. "I love your kitchen by the way. I've always liked lighter wood cupboards."

"Thanks. They're made from yellow birch." Jo remembered picking out the wood for the doors from pieces stored in a woodlot owner's garage down south. Jan was with her, but she'd stayed pouting in the car because she wanted oak.

"Nice." Sam examined one of the doors, pulling it open and rubbing her hand along its surface. "Is the wood from your land?"

"Only some." Jo leaned against the counter and folded her arms. She followed Sam's gaze up to the matching panels on the cathedral ceiling. "I couldn't get the cupboards made locally, but the birch on the ceiling is from here."

"I love the awning windows at the top of the room. They must let in a lot of light."

Jo grinned. She was proud of her home; it meant a lot for Sam to like it. "They do, especially when the sun is shining. I hope you have a chance to see tomorrow."

Sam's eyes lowered, and her hands began to fidget. "So do I."

"It's supposed to be cloudy tomorrow so there won't be any rays of sun shining through them."

"Whew." She smiled, dimples digging into her cheeks. "I thought that was my cue to move on in the morning."

"Leave tomorrow? Are you kidding? I have lots of work for you to do, remember? You're not getting off that easy."

Sam got to her feet. "That's good to know. I'm ready for my tour now."

Jo's house was solid, constructed with energy efficiency and environmental friendliness in mind. That was one thing she and Jan had agreed on, and Jo was thankful for it. The walls were insulated to standards well above the building code and the windows were triple-glazed. She'd always believed they'd stay in it for the rest of their lives. Well, she still planned to.

As they stood by Jo's dark green leather couch in the living room, Sam ran a socked foot across the wooden floor. "I love the flooring in here. Is it bamboo?"

"Yes." Jo's jaw tightened.

"How nice to have lucky bamboo in your living room," Sam said.

"I actually hate it." Jo glared at the floor. "The bamboo was my ex's idea. I'm going to rip it out and replace it with some reclaimed oak I bought last fall."

Sam smiled. "That should be nice. If I'm still here, maybe I can help."

"Maybe." Jo hated that everything seemed to remind her of Jan—even the goddamn floors. She pushed past Sam and led the way through the long hallway and down to the basement. "What are your plans for now?" she asked, clicking on the overhead light as they descended.

"To get my vehicle from the cottage. Wow, the ceilings down here are nice and high." Sam reached up, but her fingers were almost a foot away from touching.

"I wanted big windows in the basement." Jo fluffed a cushion on the couch. "My office was originally in one of the rooms down here, but when Jan moved out, I relocated it to a bedroom upstairs."

"Damn, that's a huge TV." Sam picked up the remote from the coffee table and flicked it on. "You must still spend a lot of time in this room."

"Not really." Jo preferred to be upstairs where there was much more natural light and the air was always warmer on cold days like this.

Sam flipped through a few channels on the muted TV then turned it off, putting the remote back down on the coffee table and going up to the woodstove. "This is nice." She opened the door and looked inside. "Bigger than the one at the cottage. It must make things cozy down here when you have a fire going."

"Thanks. It does, but I haven't used it in a while."

"Well we should change that." Sam went over to the couch and flopped down with her feet up, as though watching a movie. "I'll have popcorn, please."

Jo sat balancing on the arm of the couch, at Sam's feet. "I was thinking you could work in my old office, but I see now that it might be too distracting with the entertainment room so close. I like it down here. I've always enjoyed hanging out in the basement. It became my retreat while Jan and I were splitting up."

"You mean you still lived with her after she took some other woman on *your* vacation?"

"I didn't have a choice. She owned half the house, so I couldn't just kick her out."

"What a bitch." Sam sat up straight and turned to Jo with a sympathetic look. "Even I wouldn't do that to someone after dumping her."

"Is that why you're not in a hurry to head back to Toronto? So you don't have to live with your ex?"

"Sort of." She smirked then got up and followed as Jo continued the tour in the basement.

Jo brought them into her former office that she now thought of as a symbol of her second-tier status in her relationship with Jan. Even before Jan left her, Jo had been relegated to the basement.

"Nice desk." Sam ran her hand along the oak top. "A classic, especially for a senior partner in a law firm. Isn't your office upstairs now?"

"It is, but this was too heavy to move so I bought a new one. Used, of course, and just as nice. There's nothing like a solid wood desk. You can work here tomorrow, if you like." Jo sat in the chair and spread her hands over the desk, following the trail of Sam's fingers. Best to keep her in the basement.

"You're serious about putting me to work then." Sam tapped Jo's shoulder. "What other plans do you have for me?"

"You can walk my dog tonight." Jo chuckled, her need to relax and forget about Jan increasing. "Just kidding. I'll show you the rest of upstairs and you can settle in for the night."

"I'm happy to walk Mollie or do whatever else to earn my keep." Sam followed Jo out of the room.

"That's good to know." Jo took her time going up the stairs. The next part of the tour included sleeping arrangements.

"So you only have one bedroom in this house, right?"

"You wish." Jo led them down the hall, her heart pounding as they neared her bedroom. "This is my room. It has its own bathroom so the one down the hall is all yours." Jo backed away and was barely able to breathe as Sam hesitated at the doorframe.

Sam glanced inside, her feet firmly planted in the hallway. "Nice room. I love the teal green walls." She then backed away and turned to the room across the hall. "Is this where I'll be crashing?"

"Yes, this'll be your room. Help yourself to extra blankets and towels in the linen closet next to the bathroom."

"This is great." Sam went in and sat on the edge of the bed that Jan had used when she started to complain about their bed not being big enough for two. "Ooh, this is so comfortable. I'm sure I'll have some good sleeps in here." She leaned back on the pillows and scanned the room. "You chose well on your color. It's so fitting for a lesbian guest like myself who worships purple."

"I'm glad you like it." Jo smiled. Jan always hated Jo's choice of color for this room. Another check for Sam. "I'll let you get settled in now while I make a few phone calls."

Jo hurried into her room, shut the door, and flopped onto the bed, phone in a trembling hand. She had to stop this. Sam would be gone soon, and it would all seem like a dream. She dialed her mother.

"Your soup was great. Thanks, Mom."

"I'm glad you enjoyed it." The TV suddenly muted. "How's your guest settling in?"

"Fine. I think Mollie's with her now." Jo heard the clinking of her tags as Sam threw a tennis ball down the hall.

"You sound tired."

"It's been a long day." Jo yawned, the low lighting from the lamp on her night table calming. "I have a busy week ahead and I still have to call Robert to thank him for plowing my driveway."

"I have to call over there, so I'll tell him for you."

"Thanks, Mom. That'd be great. I'll let you get back to whatever you were doing."

"Okay dear, have a good sleep. I'll see you tomorrow."

Jo flopped back on her pillows and stared at the white painted ceiling. She closed her eyes and imagined Sam's hands on her breasts. The way her fingers teased her nipples and then her tongue…

Jo sat up. What was she doing? She was a planner and had to stick to her personal plan of a contented existence on her own. It was the only sustainable thing to do. She dragged herself off the bed and went in search of Mollie. She'd take her outside for a bedtime walk and cool off these emotions in the frigid night air.

"Outside, Mollie." Jo stood by the back door, leash in hands at the ready. The quick ticking of nails on the hardwood announced Mollie's enthusiasm. She rushed to Jo and nudged the leash.

"And here I thought she was content to stay in my room with me." Sam's socks glided across the floor, muting her footsteps as she followed Mollie.

"I'll keep her in my room tonight, so she doesn't bother you," Jo said.

"Don't worry about me."

"I'm not. I'm more worried about me. Good night." She stepped outside, Mollie rushing ahead, and closed the door.

CHAPTER ELEVEN

Sam slept until nine thirty the next morning. She was almost embarrassed to sneak out of her room into the shower then show up in the kitchen at ten. Jo was already having her coffee break.

"Oh man, I didn't mean to sleep so late," Sam said. The kitchen smelled of fresh coffee and was brightened with Jo's presence.

Jo bit into an apple. "What a slacker. I've already organized to have your vehicle plowed out on Friday morning."

"Gee, thanks." Sam poured a coffee and leaned against the counter, gripping her mug between two hands to keep it steady. "It'll give me the rest of the week to figure out a plan of where to go after that."

"You'll head back to Toronto, I imagine," Jo said, casually looking at her phone. As though Sam leaving meant nothing to her.

Sam shuffled her feet "No. I thought I'd at least spend the rest of the month in town and snowshoe into the cottage whenever I get a chance."

Jo continued to flip through messages on her phone. "Do you know anyone from here? Someone else you could bunk with?"

"No, but don't worry. I'll find myself a place to rent and get out of your hair."

Jo finally put the phone down. "Look, you can stay here for as long as you want. As long as you don't break my dog's heart."

Sam laughed. "I promise not to."

"Of course if you'd rather go somewhere else..." Jo looked back at her phone.

"No, no, I'd love to rent a room from you. Your place is beautiful, and I had one of the best sleeps in forever last night. And then there's Mollie. I've never had a dog before, so this is a new experience for me. If a heart gets broken, it's going to be mine."

Jo got up and poured the rest of her coffee down the sink. "There's already been enough heartbreak around here. I have a call at ten thirty, so better head back to my office and prepare."

"Hello. Is anyone home?" Sam recognized Jo's mother as soon as she pushed open the door and stepped inside. The woman was a slightly shorter, early-sixties version of Jo. Her curly blond hair was up in a bun and a puffy pink parka accentuated her femininity, but the blue eyes and soft facial features were just like Jo's.

"Hi, Mom." Mollie beat Jo to the door, her tail wagging.

"I thought I'd pop by this morning to drop off some of my homemade blueberry muffins and meet your guest." She stomped snow off her boots and put a bag of fresh muffins on the counter then gave Jo a hug.

"Mmmm. Thanks, Mom." Jo opened the bag. "They're still warm. Maybe I'll have one for lunch."

"They just came out of the oven." She turned to Sam and smiled, her blue eyes friendly. "Aren't you going to introduce us?"

"Of course." Jo stepped forward. "Mom, I'd like you to meet Samantha White. She'll be staying here for a while."

"Hi, Samantha. I'm Julia Lavigne." She offered her hand.

Sam smiled as she slid her palm into a firm shake that felt genuine. "Hello, Julia. It's nice to meet you. Your daughter has been a real life-saver for me."

"I heard." Julia released Sam's hand and patted Mollie's head when she nudged at their legs for attention. "Josephine's a real bushwhacker and sure knows her way around the forest. It's a good thing she was near Button Lake."

"And Mollie too," Jo said. "She's the one who alerted me that something was wrong. I couldn't hear a thing with my hat and hood."

"It was so cold the other day I don't know why you even went out in the first place," Julia said. "It must have been fate for the two of you to meet like that."

Jo's cheeks reddened. "Mom, I have a deadline, so I had to go out."

"I like to believe it was karma," Sam said. "Jo told me your father knew my grandfather."

"It's a small world, isn't it?" Julia put on her navy knitted gloves. "I'll let the two of you get back to whatever you were doing. It was nice meeting you, Samantha."

"The pleasure was all mine," Sam said. "I can't get over how much you and Jo look alike. She's going to age very well."

"Oh you're too kind," Julia said, blushing. "Why don't the two of you to come over for dinner tonight? Anna will be there and I'm having a vegetarian lasagna."

"Thank you, that sounds lovely." Sam turned to Jo. "Are you game?"

"For sure. Thanks again for the soup and muffins." Jo hugged her mother, exchanging kisses on the cheek. "I never turn down a free dinner at Mom's. Is six okay?"

"Perfect. I'll see you then. Bye, girls." Julia gave Mollie another pat before heading out.

"What a nice woman. You're lucky to have a mother like her."

Jo smiled. "Yes, I am very lucky."

"Does your sister look like you too?" Sam imagined someone looking just like Jo, given the similarities between mother and daughter.

"Her hair is darker, but people have said we look alike. Keep in mind, though, she's not a lesbian and neither is my mother. There's no need to flirt with them."

Sam crossed her arms, smiling at Jo's reaction. "Your mother seemed to enjoy it."

"Everybody likes to be charmed once in a while." Jo looked inside the bag of muffins and sniffed. "Mmmm. Blueberry is my favorite. Feel free to have one now if you'd like."

Sam reached for a muffin. "Thanks. Great timing for your mother to drop them off."

"Yes, considering you're just looking for breakfast now." Jo gave her a playful tap on the arm. "I have to get back to work. I'll be in my office if you need anything."

Sam sat at the kitchen table and turned on her phone. A bunch of messages popped up and she put down her muffin to see what was going on. They were all from Trish, and had subject lines full of questions and exclamation marks.

How could you do this to me?!
What am I going to do now?!
When did you lose your heart?!
I thought you loved me!!
What happened?!
What did I ever do to you?!

Sam threw her phone on the counter. She wasn't going to read any of the diatribes, not after all they'd been through. Sam put her head in her hands and closed her eyes. She moaned with regret. No. Embarrassment. How could she have been with someone like Trish, when in only a few days, Jo made her feel more alive than ever? She wanted more of whatever it was she was feeling around Jo. There'd be no more sex for the sake of sex. It was time to grow up.

Mollie came back into the kitchen, tail wagging and panting as she rested her head on Sam's lap.

Sam took comfort in rubbing the soft fur of Mollie's ears. "It's okay, girl. I've been a shit, that's all. Nothing new."

She needed some fresh air. Sunrays were bouncing off the floor and the sky was a perfect blue, beckoning her outside. The forecast of a cloudy day was wrong. Sam moved to the kitchen sink and looked out the window above it. A sparkling winter wonderland stared back. Jo's yard was buried in fresh snow and a cedar hedge separated the two-car garage from the house. The property was bordered by a spruce forest, with a large field behind the garage.

"I think we should go outside, Mollie." Sam moved to the patio door for a better view. There was a sizeable snow-covered deck with a screened-in gazebo at the far corner. A trail at the back of the yard led into the thick bush. Sam wanted to explore it, so she pulled on her parka and toque.

"Hey, Jo." Sam stood at Jo's office door, coat open and mitts in hands.

Jo looked up from her computer, and her eyes widened as she studied Sam's attire. "Heading out?"

"I thought I'd take Mollie for a little walk. I noticed a trail into the bush at the back of the yard. Where does it go?"

"It doesn't go far." She hit a few keys as though in the middle of something and Sam was interrupting. "It leads to my haven."

Haven? "I can't imagine needing a place like that with this beautiful house."

"Sometimes things aren't always what they seem." Jo sighed, her voice lowering. "There are lots of beautiful houses, but when they stop being a home, you need a sanctuary."

"Your ex—of course. I hope you see this place as a home again."

"Yes, I do, and I don't want to ever risk losing that again." Jo's fingers hovered over her keyboard. "Have fun."

"Thanks. See you in a bit."

Sam donned her snowshoes and headed down the trail. True to Jo's words, it didn't lead far. A gray wooden shed with a red door and two front windows marked the end of the path. Sam approached and looked inside. A small desk was under the window and a brown-checkered fabric couch lined the back wall. There was a wooden table with two chairs, a white-painted rocker in the far corner, and a brown shag rug in the middle of the floor.

Sam tried the door, but it was locked. She backed away, wondering how long it had been since Jo used the place and thinking she could have used something like this at her house in Toronto. Had her house ever really been a home?

Not after what she'd been feeling the last few days. She liked Jo. A lot. The woman had saved her life, but it was so much more than that. For the first time ever, Sam had met someone she could envision spending the rest of her life with.

CHAPTER TWELVE

Sam studied Julia Lavigne's well-lit house as they drove up. It was set back on a big lot in an older neighborhood in Timmins. Kind of like her bungalow in Toronto, but it looked much warmer and inviting with its orange brick instead of the colder gray of hers. Julia's blue front door decorated with a floral wreath just seemed so fitting for her. Sam was looking forward to the visit.

Jo parked in the driveway and winked at Sam. "Ready to meet the family?"

"For sure. If your sister's anything like your mother, we'll get along just fine."

"What if she's more like me?" Jo grinned as she nudged Sam's arm.

"All the better then." Sam was enjoying this. Jo was in a good mood and Sam's spirits were still high from her afternoon visit to the backyard. "We should head inside, or they might think we're necking out here."

Jo nudged Sam's arm again. "Please don't joke like that in front of them. We shouldn't even be doing this and I'm sorry for starting it just now."

"Don't worry, I'll behave." Sam walked onto the freshly shoveled driveway, a skip in her step as she headed to the door. Julia smiled and waved from the glowing kitchen window as they knocked.

Jo opened the door to a gust of garlic and cheese. "Mmmm. It smells so good in here."

"Come on in before you let all the heat out." Julia was hustling about, setting the table in the kitchen as they stepped inside. "Show Sam the basket of slippers so she can find herself a pair."

"My mother loves to knit, so you have your choice of woolen slippers to keep your feet warm on these cold floors." Jo jiggled the wicker basket as Sam slipped out of her boots.

"My floors aren't cold," Julia said. She turned off the radio news.

"I'm just teasing, Mom." Jo kicked off her boots and went up the few stairs into the kitchen, greeting her mother with a kiss on the cheek. She removed her parka and hung it in the closet across from the top of the four stairs leading into the kitchen.

Sam hopped up the stairs without selecting a pair of slippers. The floors, like the rest of the house, were nice and toasty, and Sam smiled as she handed Jo her jacket.

"Come on in, Samantha, and make yourself at home."

"Thank you." Sam went into the kitchen, her socks gliding across the shiny ceramic tiles as she greeted Julia with a hug. She stood near the small kitchen island, cluttered with dishes for the meal. "You have a beautiful place here. It smells so tantalizing my stomach won't stop growling."

"Anna's not here yet?" Jo came to stand beside Sam, her closeness comforting.

Julia lurched at the stove to silence the blaring oven timer. She opened the oven and inspected inside. "She said she'd be a bit late because she wants to run home and change first. Everything's ready. I hope the two of you have a big appetite."

"I can hardly wait." Sam took a deep whiff of garlic and cheese, her stomach growling loud enough for everyone to hear.

Julia laughed. "Jo, get Sam something to drink, would you please? I have to take the lasagna out of the oven."

"Red wine?" Jo held up the bottle they'd brought.

"Sure, thanks." Sam glanced into the living room. A large knitting bowl sat on the shiny hardwood floor beside an inviting rocker-recliner. The television remote perched on one arm of the chair and a half-finished scarf with knitting needles sticking out rested on the other.

The door burst open and a dark-haired woman stepped inside. "It's cold out there."

"Anna, why didn't you let me know you were walking?" Jo said. "We could've picked you up."

"I wanted the exercise." The tip of Anna's nose was frosty red as she removed her light blue wool coat. Sam watched as she fluffed her wavy brown hair so it hung neatly over her ears. The family resemblance was certainly there.

Julia came to the top of the entry stairs. "Why didn't you wear your down parka? That jacket's not warm enough for a night like tonight."

"It was fine, Mom." Anna's hazel eyes met Sam's as she unzipped then pulled off her tall leather boots. "Hi. You must be Samantha."

"Yes, I am. It's nice to meet you, Anna." Sam raised her glass of red wine and smiled. "I can't believe how much the three of you look alike."

"Do you think so? I always thought I was adopted because my hair's so brown while theirs is blond."

"Oh really, Anna." Jo laughed. "She's always been jealous of my blond hair. I don't know why you don't use blond dye now instead of brown."

"Hey, this is still my natural color." Anna's hands were cold as she offered one to Sam. "Are you sure you know what you're getting into by moving in with my little sister?"

"Anna." Jo hit her sister's arm. "You make it sound like we're a couple."

"Sorry. I didn't mean to imply anything." Anna's teasing grin warmed Sam as they shook hands, her grip pleasantly firm.

"Yes, you did." Jo's cheeks were now redder than Anna's nose as she winked at Sam. "Now, let's eat. I think Mom's ready."

"Yes, come on girls." Julia hugged Anna. "Ooh, you're cold. Be careful you don't get sick."

"Mom, I had the flu shot. I'm okay." Anna washed her hands in the kitchen sink.

Jo led Sam to the bathroom, where they shared the sink to wash up for dinner. Sam longed to lather her hands with Jo's, but instead relished the fact that their hips touched and eyes met in the mirror.

"Did you grow up in this house?" Sam asked as they dried their hands on the shared towel.

"I did. I can't imagine my mother ever moving."

"It seems like the ideal house for her." Sam felt it was a perfect home, too, as she followed Jo back to the kitchen. "And the way it's been kept up is amazing. We could eat off the floors it's so clean."

"What about the floors?" Julia asked as she dished out their lasagna. "Did I spill something?"

"No, Mom." Jo chuckled. "Sam was just commenting on how clean your floors are. We could eat off them."

"Oh, like in a Japanese restaurant." Julia put a basket of garlic bread on the table then sat down.

"Mom." Anna laughed. "Japanese people sit on the floor, but don't eat off it. Right, Sam? You must have eaten at a traditional Japanese restaurant before, being that you live in Toronto where there are all kinds of exotic places to eat."

"I can't say that I've ever eaten at a Japanese restaurant with floor seating," Sam said as she took her seat at the table. "I sometimes like to eat on the floor, though, especially at the cottage when the woodstove is throwing off lots of heat."

"What's a city girl like you doing up here?" Anna asked.

"And way out in the bush in the middle of winter," Julia said, dishing herself up some salad. "How long were you planning to stay there? And by yourself?"

"Mom," Jo said, sitting beside Sam, "it's really none of our business."

"No, it's fine," Sam said. "I was intending to stay for a month to experience a northern winter. If Jo and Mollie hadn't come along, I'd have only had less than a week."

"What do you mean?" Julia asked. "I thought your car was buried in snow. How could you have left?"

"Angels would have carried me away." Sam took another drink of her wine, thoroughly enjoying the ease with which Jo's family seemed to accept her.

"What?" Anna and Julia asked at the same time, their forks clinking on plates.

"I didn't know you could be so dramatic," Jo said, her eyebrows raised.

"Neither did I." Sam chuckled, realizing she'd probably drunk her wine too fast. "I almost went through the ice in front of the cottage. Luckily Jo and Mollie came along and saved me. I owe them my life."

"I'm sure you would've gotten yourself out on your own," Jo said.

"Josephine," Julia said, "you never told me Samantha fell through the ice."

"If you're going to be rescued by anyone in the bush," Anna said, "it might as well be Jo. You'd think she was part tree by the way she treks around the forest."

"Trees don't trek," Jo said. Her cheeks were slightly red. "They put down roots."

"You know what I mean." Anna took a mouthful of her lasagna. "This is really good, Mom."

After dinner the four of them cleaned up the dishes then retreated to the living room. Sam sat in the comfy recliner, knitting needles and TV remote quickly gathered up by Julia. Jo sat on the matching blue couch, between her mother and sister. All four sipped on tea.

"There you are." Julia held out her hands as a large black and white Persian cat strolled into the room.

"I didn't know you had a cat," Sam said as she snapped her fingers. "Here, kitty."

"His name's Felix and he's not very sociable," Julia said. "I'm surprised he's even come out tonight."

"He's a grouch and scratched Mollie when she was a pup," Jo said. "She's terrified of him now so I can't bring her over here."

"That's too bad." Sam yanked her hand back as the cat approached.

Anna laughed. "Mollie's a big chicken. Felix won't hurt you." She patted her knees and the cat jumped up, its tail almost hitting her nose as it circled. "Nice boy. Come sit with Auntie Anna."

"Isn't she your mother's cat?" Sam teased. "I thought you were Jo's sister instead of Julia's."

Jo and Julia burst out laughing.

"You thought right." Anna snickered, her cheeks reddening as she wove her fingers through the long fur on Felix's back. "Jo's made it clear she's never going to have kids and I want to be an aunt."

"You're Mollie's aunt," Jo said.

"I know," Anna said, "but Felix is just a cat and I don't like to think of Mom as having any more kids."

"True enough." Jo looked at her watch. "Well, Sam, I think we should get going. It's been a long day and I don't want to leave Mollie on her own for much longer."

They left shortly afterward, and spent the fifteen-minute drive home chatting about what groceries they needed. Sam shivered, but not from the cold air engulfing the truck cab. Her jitters were about wanting Jo, and the family life she could offer, more than she'd ever wanted anything before.

CHAPTER THIRTEEN

Jo tasked Sam with getting grocery items while she met with a client at ten the next morning. She'd had a good night's sleep and felt well rested. The dinner at her mother's had been quite enjoyable with Sam there; Jo was pleased her mother and sister seemed to like her.

Sam fit in with her family as though they'd known each other for years. Or maybe it was the chemistry. Her mother and Anna had known Jan for years, but in just one dinner, Sam's visit was much more relaxing than any she'd ever remembered having with Jan.

Jo let Sam drive her truck into town this morning. When she'd perched behind the wheel and her dimples lit up, Jo knew Sam was enjoying herself. It almost felt domestic, the way Sam dropped her off then was waiting with groceries when Jo's meeting finished. She liked having Sam as her houseguest.

"How much do I owe you?" Jo asked as Sam turned into the driveway.

Sam eased the truck to a stop. "Don't worry, I got it. It's the least I can do, considering I'm bunking at your place."

"Thanks." Jo jumped out and slammed her door. She knew Sam wouldn't be around for long, but *bunking* made it sound so transient. How could she have forgotten Sam was only here to avoid the woman she'd just dumped?

"Here are your keys." Sam's hand had a slight shake to it as she held them out. "I loved driving your truck. It made me feel special, considering I don't imagine you let just anyone behind your wheel."

"It's a work truck. Anyone I'm working with can drive it." Jo grabbed the keys and unlocked her front door. Mollie burst outside and ran up to Sam.

"Hey, girl, I bought you some treats." Sam played with Mollie, teasing her with little lunges and bringing on vigorous tail wagging that thrilled even Jo. "Why don't you go ahead inside and I'll bring in the groceries? I know you're busy."

"Thanks, that would be nice." Jo hurried inside, rustling up a cup of tea and a banana for a snack to take back to her office before joining in the fun. She'd hoped to escape before Sam came inside, but the door opened and Mollie bounded in. Sam followed, her face flushed as she struggled to carry all of the bags at once. Jo knew she should help, but needed to get away before having another domestic bliss moment.

"It'd be great if you could put cold stuff in the fridge for me," Jo said, avoiding eye contact as best she could. "I can put away the rest later."

"No problem. I'll see if I can figure out where everything else goes." Sam kicked off her boots and carried the bags into the kitchen.

"Thanks," Jo said. "I'm going to be focused on my work for the next several hours, so help yourself to whatever you want for lunch."

"How about if I make us some egg salad sandwiches?"

"That would be nice." Jo let her eyes wander toward Sam, hinted at a smile, then swung around and left.

Jo closed the door on her office and plopped in her chair. Elbows resting on the desktop, her head fell into her hands.

She had to concentrate. The public open house for the forest management plan was only days away and there was so much to do.

She'd promised to deliver a ground validation report of a small stand of old growth white pine located in the middle of the proposed harvest area. Her clients wanted recent pictures included in the report, which meant a drive out to the site early the next morning.

The only problem was she couldn't stop thinking about Sam and how good it felt to be around her. The way she smiled, her playful interactions with Mollie, her attentiveness to Jo's needs. Offering to make egg salad sandwiches for lunch even though Jo had just been short of rude to her by rushing away and not helping with the groceries. At a crucial time when she needed to focus on her work, most of her energy was being used to fight off her growing attraction to the woman.

While a day in the bush on her own seemed like the best remedy for her distracted mindset, Jo yearned to invite Sam along. She'd think about it and make a decision later, depending on how good those egg salad sandwiches were.

A scratch at her door announced Mollie, bringing Jo back to reality and the need to return her focus to work. Mollie found her favorite sunny spot in the middle of the floor and settled in for a nap, as though things were back to normal. Jo resolved to continue working like nothing was different too.

An hour later, Jo flinched back to reality at the tap on her door. She'd managed to lose herself in her work, deep in developing her slide presentation for the open house.

"Hey, Jo. I have some lunch for you. Is it okay if I come in?"

"For sure." Jo stretched her back then twirled around to watch Sam confidently carrying a garnished plate of food to her desk. "It looks like you've been busy."

"I'm sure not as busy as you. Sorry, Mollie, I didn't bring anything for you." Sam skirted by the jumping dog, holding up the plate to show Jo. "I boiled four eggs, mixed them with mayonnaise and a bit of salt and pepper then slathered the mix onto sandwiches. I put some baby carrots, a few pieces of cheese, a handful of almonds, and green grapes to round out your lunch. I hope you like it." She put the plate down, her arm brushing Jo's shoulder as she leaned forward.

"Oh wow, this looks yummy. Thank you." Jo stood, avoiding Sam's eyes. "Can you watch my food so Mollie doesn't help herself while I skip out to wash my hands?"

"For sure." Sam's dimples teased with a smile. "I'll keep your chair warm for you."

Jo needed to get out of there before she lost it and did something like hug Sam for the lunch. She deserved one for sure, presenting that plate as though Jo meant the world to her.

When she got back, Sam was bent over, rubbing Mollie's belly. She looked so sweet, her sweatshirt pulled up at the rear and exposing her lower back. "Not only looking after me with an amazing lunch, but also taking care of Mollie with a nice massage. I could really get used to this." Her cheeks burned as she realized how that must have sounded. "Sorry."

"No need to apologize." Sam stood, pulling down her shirt at the back. "I should let you get back to work."

"Thanks." Jo sat into Sam's lingering warmth. "I have to go to the bush tomorrow morning. Would you like to come along for the ride and a short walk on snowshoes? It's supposed to be cold, but sunny."

Sam smiled as she backed out of the room. "I'd love to. You can tell me more over dinner. Would you like me to close your door?"

"Dinner." Jo sighed. "I haven't even thought of it."

"Let me worry about that." Sam's eyes sparkled. "I'll cook up a batch of brown rice and stir-fry some of my leftover vegetables from the cottage that we need to eat up. How does that sound?"

"Perfect." Jo turned back to her laptop. "And yes please, close the door."

Jo dropped her head with the click of the door latch sliding into place. Things were becoming too ideal with Sam around. She would most likely be back to her life in Toronto next week at this time. Jo had to keep that in mind, front and center.

She took a bite of her sandwich, savored the taste, and then forced her thoughts back to the task at hand. Deadlines aside, work helped Jo avoid thinking about how much she wished Sam could stay longer. Forever even. If only the woman was trustworthy.

Sam stood at the kitchen sink window, watching chickadees as they flitted around the cedar hedge near the garage. She thought about returning to Toronto. She could easily crash with a friend until Trish moved out of her place, but she wanted to spend more time with Jo. There was just something about being around Jo that felt good, like she brightened life. Sam's place back in Toronto was just a house to her—a building to live in. Jo's place was so much more than that. It was warm, welcoming and had a sense of family. It was a home. It made Sam feel comfortable, as though she belonged.

Sam was about to turn away from the window when a truck pulled into the driveway and a handsome young man jumped out. He flung open the side door on Jo's garage and was inside before Sam could react.

"Hey, Jo, someone's in your garage," Sam called out. She jumped into her boots and grabbed her parka to find out what was going on.

Mollie barked and followed as Jo came to the kitchen window. "That's Robert's truck. He must be here for his gloves. I'll go out too."

Mollie slid through their legs and got outside first. Sam bolted to grab her collar and attached it to the leash.

"Hey." A clean-cut, well-dressed young man came out of the garage, pulling the door locked behind him and holding up a pair of black leather gloves. "They were on the plow seat, just where I figured I left them the other night."

"Good," Jo said. "It's too bad I didn't know yesterday, or we could have given them to your mom at dinner."

"I had a few minutes to kill before my dentist appointment. You must be Sam." He smiled and held out a hand.

"Sorry, I'm forgetting my manners," Jo said. "Sam, this is Robert, my kind nephew who plowed the driveway for us."

"Nice to meet you Robert." His aftershave wafted in the air ahead of him, and he folded Sam's hand into a firm shake. "Thank you for making it so much easier to get in here the other night when we were both exhausted." Yet another caring family member—Jo was lucky.

"Anytime." Robert bent over Mollie and rubbed around her ears. "Hey girl, are you behaving yourself?"

"Of course she is," Jo said.

"She's the best," Sam said. "Jo's fortunate to have her."

Robert put the gloves on, his breath blowing clouds into the cold air. "I heard you're lucky the two of them came along when they did."

"I am indeed." Sam looked at Jo and smiled. Her hero. "They saved me for sure."

"Well, I'd better get going." Robert moved toward his idling truck. "It was nice meeting you, Sam. Safe travels if I don't see you before heading back to Toronto."

"Thanks." Sam forced a smile.

"Don't worry about me for dinner," Jo said as they headed back inside. "I'm not very hungry. I'll probably just get myself a snack before bed."

"It's no bother." Sam kicked out of her boots, stepping in a puddle and wetting her socks. "I promise not to put any meat in my stir fry."

"No, please do. Use up the beef you have left otherwise I'll have to throw it out once you're gone."

Sam stood alone in the kitchen, abandoned even by Mollie. Her feet were wet and heart heavy as she pondered her situation. It was expected she'd be leaving as soon as her vehicle was plowed out. Was that based on a desire for her to leave or an assumption she would never stay? Sam knew her own history of not sticking around for long so what did it matter if Jo wanted her gone before she was ready to leave? She spent the rest of the day struggling to decide when best to depart.

CHAPTER FOURTEEN

Jo crept around the kitchen in the fading darkness of early morning, making herself a coffee and grabbing the second to last blueberry muffin before heading to her desk. She'd avoided Sam for the rest of the day yesterday, choosing instead to bury herself in work and hide out in her office. Jo had really wanted to be near Sam, get to know her more and enjoy her companionship. Sam would be gone soon, though, and she needed to protect herself.

Mollie kept her company for most of yesterday afternoon, sprawled on the wool rug in her office, but abandoned Jo just before dinner. Sam had offered to take her outside for a short walk and she eagerly accepted. Jo yearned to join them, too, needing some fresh air on an otherwise stale afternoon, but she refused to indulge. She stayed closed up in her office, focusing on her work long into the evening until Sam had gone to bed. Only then did she emerge, tiptoeing to her bedroom for a restless night of wishing they were back at the cottage and Sam was in bed with her.

The morning air outside was frigid, even too cold for Mollie. She'd hurried outside for a quick pee then rushed right back in. Jo knew they'd have to wait until later in the morning before heading to the bush, when the sun would at least offer some relief against the frosty winter air. The trip would be all business and even then, she wasn't sure if she'd be able to capture all the pictures she needed for Saturday. She at least hoped to get a few good pictures of Sam.

By the time Sam stirred, Jo had already been working for two hours and was ready for a break. Sam was playing with Mollie in the kitchen, squeaks from a stuffed toy, ticking nails against the floor, and the occasional laugh sure signs they were having fun. Jo wished things were different. That Sam lived in Timmins and was interested in settling down. No such luck. She closed her laptop, grabbed her empty mug, took a deep breath, and headed out to the kitchen.

"Good morning." Sam was spreading peanut butter on some toast.

"Hey." Jo rinsed her mug. "It's freezing out there this morning. I'll understand if you'd rather stay here, where it's nice and warm."

"I'm looking forward to it. I know you'll keep me warm, considering you're such a good bushwhacker."

"You think so, eh?" Jo sifted through her assortment of herbal tea, her face straight as though totally engaged in selecting the right one.

"Of course I do." Sam touched Jo's arm. "I know I can trust you with my life out there."

"Would you like some tea?" Jo continued as though Sam's touch meant nothing, although her heart was thumping. "How about some raspberry, or maybe chai?" She held up a few choices.

"No, thanks." Sam stepped away, her socks dragging on the cork floor. "I can get a hotel room in town if my staying here is becoming an inconvenience."

"It's not. I'm just very busy with my work." Hot water splashed against her hands as she washed out her mug.

"I feel like I'm disturbing you."

"You're not." That was a lie—Jo was definitely disturbed.

"I hope you'll let me know if I am then." Sam tapped her knee to call Mollie. "Come here, girl."

"The road into your cottage will be plowed out Friday. You might as well stay here until you head back to Toronto." Jo stared out the kitchen window as though looking at something important when all she wanted to do was return to her office before starting to cry.

"What if that's not for a few more weeks?"

"I thought you'd want to head home as soon as your vehicle is free," Jo said. "Especially with this deep freeze we're having right now."

"I'm warm when I'm with you." Sam was suddenly at the window, brushing up against Jo's hip as she leaned over the sink to look outside. "Are there more birds in your hedge?"

Jo took a step back. "No. We should probably get going shortly so we can return early this afternoon. I need to finish my slide presentation."

"Sure." Sam returned to the table. "Whatever you say. I'll follow your schedule."

They left soon afterward. Jo's truck was warm and the ride picturesque. She loved being in the bush on sunny days like this, and Sam kept oohing and awing as they drove by many wintery vistas. The landscape sparkled like diamonds on the snowy drive through narrow roads and mature trees. A few times Jo had to pull over to let a fully loaded logging truck pass by. The sweet aroma of fresh-cut pine in winter always reminded her of Christmas. The drive seemed shorter than Jo remembered, and they were soon at the site.

"It's only a short walk in off the road," Jo said as she stopped the truck. "I'll let you out here then pull up tight against the snowbank in case someone wants to get by while we're in the bush."

"Sure." Sam jumped out, hugging herself in the cold air as Jo squeezed the passenger side of her truck up against the snowbank. Sam had forgotten her toque on the seat and leaned into Jo's door as soon as it was opened.

"I figured you'd want this." Jo reached for the hat, careful to keep her fingers away from Sam's as she handed it over.

"It's freezing out here." Sam pulled her toque on then squeezed in beside the open door and eased it in against her back.

"Here, take my seat and jump inside until we sort ourselves out." Jo felt sorry for Sam in the cold. She struggled across the middle console, pinching her knees while trying to keep her boots in the air as she slid into the passenger seat.

"Oh my God, it's cold." Sam jumped into the driver's seat, slamming the door shut. "Is it just me and my southern blood or are you freezing too?"

"Have a sip of hot tea." Jo opened her vacuum bottle and offered the steaming beverage to Sam. "Sorry, but I forgot to bring an extra cup. We'll have to share. I hope that's okay."

"For sure." Sam took the thermos and sniffed the steam. "Oh, this feels good." She took a sip then flinched. "Ouch, it's boiling. I think I burnt my tongue."

"Then I guess you'll have to stick it in the snow." Jo fidgeted with her camera.

"As long as it's not yellow." Sam took another sip then handed the bottle to Jo and winked.

"Thanks." Jo took a sip of her own, careful to keep her tongue aside and lips away from where Sam's had just been. "It's not that bad." She put the lid back on. "Okay, let's head out and get this done."

The frigid air and frosted trees made them hustle through the dense bush, twigs snapping and grabbing onto their snowshoes as they searched for the small stand of old growth white pine marked as a value to be preserved from harvesting. Sam spotted the bright orange flagging tape first, waving an arm to point the direction.

"You have a good eye," Jo said. "I was the one who marked it so I can't believe you saw it first."

"You did a good job of marking it then," Sam said.

"Will you model for me while I take the pictures?" Jo looked for the best angle to capture the trees.

"That depends. It's too cold to take any clothes off."

Jo swatted at Sam's arm. "Not that kind of modeling. I need to get some perspective on how big the trees are."

"So you're just using me today." Sam smiled.

"Why not? I may as well take advantage of the situation before you try to take advantage of me."

"Is that an invitation?" Sam tilted her head toward Jo and blinked, her lashes covered in frost.

"Of course not." Jo frowned, avoiding Sam's eyes and blaming herself for the flirtation. She really needed to keep to her boundaries.

"Will you let me take a picture of you and Mollie?"

"To remember us by?"

"I'll never forget you. Picture or not." Sam smiled then confidently made her way to the old growth stand for the photograph. Once there, she turned around and waved. Jo snapped a picture. It would be a good one to remember Sam—a wave goodbye.

CHAPTER FIFTEEN

Jo hurried to take the required pictures, and then they sped home so she'd have the better part of the afternoon to put the presentation together. Sam spent the rest of the day curled up on the basement couch, the television on and channel surfing. She couldn't concentrate on anything and her stomach was starting to feel a bit upset. By the time Jo popped into the rec room, Sam was feeling drowsy and slightly fevered.

"I think I'm coming down with the flu or something," Sam said. That had to be it. There was no other reason she'd be feeling like this.

"Shit. I hope I didn't push you too hard this morning." Jo put a hand on Sam's forehead, her touch warm and soft. "Yep. You feel pretty hot."

"I was hoping to hear you say I'm hot." Sam closed her eyes and forced a smile.

"What do you think, Mollie? Should we throw some cold water on her?"

"Go ahead. I deserve it." Sam put her feet on the floor and struggled to sit up. "Wow, the room's spinning."

"Lie back down and I'll get you a blanket."

"Maybe I should just go up to my bed." Sam stood, her knees wobbly and feeling dizzy. "Oh God, I think I'm going to be sick."

"Here, use this if you're going to puke before you get there." Jo swung around and grabbed the small red and black fleece throw from the arm of the couch. She tossed it at Sam.

"Thanks." Sam buried her face in the fleece and rushed to the bathroom, slamming the door shut behind her in embarrassment. She hovered over the sink and studied her pale reflection in the mirror as her stomach churned. What was going on? She never got sick.

"Are you okay in there?" Jo tapped at the door, concern in her voice.

"I'll be fine." Sam dropped into the chair beside the shower stall, wondering if she'd ever be fine with her life again after meeting Jo.

"Okay. I'll be up in my office if you need me. Just shout." Jo's footsteps echoed up the stairs.

Sam's head dropped into her lap and she forced fingers through her hair, clutching her skull as though trying to squeeze out her distress. Falling for Jo had taken her by surprise. This was not her style. Was she really sick?

Sam's life was in Toronto, always had been, and she knew Jo's would forever be here, hours away in this northern nether region of Ontario. No wonder Jo was such a mess in this land of romantic desolation that Sam had chosen to exile in after dumping Trish. How ironic to meet the one person up here who could define her destiny. Could this be her land of opportunity? She needed to pull herself together and find out.

Jo focused on the morning's pictures, studying each one to see if there was sincerity in Sam's smile. She wanted to believe Sam was feeling the same strong pull that was keeping her distracted and dreading the end to whatever this was between them. And now Sam was feeling sick. Could it be a way to prolong her stay in Timmins?

Jo needed to stop thinking like this, because her increasing attraction to Sam was at risk of wreaking havoc on her otherwise tolerable life. Sam's life was in the city, and Toronto was so far away. A long-distance relationship would not be practical to even consider. A nine-hour drive each way in winter was too long, and flying back and forth on weekends would be prohibitively expensive. She loved the north and had promised to stay near her family. The only thing to do was help Sam get her vehicle out from the cottage then start preparing for the end of this winter diversion of lust and longing.

Later, as Jo put the finishing touches on her slide presentation, Mollie's squeaky toy started to sound. Sam was playing with her. Jo smiled as she pictured Mollie's excitement at pulling on the stuffed rooster. A break was long overdue. Jo headed to the basement.

"I'm happy to see you're feeling better." Jo perched on the arm of the couch near Sam's feet, as she lay cuddled up under the fleece throw.

Sam straightened up and patted the sofa cushion beside her. "Here, sit down, there's lots of room."

"Thanks, but I'll keep my distance. I can't afford to get sick." That was her excuse and she was sticking to it.

Sam rubbed her stomach. "It must have been something I ate. Probably that chicken I brought back from the cottage."

"Ah, that explains it. See, if you were vegetarian, you wouldn't have to worry about food poisoning from meat."

"No, just E. coli from fresh leafy greens." Sam smirked.

"Maybe we should have grilled cheese sandwiches for dinner, then." Sam had been kind in looking after her the other day with those egg salad sandwiches. Time to return the favor. She could probably use a bit of mothering, and it might help to make her feel better. "I'll whip up some tomato soup to go with them. How does that sound?"

"Perfect." Sam leaned forward to pat Mollie. Sam's hair was still damp from showering, and the scent of her peach shampoo teased Jo's nostrils. "Just like how I'm feeling right now. I'm so glad we met."

Jo looked away, focusing on her hands as they fidgeted in her lap. "I got confirmation from the grader operator he'll be out on your cottage road by two on Friday afternoon. We'll follow him in then get the rest of your stuff before heading back out."

"Perfect again." Sam's dimples brightened her smile. She could be so damn charming. "How much do I owe for that?"

"Nothing. He had to go out there anyway so it's no big deal." Jo's knees wobbled as she stood and readied to head back upstairs.

"It is a big deal for me. Everything you've done for me is a big deal and I'll never forget it."

"The pictures turned out great. I'll send you some for your memories."

"That would be nice." Sam came to stand near her, and gently took Jo's hands.

"I'll get supper going." Jo pulled her hands away then rushed up the basement stairs, heart thumping and breathing uneven as she escaped before changing her mind. The last thing she needed right now was to be close to Sam.

Dinner was ready by the time Sam came into the kitchen. Jo had set the table and all she had to do was serve up. She'd forced her thoughts back onto work and knew it was better this way. Her concentration needed to be on the job.

"This looks good." Sam took a seat and inhaled the steam coming off her hot soup. "Thanks for looking after me."

"Careful you don't burn your tongue." Jo tried to say it like a tease after the episode with the tea, but the words came out serious, like she was mothering Sam again.

"I will. I learned my lesson this morning." Sam smiled as she slurped, her lips barely touching the spoon.

"You might want to add a few soda crackers." Jo pushed the box toward Sam.

The rest of the meal consisted of light conversation and heavy sighs, mostly from Jo. She blamed it on her work and stress over the upcoming open house. Sam suggested she clean up the kitchen while Jo finalized her slide show. They agreed to meet in half an hour by the TV in the basement, where Jo would walk Sam through her presentation.

Mollie followed Jo to her office and sprawled on the beige wool rug by the desk. Jo knelt beside Mollie and rubbed her exposed belly, Mollie's tail thumping against the carpet. Jo was happy for their companionship. She could trust Mollie; she loved the way her dog delighted at her presence. She always felt in control with Mollie—dogs couldn't play mind games. She buried her face in Mollie's fur. Life without her dog would be untenable. Otherwise, she'd fall apart. Like she did when Jan left.

"Well, girl, I'd better get up off the floor and make sure my presentation is ready to go." Jo kissed Mollie then went in search of Sam.

Sam was excited to learn more about Jo's work. She'd always loved being in the bush and wanted a better understanding of forestry. She plopped on the basement couch in anticipation of sitting close to Jo during the presentation.

"Sorry I don't have any popcorn." Jo placed her open laptop on the coffee table in front of the couch and set it up to wirelessly project the slides on the television screen. "Thanks for being my audience during this dry run."

Sam rubbed her hands together. "It'll be just like the movies. I can't wait for the show to start."

"Don't get too excited. People always seem to get bogged down by intricate planning. I'm sure Mollie will be happy for some extra attention if you get bored during my talk."

"That's not going to happen. I may pet Mollie every now and then, but I'm super-interested in learning more about you and your work." Sam straightened up and leaned toward Jo.

Jo started off with an overview description of the ten-year forest management planning process. Sam saw passion take over almost immediately. The way Jo described the different stages with her hands, pointing to the slides and even pacing in front of the screen. By the end of it all, Sam had a much better understanding of Jo's work and wanted to know more.

Jo's level of competence was impressive, and Sam loved the way her voice rang out with enthusiasm for forestry. She was especially interested in the legislative framework guiding the process. She wanted to hear more about long-term management considerations to protect forest resources and land values for local cottagers like her.

"Developing a forest management plan is such a long process." Jo's cheeks had flushed, and she looked so cute as a strand of hair stuck out over her ear. "From start to finish we're legally obligated to abide by all kinds of regulations to ensure the sustainable development of our forest resources."

"As a cottage owner, I'd insist that my view of the forest isn't going to be wiped out by a nearby clear cut."

"For sure. We hope lots of cottage owners will come out Saturday and voice their concerns. These public open houses are an important part of the process and I always look forward to getting everyone's views." Jo took a seat beside Sam, drawing her legs up on the couch.

"What's your role in all of this?" Sam shifted, conscious of their legs almost touching. "Whose side are you on?"

Jo edged away. "I've been hired as an independent. My role is to ensure the sustainable development of this forest area by supporting all parties."

"How do you expect to do that?"

"By making sure all voices are heard. As my concluding slide says, the main goal of this forest management plan is to ensure the social, economic, and environmental needs of present and future generations are met. My role is to help facilitate that process."

"Who's paying your salary?"

Jo leaned forward to shut down her computer. "I have small contracts with a lot of the stakeholders. The government, the forestry company, a few cottage associations, and even one of the First Nation communities impacted by this harvest are clients of mine. That's why I love being independent. I don't like to take sides."

"Then why do you have such a strong position against letting your guard down around me?" Sam tried to move closer, but Jo stood up and backed away.

"Dammit, you don't get it, do you? I need to know there's a plan because without one, this forest would be fucked. What's your plan after Friday, when you can leave?"

"I want to be at your open house on Saturday. I want to spend more time with you, like this. I really enjoyed learning more about your work and want to…"

"It's getting late, Sam." Jo grabbed her laptop and marched to the stairs. "I have a lot more to do tomorrow to wrap things up for the open house."

"Jo, wait." Sam rushed to her side, but didn't touch her. "Please don't be upset."

Jo sighed. "I'm sorry. On Friday we'll head out in the early afternoon to get your vehicle and plan to be back by five. My mother's invited us over for dinner then, and I accepted. I hope you'll come along."

"For sure. I like your family." She paused, watching as Jo's eyes looked everywhere but at her. "I hope you have a good night's sleep."

"Thanks. You too." Sam watched Jo trudge up the stairs then listened as she went right into her bedroom and closed the door.

CHAPTER SIXTEEN

Jo followed close behind the big yellow grader as it plowed the way into Sam's cottage. Mollie slept on the backseat while Sam helped Jo navigate her truck through the narrow road.

"I see why having four-wheel drive can be handy up here," Sam said as she monitored her side of the vehicle to ensure they weren't getting too close to the ditch. "Thanks again for doing this, especially when you're so busy preparing for the open house tomorrow."

"No worries." Jo was gripping the wheel, her jaw tight and eyes focusing on the path of the grader. "It's a nice break for me and a good opportunity to get your vehicle plowed out."

"Everything about you seems to be a good opportunity for me. I wish I could do something to help you."

"So you're not remembered as an opportunist after you leave?" Jo meant to tease, but her words sounded sarcastic.

"If that's what you want to believe." Sam leaned her head against the passenger window and sighed.

When they got to Sam's cottage, the grader stopped, and Jo jumped out to exchange a few words with the operator, shouting over the roar of the idling engine. The driver was a middle-aged man with a beard, and Jo spoke in French with him to express her appreciation for taking a small diversion into Sam's cottage. It had been a while since she'd used her French and quite a few English words were mixed in. She almost felt ashamed at letting her French language skills slip. If she were to ever move anywhere else, she'd choose some remote community in northern Quebec where everyone spoke French. It would be much more appropriate than moving to Toronto.

Sam had stayed back at the truck with Mollie, but she suddenly appeared at Jo's side just as they'd finished their conversation. The grader engine revved as the blade dug into the snow.

"Thank you." Sam smiled and waved at the operator as he pulled away.

"Go ahead inside and gather up the rest of your things," Jo said. "I'll park and let Mollie out for a run."

Sam tapped Jo's arm. "I didn't know you were bilingual. You don't even have an accent when you speak English."

"I do when I speak French," Jo said. "At least, that's what I'm told by a lot of Francophones."

"What about your mother and Anna? Why don't you speak French with them?"

"I do sometimes, but we've gotten so used to speaking English with each other that we hardly ever speak in French. Come on, let's get a move on. I want to get off this road before dark."

"You can head back now if you like," Sam said. "I don't want to hold you up any more than I already have."

"We're driving out together. The road is treacherous. I'll need to pull you out if you slide into the ditch."

Sam stepped closer and looked at Jo with sparkling eyes. "You're so good to me, Jo. I really appreciate everything you're doing. Thank you."

Jo backed away from her. "You're welcome. I'll see you at the cottage in a few minutes." She swung around and trotted toward her truck.

Jo was afraid to step back into the place where they'd exchanged orgasms only a few days before. She'd thought about it during the drive out, remembering how good it felt and wondering if it would be so bad to do it again. No, she couldn't let it happen. Her feelings for Sam would become much more than just attraction. That would be a disaster because there was no future for them. She had to focus on serious business, like getting Sam's vehicle out of there. She got the shovel out of her truck and began to dig through the snow, knowing she needed to be in good form for the open house tomorrow. No fooling around allowed. Her boundaries were set.

Sam's breath burst out in cloudy puffs as she hurried around the frozen cottage to gather the rest of her clothing and food to transport out. A small electric heater hummed on high, but the air remained frigid, and there was no time for a fire in the woodstove.

"Your vehicle's cleared off and ready to go." Jo stepped inside, Mollie right behind. "My truck's beside yours in case you need a boost."

"I hope not. I have a block heater and plugged it in as soon as we got here."

"Good move. You're learning how to think like a northerner."

"And just how does a northerner think?" Sam smiled as she rubbed Mollie's cold fur.

Jo removed her mitts and wedged them under her left arm. "We always have to stay one step ahead of the weather. Why don't you give me your keys and I'll get it going for you?"

Sam smacked her head. "Oh fuck, I forgot my keys."

Jo's face reddened. "You, what? How could you forget your keys? You'll never get your truck out now."

Sam had wanted to tease Jo, lighten up the mood a bit, but Jo's reaction made her cringe. As if the woman didn't have enough stress in her life. Sam reached into her pocket and dug them out. "I guess it was a bad joke. I'm sorry."

"Jesus Christ. I should slap that hand of yours." Jo grabbed the keys. "I'll get it started while you finish up in here. Come on, Mollie."

"I'll hurry." Sam meant it too, as she rushed around gathering her belongings. It was the least she could do for Jo right now.

Jo's cheeks were flushed when she came back inside. Sam had her things by the door, all packed up and ready to go. There was a large black duffel bag on wheels, a few boxes of food: cereal, condiments, crackers, a brick of mozzarella cheese, four loaves of brown bread, frozen vegetables, packages of beef and chicken, two bottles of chardonnay and two of merlot, and a case of diet ginger ale. She was set for the month.

Jo struggled to pick up the bag. "A good thing your bag is on rollers. It weighs a ton."

"Let me help you." Sam grabbed one end and they carried it out together. "We can put it in the backseat."

"Nice set of wheels, by the way." Jo wedged her end of the suitcase onto the seat of Sam's warming vehicle. "Fitting for a lawyer from a big city like Toronto."

"You think so, eh?" Sam pushed, but her end of the bag wouldn't move onto the leather backseat of her new vehicle.

"Yep," Jo said as she went to the other side to pull.

"Just like your truck is fitting for a forester from a small town like Timmins?" Sam slid the bag all the way in as Jo tugged.

"Not at all." Jo shut her door and came around the vehicle. "My truck is a tool of my trade, not some status symbol like driving an expensive SUV in the city."

"Are you judging me?"

"Maybe." Jo walked past her toward the cottage. "I'll put your stash of wine in the cargo space where you can't access it."

"I thought we could share a bottle tonight for our anniversary."

Jo swung around. "Anniversary?"

"One week ago today, you and Mollie rescued me." Sam tried to close the gap between them.

"You mean your anniversary." Jo continued to the cottage and flung the door open. "You should look at this as a new beginning in your life. A chance to change your ways."

"Ouch," Sam said. "I'm not like that. I've always been monogamous in my relationships."

"Then why do you have such a one-track mind?" Jo's big mitts jammed against her parka as her breath sent clouds into the cold cottage.

"Is that how you see me? I'd love to have a long-term stable relationship with someone, but it's never worked out. They're not for me, I guess."

"Trying to have a fling with me will never get you the type of relationship you say you want."

"I know." Sam knew Jo didn't trust her. Probably never would. She sighed, afraid her voice might crack if she said anything else.

"Look, I find you attractive." Jo shook her head. "But I can't go there with you."

"I know." Sam turned away, afraid Jo might see the tears in her eyes. Time was running out and she really wanted to prove to Jo that this was different for her.

"I'll take these out now." Jo picked up the box with the wine and carried it outside.

Jo was waiting beside her truck with Mollie as Sam locked her cottage door for what would probably be the last time this winter. She felt defeated, wishing she could start over again with Jo. Why did she have to be such a jerk on that first day?

"Everything's locked up," Sam said as she petted Mollie.

"I'm sorry for sounding standoffish back there," Jo said, "but you'll be leaving soon and I'm afraid of getting too attached."

"Jo, you saved my life. We're already connected as far as I'm concerned. I don't want to hurt you. Ever."

"Good." Jo kicked her feet together, knocking snow off her big insulated boots. "You'll be gone by next week at this time anyway."

Sam crossed her arms. "Says who? Are you trying to get rid of me?"

"Well I thought…"

"You thought wrong. You're supposed to put me to work. I've had enough sitting around. I want to start reviewing whatever legal files you're thinking of."

"What about your job in Toronto?" Jo opened her rear truck door and Mollie jumped onto the backseat. "I can't afford to pay you what you're used to."

"You've already paid me more than enough. Besides, this isn't about money. I don't have to be back at work for another few weeks, so my services are yours until then." She'd beg to stay, if she had to.

"We'll talk about it later. We should get moving." Jo got behind the wheel of her truck. "I'll go first, but won't leave you behind if you get stuck."

"Thanks." Sam shut Jo's door then hurried to her warm SUV. She would follow Jo on this drive home, and perhaps anywhere after that.

CHAPTER SEVENTEEN

They made it back into town in good time. Sam unloaded her vehicle while Jo went straight to her office to finish a few details for the open house. She couldn't stop thinking about Sam. The way her eyes misted when accused of just wanting a fling, as though hurt at the suggestion. Could there be something more there? Sam wanted to stay longer even if she did make it clear she'd be heading back to work in a few weeks. Why wouldn't she just hightail it back to Toronto now, where she could have all kinds of flings?

Jo heard the basement stairs creaking, Mollie's tags clinking as she followed. Sam must have finished unpacking and was heading down to watch TV. She looked at her watch. It was almost five and time to head to her mother's for dinner. She called out to let Sam know she was ready to go and they left shortly afterward.

When they arrived, it was already dark, and Anna came to the door to greet them.

"Hurry in so you don't let the heat out." Anna gave each of them a hug as a buzzer went off in the warm kitchen and her mother took a casserole out of the oven. "You both look so tired and hungry. It's a good thing Mom's cooked a yummy dinner for you."

"Great! I'm *starving*." Jo kicked off her boots then went to greet her mother near the blasts of heat still coming from the open oven.

"Hi, dear." Her mother closed the oven door and gave her a big hug. "I made your favorite. There'll be some leftovers for you to take home."

"Mmmm. Macaroni and cheese." Jo could already taste the creamy dish with its hint of garlic. It was her mother's specialty and she'd never grow tired of it. "Perfect. Thanks, Mom. I can hardly wait to dig in."

"How's Sam?" Her mother looked over her shoulder while wedging a serving spoon into the cheesy dish.

"I'm great. Homemade mac and cheese is one of my favorites too." Sam rubbed her hands together as she approached the kitchen island and leaned against a stool.

"Can I get anyone a glass of wine?" Anna held up a bottle of chardonnay.

"Shoot," Sam said. "I forgot my bottle at home...I mean at Jo's."

"There was no need for you to bring wine," her mother said. "One bottle is enough for dinner."

"She had a bunch of bottles stashed at the cottage," Jo said to distract from Sam's comment about her place being home.

"So you're a bit of a lush then?" Anna raised her eyebrows toward Sam and hinted at a smile.

Sam laughed. "Hardly. There were only four bottles, and they were meant to last at least a month."

"We brought them back in this afternoon," Jo said. "Along with her vehicle and the rest of her stuff."

"I'm glad to hear you got everything out of there." Her mother handed her a bowl of buns. "These can go on the table." She turned back to Sam. "It's a good thing you ran into Jo. She has the connections when it comes to needing a bush road plowed."

"Yes indeed. If you'll excuse me, I'll wash up for dinner."

"Everyone can start dishing up now," her mother said. "I steamed some fresh broccoli for our vegetable."

"Thanks again, Mom." Jo washed her hands at the kitchen sink then scooped a big blob of mac and cheese onto her plate before plunking down at the table.

"Are you ready for tomorrow?" Anna tossed the lettuce salad and put some on her plate.

"Pretty much, but I want to go over my notes again tonight to make sure I have my facts straight." Jo reached for the salad, ignoring Sam as she sat down beside her.

"She's put together an amazing presentation," Sam said, her hands still damp and smelling like her mother's lavender soap.

"I'm anxious to see it," Anna said. "Mom and I'll pop by the open house around two tomorrow."

Jo rolled her eyes. "You really don't have to come. It's not like it's some school project that families have to support."

"Josephine, you're too modest." She hated it when her mother used her full name. It reminded her of being scolded as a child. "I'm looking forward to being the proud mother of a professional forester at this event."

"Will you be there, Sam?" Anna held a full fork of pasta midway between her plate and mouth.

"I wouldn't miss it for the world. It'll be a great learning opportunity, especially since I'm going to be doing some work for Jo next week."

"You are?" Jo cringed as her mother spoke, a big smile accompanying her chipper tone. "That's nice. What will she have you doing?"

"She wants me to cast my lawyer eyes on some of her files involving legal jargon." Sam broke a piece off her bun and began to dip it in her plate, her elbow almost hitting against Jo.

"So she's going to take advantage of you?" Anna grinned from Sam to Jo.

"Of course not," Jo said. "Sam doesn't have to hang around for that."

"I'm doing it because I want to," Sam said. "It's the least I can do, considering everything Jo's done for me."

"You're not indebted to me. You can leave whenever you want." Jo took more salad without offering the bowl to Sam before putting it back.

"I know."

The rest of the meal was relatively quiet as everyone was hungry and tired. Jo got ready to leave right after the dinner dishes were put away.

"Don't forget to take some leftovers with you," her mother said as she filled a glass-lidded bowl with pasta. "You can have some for a quick lunch before your busy afternoon tomorrow. And there's enough for Sam too."

"How kind," Sam said as she slipped on her boots. "Between you and your daughter, I feel so well taken care of."

"It's good to know your needs are being met." Anna winked at Jo.

Jo just wanted to get out of there. "Thanks for dinner, Mom. If you change your mind about coming tomorrow, don't worry about it. I won't be insulted."

"Maybe you wouldn't be insulted, but I'd be embarrassed not showing up." Her mother handed her the food and kissed her cheek. "Have a good sleep, dear, and try to relax."

"I have a lot on my mind right now," Jo said. "I can't wait until tomorrow night."

"Is Sam taking you out to celebrate?" Anna asked.

"Now that's a good idea." Sam almost chirped with excitement. "The two of you have to join us. It'll be my treat for all the good hospitality you've shown me."

"Oh, you don't have to do that," her mother said. "It's been a pleasure having you around and I hope you'll stay for a while."

"I'll be too tired to go out tomorrow night," Jo said matter-of-factly, in an effort to put an end to it. "Thanks for dinner, Mom. I'll see the two of you tomorrow."

Her truck was freezing inside as she backed it out of the driveway. They both shivered as the heater blasted on high and blew out air from the cold engine.

"You don't have to impress my mother, you know." Jo gripped the wheel.

"Is that what you think I was trying to do?"

"Wasn't it obvious? Making it sound like I'm taking care of your needs? Did you see the look Anna gave me? I'm going to have to pay for that comment when she gets me alone. What were you thinking offering to treat them to dinner with us when I'm going out of my mind with my work?"

"I'm sorry to have upset you, Jo." It bugged her that Sam's voice was so calm. "I'll try to be more careful in the future."

"That's all you have to say?" The words just blurted out. "Apologizing for upsetting me? Well there's no need to apologize for that. I'm fine and not worried about a future we don't have together."

"Yes, you are worried, or you wouldn't be so agitated."

"Don't try to analyze me." Jo stared out the windshield, her jaw tight. "If you must know, I'm fucking stressed right now. I have a big day ahead of me and nothing to wear tomorrow."

Sam burst out laughing. "You have a good sense of humor, Jo. I like that."

"I'm serious." She stifled a smile, suddenly relaxing with Sam's reaction. "I haven't had time to wash my favorite outfit and want to be comfortable with what I'm wearing."

"That's an easy fix," Sam said. "I'll put a wash on for you as soon as we get home."

"There you go again."

"What?" Sam's shadow shifted, and Jo knew she was being watched.

"Referring to my place as home when it's just a short-term place for you to stay. Your home is in Toronto."

"My house is in Toronto."

"So is your life."

"You mean my job." Sam's shadow shifted again, and Jo glanced to see her looking out the side window. "I want to live for the moment. I feel like my life is here right now, and I want us to have fun together."

"I'm a planner. I need to have things mapped out. I want to know where I'm going and that things are stable, especially where my life is concerned."

"Stability." Sam almost spat out the word. "It only works if you've found the love of your life or can exist in a tolerable state of unfulfilled passion."

Jo turned into her driveway and brought the truck to a racing stop. "Is that what you think I'm doing? Living in a world of denial?"

"You tell me." Sam undid her seat belt and turned to Jo. "Just because you have a plan in place doesn't mean it's the right one."

"And not having one is better? I'm not like you. I need to have a plan. Always."

"Always is a strong word, just like never." Sam leaned into the center console, her arms folded. "I think we're a lot alike. We certainly have two things in common: we're extremely attracted to each other and both scared as hell."

Jo flung her door open and scrambled out of the truck. "I need to let Mollie out."

CHAPTER EIGHTEEN

Citizens clustered in front of the monitor playing Jo's slide show, watching with interest. Attendance at the forest management plan open house was good. A number of concerned residents also studied the large maps and photos displayed around the room.

Jo was busy working the floor, laughing and talking with as many stakeholders as possible to get their views on what was being proposed for the block of Crown land slated for harvesting. She wore black wool dress pants, a royal blue sweater that brought out the beauty of her eyes, and black leather lace-up shoes—casual, but professional. Jo was undoubtedly the leader in the room.

Sam stood in a corner, admiring Jo from afar and impressed with her ability to address concerns. As Jo flawlessly flowed from one conversation to the next, her opinion was in high demand. Both government and company officials seemed to gravitate toward her when discussions with members of the public became heated and voices were raised. Jo was obviously their issue manager and problem solver.

Sam was awed and touched by Jo's modesty. Clearly an expert in her field, Jo gave her full attention to each individual she spoke with. She greeted everyone with a beautiful smile and lengthy handshake to make a personal connection. Sam felt a connection too, her stomach twirling each time Jo looked her way.

Julia and Anna entered the hall together, both undoing scarves and coats as they navigated their way toward Sam. It was just after two in the afternoon and the forum had been underway for a little more than an hour.

"Looks like a good turnout," Julia said as she gave Sam a quick hug. "Jo was worried the place would be empty."

"She's amazing," Sam was pleased with Julia's warm hug, sensing the woman really liked her. Maybe even thought she was good for Jo. "The way she set things up this morning and is taking charge of the room right now is impressive. She'd make a good defense lawyer."

"My little sister's always had a way of reaching out and being good at whatever she does," Anna said, draping her coat over a chair.

Julia put her coat on top of Anna's. "I'm going to have a look around. I see a few people I want to say hi to." She headed across the room.

"Jo's finally gotten her life back together and it's nice to see her spending time with you," Anna said, guiding Sam over to the refreshments table. "Please tell me you're going to stick around for a while."

"That's the plan." Sam kept her eyes on Jo.

"It's good to hear you're a planner too," Anna said as she got a coffee, her spoon clinking against the mug.

"I'm not, really." Sam turned to Anna, sensing a hesitation in the way she stirred her coffee longer than necessary. She put her water bottle down on the refreshment table to tidy up a few stray napkins and used sweetener packets. "I met your son the other day. He's very polite. You've done a good job raising him."

"Thanks." Anna's spoon finally clanked into the metal canister labeled for dirty ones. "Jo has always planned out her life and likes to be prepared for what could be ahead."

"Yes, I know that having a plan in place is important to her." Sam picked up her water bottle and took a drink, knowing she'd just been warned.

"Good. I'd hate for my little sister to get hurt."

"Me too. Is there anything else you want to say to me while we're alone?"

Anna patted Sam's arm with her free hand and smiled. "I think you're great for Jo right now. Her eyes haven't lit up like that in a long time. I can see sparkles in yours when you look at her."

"Meeting Jo has been one of the best things to happen to me in a long time." Sam smiled as she peered across the room, where Jo was by herself tidying up some papers next to one of the binders.

Anna tugged at Sam's sleeve. "Come on with me while I go say hi to her."

"Hey you two." Jo beamed as they approached. There had been a small break between conversations with stakeholders so the timing for a quick chat was good.

"Good job, sis." Anna hugged Jo. "The place looks great and everyone seems engaged."

"Thanks. Sam, if you're getting bored you could probably leave with Mom and Anna. I can pick you up afterward at Mom's."

"For sure," Anna said. "I have my car. I'm dropping Mom off at home after this. I'm sure she'd love the company."

"I'll be fine," Sam said. "I'm really enjoying this. I've always loved people watching. The dynamics in the room are quite interesting."

"In what way?" Jo's head tilted toward her.

"Just look at everyone," Sam said, waving the water bottle around as she spoke. "They're all so engaged, whether it's with the displays or in conversation."

"Sam's right," Anna said. "Even Mom. Look at her over there by one of your maps. The way she's talking and pointing at it, you'd think this was her show."

"That's what I find so impressive about all this," Sam said. "Everyone seems to be having their say, whether they're dressed in business suits or wearing snow pants and flannel shirts."

"That's how these open houses are supposed to work," Jo said. "We want to hear from all stakeholders."

"Of course you do," Sam said, "but open houses for public consultation can be challenging to pull off. Kudos to you for doing such a good job here."

"Thanks, but putting this together had a lot more players than just me. We're a good team."

"And you're a good leader."

"Oh, I don't know about that." Jo shuffled a few papers.

"Well, I do, because it's been obvious since this show got on the road." Sam crossed her arms. "You're clearly the leader this afternoon and in high demand for your opinion."

"I'm just the hired help. Look, I should get back. Let me know if you change your mind about leaving."

"I won't." Sam flashed a smile and winked at Jo before turning away.

"See what I mean?" Anna said.

"About what?" Sam followed her to the computer displaying Jo's electronic presentation.

"It's like I didn't even exist back there once the two of you got talking. There was enough eye twinkling and sparkling to put on a fireworks display."

The open house ended at four, but people stayed around chatting until almost five. Sam sat patiently in a corner while Jo ushered the last of the stragglers out of the room. Cleanup would be done on Monday morning, so Jo locked the doors to the community center and they headed home for the night.

"I'm exhausted," Jo said as she sat in the passenger seat of her truck. "I'm so glad it's over."

"You should feel really good about this afternoon." Sam pulled out of the parking lot, grinning at Jo relaxing against the headrest. "I ordered us a pizza for dinner."

"Sounds great. Thanks. I think I'll have a hot bath after supper to help unwind."

"That sounds like a good plan. I bought some bubble bath the other day." Sam had picked it out in hopes Jo would enjoy it in her deep bathtub. "I think you deserve a little treat tonight."

Jo closed her eyes. "Thanks."

The vegetarian pizza wolfed down and Mollie content on the living room rug, Sam handed Jo the bottle of pink bubble bath. "I hope you like the smell of strawberries."

Jo opened the lid and put the bottle to her nose, the mixture almost sweet enough to taste. "Mmmm. It smells nice."

"Let me know when you're covered in bubbles and I'll bring you a glass of red wine."

"Thanks." Jo kept her gaze glued to the bottle, her hands trembling as she read the label. "Strawberry and kiwi fragrance. Sounds nice. I can take my glass of wine now, so you don't have to deliver it."

"I need to open the bottle and want to let it air a bit before pouring. If you're worried about me seeing you naked…"

"I'll be covered in bubbles. You won't see anything." Jo shuffled toward her bedroom, letting on that Sam seeing her in the tub meant nothing. "A glass of wine would be nice, if you can drop one off without expecting anything else."

By the time Sam tapped on her en suite door, Jo was luxuriating in a hot strawberry-and-kiwi-scented bath. She'd used more than half the bottle and her tub was overflowing with bubbles.

"You're safe to come in now." Jo stifled a giggle, nervous with excitement. What was she doing?

"Am I?" The door slid open and Sam's eyes glowed in the candlelit bathroom as she studied the bath big enough for two. Jo was covered up to her neck in bubbles. She noted a slight tremble in Sam's hands as she knelt beside the tub and put the glass of red wine on the edge.

"I'm glad to see you have your clothes on." Jo was half hoping Sam would be naked.

"There are lots of bubbles." Sam dipped a finger in the white foam. "I should have watered the bottle down before giving it to you."

"Then I wouldn't have let you in," Jo said, conscious of Sam's fingers swirling close to her breast.

"How's the water temperature?" Sam's hand slid under the water, brushing up against Jo's skin and working its way down.

"Hot." Jo's breath caught. "Sam, please don't…"

"Sorry." Sam's hand retreated, her fingers folding into a fist. "I shouldn't have…"

"Please don't stop." Jo's boundaries came crashing down. Feeling Sam's touch was all that counted as her uneven breathing transformed the moment. Hips lifting off the tub bottom, nothing else mattered. "I want you to touch me. I need you to touch me."

"Yes. Oh yes." Sam's fingers slid down Jo's stomach, through her tuft of hair and into the center of her arousal. "You feel so good, Jo. You make me feel so good. I want to make love to you."

"Your fingers are magic." Jo held her breath, hips thrusting in the water and climax clawing its way to the top until she let out her breath in a sustained moan that brought Mollie rushing into the room.

"You're beautiful." Sam leaned in for a kiss on the lips, but Jo turned away.

"I can't Sam." She started to cry, feeling like she'd just betrayed herself for a quick thrill. "You're leaving soon, and I can't handle anything more. Please leave me alone now."

"I want to make love with you, Jo." Sam's voice was shaky.

Jo tucked her chin in her shoulder next to the wall, hiding her face in shame. She fought off tears, the pain in Sam's voice not really registering.

"I'm going for a shower then getting into my bed without any clothes on," Sam tenderly kissed Jo's back. "Please sleep with me tonight. I need you."

By the time Sam closed the door on her way out, Jo knew she'd just been horrible. She owed Sam.

CHAPTER NINETEEN

Sam had tears in her eyes as the shower's warm water soaked her face. Weak knees, knotted stomach, and aching groin, she lathered peach shampoo in her hair as though massaging her scalp would somehow alleviate the pain of desire. What she really needed was a cold shower to dampen the longing for Jo that was threatening to burn up her insides.

What was she doing, falling for this woman so far away from home? The way Jo had handled herself at the open house deserved an award for professional excellence. Sam knew she was good at her job, too, always demanding attention from everyone in the courtroom as she argued her case, but not like Jo, who didn't have to prove anything.

People gravitated to Jo, captivated by her and her knowledge. It was as though Jo was the judge in that forum. Her decisions set precedence amongst the forest stakeholders as they tried to reach consensus.

The shower door clicked open and Sam froze, shampoo and water blinding her. A gust of cool air wafted into the stall then Jo was there, her hands sliding over Sam's breasts and body.

"Thank you for today, Sam." Jo's warm body wrapped around Sam from behind, her hands sliding down her stomach and between her legs.

"Oh, Jo." Sam tried to turn around, hardly able to breathe.

"Just relax," Jo whispered, her lips brushing Sam's ear as adept fingers coaxed an orgasm. "I want you to experience the thrill you just gave me."

Sam clung to the shower wall, both hands gripping the slippery tiles while Jo's fingers circled as though folding in whipping cream for a decadent recipe. Sam stopped breathing, her body consumed with Jo's touch. She wanted this woman—more than anyone before. When Sam came, it was sudden and hard. Her legs wobbled, and she collapsed into Jo, strong arms keeping her from falling to her knees.

"You're...amazing, Jo." Sam could barely breathe, her feelings for this woman so raw, pure, and blissful. She had to say something. "This afternoon...I was so proud of you...and now... That was incredible. I think I'm..."

"I need to walk Mollie." Jo let go and was gone before Sam could stop her.

Sam leaned against the shower wall, her legs wobbly and barely able to hold her up. Again, Jo had touched something in her that no woman had ever reached before. All without so much as a kiss on the lips, yet full of an intimacy that was surely reserved for those in love.

By the time Sam finished in the shower, Jo was already outside with Mollie. She thought about getting dressed and following them into the cold, but decided to give Jo some space. Or maybe she was the one who needed a bit of time on her own.

She'd almost told Jo she was falling in love with her. They'd only known each other for just over a week and yet she felt closer to Jo than lovers she'd spent years with.

But her life was in Toronto, and beckoning her back. She missed the adrenaline rush of commanding the attention of a courtroom. The senior partner in her firm had sent an email saying they were swamped and hoped she could return sooner than expected. Maybe it would be best if she planned to leave early next week before Jo kicked her out. Or she couldn't leave.

Sam fired off an email to Trish giving the heads-up she may be back at the house in a few days. Her heart pounded at the thought of leaving so soon, but she had to keep some semblance of her professional self intact. She dreaded sharing the place with her ex, but would have to put up with it until the week before Valentine's Day, when Trish was to move out.

Sam would demand the master bedroom. After all, she owned the house and she wasn't in the mood to mingle with an ex. She'd only need to add a microwave to complement the en suite bath and television to make her room more like a bachelor apartment than the home it was supposed to be. One that she hoped Jo would visit.

Sam was sitting on her bed, about to settle in for the night with one of Jo's books on forest management planning, when the outside door burst open with a whoosh. Stomping feet rushed into the kitchen.

"Sam!" Jo cried out. "I need your help! Mollie's been hit by a car!"

Sam threw the book down and ran to the kitchen. Jo's face was covered in tears and her breathing was heavy as she rummaged through the closet.

Sam's heart pounded as she raced to the door. "I'll get on my boots. Where is she?"

"In the snowbank at the road. Can you bring a light?" Jo grabbed an old jacket and rushed back outside, leaving Sam to follow on her own.

Mollie's eyes were closed, but she was breathing when Sam got to her side. Jo had placed the jacket over Mollie. "It's okay, girl." Tiny balls of ice were forming on Jo's eyelashes, tears freezing on her cheeks as she leaned over Mollie. Her red-knuckled bare hands were on Mollie, traveling her body in the search for injuries.

"Is she going to be okay?" Sam slid to her knees.

"She has to be." Jo's voice trembled. "Hang in there, Mollie. We're going to get you help."

Sam shone her light around Mollie's head and noticed a small patch of blood in the snow. "She must be bleeding. There's a bit of blood in the snow by her mouth."

Jo sniffed as she leaned over to have a look. "How did I miss that?" She examined Mollie's head and mouth. "I think she just bit her tongue on the impact. Can you shine your light closer?"

Sam leaned closer as Jo's fingers held up Mollie's jowls to have a better look. "Is there an emergency vet line we can call?"

"Yes, but I'll have to go back to the house and get the number." Jo jumped to her feet. "Can you stay here with her while I run back?"

"Of course. I won't leave her." At least they were well off the road, lit up by Sam's phone in case a vehicle came by.

Heavy footsteps raced up the driveway. Sam stared at Mollie in shock. She lay against the side of a snowbank, her eyes closed and almost lifeless except for her shallow breathing.

"Hey, girl," Sam whispered at her ear, afraid to touch her in case she had broken bones. "It's going to be okay. Please don't die. Jo needs you."

The roar of Jo's truck engine starting and a flash of headlights beaming down the driveway signaled they would be heading into town. Jo jumped out of the vehicle, phone against her ear and talking as she opened the rear door. "Okay, we'll meet you there as soon as we can."

"Do you have a board or something to put under her?" Sam asked. "It'll be easier to lift her and helpful if there's broken bones."

Jo knelt beside Mollie, kissing her head. "I don't have one in the truck. I didn't feel any broken bones. We can slide her onto my coat and lift her together, like a stretcher. I'll climb in with her and stay in the back while you drive, if that's okay."

"Her eyes are opening." Sam smiled, a sob escaping. "Hey, girl. You're such a good dog, Mollie. You helped save my life and now I'm going to help save yours."

"She's not going to die." Jo's face hovered over Mollie's glistening right eye as she carefully tucked her coat underneath the dog. "Good girl, Mollie. Just a little bit more and we'll get you settled. Ready, Sam?"

"Just say when and I'll follow your lead."

They cradled Mollie in Jo's parka and lifted her. Jo stepped in backward, sliding Mollie toward her along the seat and supporting the dog's head in her lap. Sam closed the door and took to the wheel.

"I don't have my wallet," Sam said as she eased the truck forward.

"Neither do I," Jo said. "We'll have to call my mother. Her number's programmed into the truck."

By the time they arrived at the vet's office, Julia was waiting for them in the parking lot. She got out of a small car and huddled under the hood of her bulky jacket. She opened the rear truck door as soon as Sam brought it to a stop.

"You poor girl." Julia reached inside and touched Mollie's fur. "I think the vet's here already. There are lights on and another car's in the parking lot."

"We need to get her inside," Jo said. "Sam, can you help me? And Mom, can you let the doctor know we're here?"

Mollie stood up, wiggled her way past everyone and jumped out of the truck then began to sniff around the parking lot.

"Mollie!" Jo leapt toward the dog, grabbed onto her collar and gripped it. "Sam, can you get me her leash please?"

"She must have been knocked out," Julia said. "How did this happen? How could a car hit her? I know you're always so careful with her."

"I feel so guilty," Jo said, her voice shaking. "I let her go for a run. There must have been a rabbit and she chased it out to the road just as someone was speeding by. I heard an awful yelp and by the time I got to her, the vehicle was gone and Mollie wasn't moving."

"It wasn't your fault," Sam said, hooking up Mollie's leash. "Blame the bastard who hit her and didn't even stop. Did you see who it was?"

"No." Jo shook her head, tears glistening in the light. "It was too dark and all I cared about was getting to Mollie."

"Of course. Let's get her examined by the vet." Sam put an arm around Jo as they went inside.

CHAPTER TWENTY

Jo sighed in relief, gripping Mollie's blue flat collar as they left the vet's office. Mollie was going to be okay. She only had a slight concussion and small bump on her head. Aside from a hefty bill, the vet determined that the injury was minimal and Mollie was sent home.

"Would you like to come over for a cup of tea?" her mother asked once they were outside. It had started to snow, and their vehicles were dusted.

"Mom, I can't bring Mollie there unless you have Felix locked up. Especially tonight of all nights."

Her mother brushed a mitt across the layer of snow on her car. "I'll keep him in my bedroom. What do you think, Sam?" She grinned. "Or are you ready for bed, considering you're in your pajamas?"

"I was hoping nobody noticed." Sam reached inside Jo's vehicle for the big snowbrush and began to clean off Julia's car.

Jo carefully helped Mollie onto the backseat of her truck and closed the door. "I think we should just head home. It's been a long day and I'm exhausted."

"Of course, dear." Her mother gave her a reassuring hug and kiss on the cheek. "I heard a lot of good things about you this afternoon. People really appreciate how you care about what happens to the forests around here."

Jo pulled her coat closed, the cold air bringing on a chill. "Everyone I spoke to cares about the sustainability of our forests. Whether it's cutting trees to create jobs or leaving stands to protect wildlife habitats. We're a resource town and have to preserve the wealth in our bush."

"Said so eloquently." Sam smiled as she put the snowbrush away. "Would you like me to drive us home?"

"Yes, please." Jo opened the door and got in beside Mollie. "I'll drop by tomorrow, Mom, and pay you for the vet bill."

"Oh, there's no hurry for that." Her mother reached in and stroked Mollie's back. "I'm so glad you're okay."

Jo put an arm around Mollie. "Me too. Thanks so much for meeting us here, Mom. Drive safely." Jo closed her door and soon they were all on their way.

"How's Mollie doing?" Sam's voice was almost a whisper as she drove.

"She's falling asleep." Jo yawned, fighting off exhaustion. "So am I. Consider yourself lucky you already have your pajamas on and can just jump into bed."

"I guess." Sam paused, her eyes sparkling in the rearview mirror as the lights from another vehicle glared by. "If only it was your bed I was getting into…"

"Sam." Jo sighed, closing her eyes. She wanted to forget the last few hours. "I can't go there right now. You know that."

"No, I don't." Sam eased the truck to a stop in front of Jo's house and put it into park, but left it idling. Her hands stayed on the steering wheel. "What happened in the shower tonight was just so amazing, like the last time at the cottage. I can't stop thinking about you."

"I don't have anything more to give right now." Jo avoided Sam's gaze in the rearview mirror. "I really like you, Sam, but that's not enough."

"Not enough for what?" Sam turned around, her head between the two seats as her arms rested on the console.

"To make love with you." Jo felt numb as she finally answered and opened her door. "Ready to head inside, Mollie?"

"Are you afraid to fall in love with me? Or have you already?" Sam reached over to touch her, but Jo leaned away.

"Is that what you want? Just before going back to Toronto? Is that what turns you on? Loving and then leaving?"

"No, Jo. That's never what I've wanted. I've always longed for more. It's just that I've never met anyone like you before and…"

"Look, Sam, I almost lost Mollie tonight." Jo sniffed, her head down as she avoided Sam's eyes. "I don't know what I'd do without her. I can't handle anything more right now. I can't." Jo jumped out of the truck and marched to the house, Mollie in tow.

When Sam got inside, Jo was sitting on the living room area rug, petting Mollie, and staring at the bamboo flooring. Sam stooped to her knees, kissed Mollie, and then reclined near the edge of the mat. Her fingers nudged Jo's.

"I'm here for you tonight, Jo." She moved her hand back. "This isn't about sex or love or anything else. I'll just hold you if that's what you need, or leave you alone if you want. But whatever happens tonight, please know that I care a lot about you and…" Sam's voice started to shake, her hand grasping Mollie's fur. "I'm sorry. It was my fault she got hit tonight."

"You weren't even outside with us." Jo shifted, but kept her hands on Mollie. "How can you say that?"

"I pushed you. Call it hormones if you like, but I'm so attracted to you, and I know I upset you. Those bubbles broke me. When I saw you covered in them, I just had to touch and feel to see if you were as aroused as me. I always have to push the limit, even when I know things could be risky."

"Is that why you were on the ice, believing you could walk on water that's not quite frozen?" Jo glared at Sam. "What the hell were you thinking out there, putting your life in danger like that?"

"I don't know." Head drooping, Sam tried to hide her tears. "I felt like shit and needed some fresh air. I wasn't thinking. Or maybe I didn't care."

"Just like tonight, and all the other times you've tried to seduce me? Am I your fresh air?"

"Yes." Sam saw pain in Jo's eyes, her words not coming out right. "I mean no. It's not like that with you. Meeting you has been one of the best things to happen to me."

"Give me a break. You started making advances almost from the moment we met. I was one of the best things to happen to you that day because I pulled your sorry ass off the ice. And after that, I was forced into your bed, stranded in the bush with no way out. Another checkmark for you."

"No. It's not like that." Sam touched Jo's fingers again, desperate to convince her. "I'm really falling for you Jo, and Mollie. I love her and…"

Jo pulled her hand away. "Lots of people love my dog. Maybe you should get your own golden retriever once you get back to Toronto."

"Jo, please." Sam tried to find the blue eyes. "That's not what this is about."

Jo stood. "This is my living room and not some courtroom where you're trying to convince a jury. I won't be persuaded into having a fling with you and then sentenced to another heartbreak once you leave."

Sam sprang to her feet. "That's not what I want. Breaking your heart is not part of the plan. Re-igniting a fire in your heart is."

"Fuck you."

"That's the second time you've said that to me." Sam's jaw tightened with frustration. "If you really wanted me to fuck off, you'd have sent me on my way by now."

Jo swung around. "Are you willing to quit your fancy job in Toronto and move to Timmins? So we can be together?"

"What about you moving to Toronto?"

"Never. I'm not leaving my family. I don't need to start a fire in my heart because it's fine the way it is."

Sam moved closer, hands at her sides and resisting the urge to do more. "Oh, Jo, you of all people should know that's not good enough."

"Yes, it is." Jo backed away, her lips trembling.

"You've shown nothing but caring since I met you. You're genuinely concerned about Mollie, your mother, Anna, and even me. I've felt more caring since I met you than I ever got from my own mother. You, your dog, and your family make me feel special in a way I've never felt before. I like it, and I like being with you the most."

Jo played with her hair, shaping it into a ponytail then letting it drop as she looked away. "Look Sam, I like you, too, and so does my family, including my dog. I wanted to stop you tonight, but it was too late. I knew you'd try something if you came into my bathroom with a glass of wine and I let it happen. I let you do what I was planning to do to myself and it was wrong of me. I'm sorry."

"I bet it felt a lot better than if you'd done it yourself." Sam wiped her nose, hopeful they could work this through. "The little visit from you in my shower sure did for me."

"Can we just put this behind and be friends?" Jo yawned. "It's been such a long day and I want to start out fresh tomorrow."

Sam was desperate to keep things amicable with Jo. She just wanted this awkwardness to end. "Sounds good. Let's shake on it and I'll make you some pancakes for breakfast."

"That would be yummy." Jo smiled as her warm hand folded into Sam's. "Nice pajamas, by the way. I'm glad you kept them on tonight. The polar bears fit in quite well at the vet's office. And so did you. I really appreciated your help tonight. Have a good sleep."

CHAPTER TWENTY-ONE

The snowmobile sliced through fresh snow, Sam clinging to Jo as they broke trail along the pristine surface in the middle of a large meadow. If ever there was a winter wonderland, Sam had found it. A fluorescent-blue sky highlighted clear weather, a shining sun brightened the day, and glittering fresh snow created a field of diamonds. But what made it even more magical was holding onto Jo as they sped through this frosty paradise.

Breakfast included blueberry pancakes, real Ontario maple syrup, coffee, raspberry yogurt, and a touch of happiness. Mollie seemed to be herself, and Jo acted as though everything was back to usual, if ever there was a normal with them.

It was a beautiful Sunday afternoon, so Jo had offered to show Sam how much fun the great outdoors could be this far north. Even when the temperature was at its most frigid and nearly everyone wanted to stay indoors, Jo seemed in her element with the fresh frigid air, glistening snow, and gorgeous blue sky. Sam snuggled closer to Jo's back. She could get used to this.

Jo pressed the throttle as they veered into a turn and began to sink. The track started to spin, and the machine bogged down to a stop, half buried in the fresh drift. Sam fell into Jo and they both ended up on the ground beside the stalled machine, covered in snow.

Jo laughed, removing her helmet. "Sorry. I should have known better than to try making a curve that tight. We'll have to dig ourselves out."

"I can't believe how reckless you were at the controls." Sam clung to Jo's back, spooning her in the snow.

"You can let go now." Jo moved to get up. "There's nowhere else to fall and you'll soon feel a chill if you stay there like that."

"How are we going to get ourselves unstuck?" Sam struggled to her feet, her bulky boots and borrowed snowmobile suit restricting movement in the deep snow.

"You tell me." Jo retrieved a small folding shovel from the snowmobile and began to hurl snow.

"It looks like you've already figured it out." She pulled up her visor and smiled. "That was fun."

Jo stopped digging. "I'm glad you think so. Now let's see if we can get ourselves out of this mess and head to some groomed trails."

"Tell me what you need me to do," Sam said, wishing for much more enlightenment than just getting the snowmobile unstuck.

"You can help push the machine if necessary, but otherwise stand back while I take a run for it." Jo straddled the seat and started the engine. She squeezed the throttle, the motor roaring and exhaust fumes rising as she bounced on the machine to make it go. Her ability to face adversity was admirable, like a goddess, or a warrior. If only Sam could somehow prove that she wanted so much more than a casual fling with this special person. Time was running out.

The track spun, sending snow upward, as though trying to reverse nature and hurl it back into the sky. Body swaying, Jo rose out of the hole and whirred across the field to create one large circle as she swung back to Sam.

"Jump on." Jo shouted over the roaring engine. "I want to take you for a ride through our beautiful bush before you head back to your concrete city."

Sam snuggled up behind Jo, comfortable in being taken for a ride. She closed her eyes and held onto the moment, Jo's body tight against hers as they headed for the trails.

Her return to the city was getting closer; she dreaded telling Jo about her plans to leave early Wednesday morning. That meant a little more than two days and three nights were left to share a proper kiss and make love. She desperately needed to do this, to somehow have a breakthrough that could open a whole new world of possibilities.

Jo slowed the snowmobile as they pulled into an unbroken trail, thick with overgrown branches smacking against them as they meandered through the trees. Sam hoped Jo was taking her to some special oasis, hidden from the path where they would have the place to themselves. Sure enough, the bush opened up—their own private sanctuary.

"Wow, this is nice." Sam got off and stood by the snowmobile, sipping steaming tea from a cup Jo offered her. She stared out at the natural opening bordered by a dense stand of snow-tipped cedars. "Is this a small lake in summer?"

"No, it's covered in grass and moss. It's a bog, actually." Jo sat sideways on the black vinyl seat, her feet resting on the running board, holding her mug of tea on her knees. "I wish I could show you in the summer. It has one of my favorite plants in it."

"Oh, and what's that?" Sam kicked the foot of Jo's boot.

"The pitcher plant. It's so neat. It has this amazing ability to make ice cubes in the fall."

"Ice cubes in the fall?"

"Its leaves are like little cups and fill with water." Jo squeezed over and motioned for Sam to sit. "Indigenous peoples used them as drinking cups when they were out in the forest."

Sam grinned as she snuggled in beside Jo. "It's too bad there's so much snow right now or I'd try drinking my hot tea from one of the leaves."

"If you did, you might get some extra protein in your drink," Jo said. "Pitcher plants are actually carnivorous. They eat bugs."

"No shit. How can they do that?"

"They trap insects in the stiff hairs at the top of the leaf openings then push the bugs down and release secretions to dissolve them."

"What do they look like?"

"Kind of like a vagina, if you ask me." Jo's response surprised Sam, especially the way she stood up and laughed. "I've never said that to anyone before, usually because I'm always out here with guys, but they kind of do. There's stiff hair at the top and the hole is smooth."

Sam was at a loss for words, wondering if Jo was joking or trying to flirt. She stood and tossed the rest of her tea in the snow then faced Jo. "Have you ever had a vagina ice cube?"

"Yes, I have, and they're delicious, bugs and all." Jo put on her helmet, but Sam caught her blush.

Sam smiled as she pulled on her helmet. "Thanks for bringing me here. I can just imagine how beautiful it must be in the summer. I hope you'll bring me back here again in July or August."

"If you come back, sure." Jo jumped on the machine. "I think we should head home now and check on Mollie."

"Yes, please." Sam climbed on and wrapped her arms around Jo. "I have to pee so the sooner we get there, the better."

"Hang on then! I can't have you wetting yourself in my new snowsuit." Jo started the engine, took one loop in the bog to turn the machine around then headed toward home.

Sam clung to Jo, more determined than ever to kiss her when they got back. Maybe they'd even make love; Jo's reference to the vagina plant seemed almost like she was thinking of it too.

Mollie was outside when they roared up to the house, Anna and Julia stood in the kitchen window. Sam's heart sank.

"Hey, Mollie." Jo rushed to the dog, removing her helmet on the way and shaking those sexy blond curls Sam ached to touch. "How are you feeling?"

"She's looking much better." Sam knelt beside Jo and kissed the top of Mollie's head. "I didn't know your mother and Anna were coming over."

"Neither did I," Jo said. "Oh, Mollie, I'm so glad you're okay." Jo gave the dog a hug, then stood up and looked at the house. "How nice of them to drive out for a visit. They probably wanted to check on Mollie. I'll invite them to stay for dinner. I have a frozen lasagna I can put in the oven."

"Sounds good." Sam followed Jo inside, discouraged at the sudden change in dinner plans. She needed to know how Jo felt, and she certainly couldn't do that with family around.

CHAPTER TWENTY-TWO

Jo removed the vegetarian lasagna from the oven, her thoughts nowhere near the meal she was preparing. Sam sat at the kitchen table, chatting away with her mother and sister, relaying how much she'd enjoyed the snowmobile ride. It seemed so genuine, the way her animated voice described getting stuck, and then raved about the cedar bog.

The caring way she had helped with Mollie—Jo shuddered to think of what would have happened had Sam not been there. Then there was their discussion before bed last night. It was as though Sam was trying to profess her love, almost begging for a chance. Maybe she really was interested in forging a relationship.

Anna approached Jo, rolling up her sleeves to wash her hands at the kitchen sink. "I'll slice the garlic bread."

"That'd be great."

Her mother's chair slid out from the table. "What can I do to help?"

"You can toss the salad," Anna said. "I'll bring it to the table so you can stay sitting with Sam."

"You must think I'm a lazy slug." Sam had her feet up on a chair.

"Not at all." Jo's mother stirred the salad, utensils clinking against the bowl. "I know what snowmobiling in the cold can do to your body if you're not used to it." Her mother really liked Sam. She'd never used that nurturing tone with Jan. "I bet you're anxious for bed tonight."

Sam straightened, her feet dropping to the floor as though caught being naughty. "Yes, I am." Her voice had a slight squeak as she ran a hand through her hair. "I'm relieved Mollie seems to be back to normal."

"Thank God." Her mother smiled as she bent over to pet Mollie. "Poor dear. Nana's glad you're feeling better after being smacked by that big, bad truck. Josephine, did you notify the police about the hit and run last night?"

Argh. Why did she have to use her full name?

"She refused," Sam said. "I tried to get her to call this morning, but she still blames herself."

"Were you driving the truck that hit Mollie?" The slight click of Anna's tongue added aggravation to her ridiculous question.

"Of course not." Jo jabbed a knife into the lasagna. Everyone was ganging up on her. "I had her outside without a leash. I should have known better, especially since she gets so crazy when there's a rabbit around."

"You should have at least reported it." Anna brought the bread to the table. "I hope the bastard has a big dent on his truck."

Jo shoved a spatula in the lasagna, breaking apart the first piece as she lifted it onto a plate. "From now on, Mollie will always be on her leash. I'm through taking risks. It's not worth it if she could be gone just like that." She snapped her fingers. "Everything's ready."

"This smells so good, Jo." Sam approached the stove, her voice cheery as though clueless that Jo's snapping fingers were meant for her. "I can hardly wait to dig in." Jo kept her focus on the lasagna. Sam's words weren't about the food at all.

"Me too," Anna said as she took her piece and shuffled back to the table. "There's something about these cold days that brings on a healthy appetite. We can't stay long, though. I have a big week ahead at work."

Jo plopped a piece on Sam's plate, then took the broken piece for herself and headed to the table. She plunked her plate down in the vacant spot beside Sam and sat. "Dig in everyone."

"Let's start with a toast." Her mother held up her wine.

"Yes, let's make it to Mollie." Sam raised her glass, her arm hovering near Jo. "I'm so relieved she's okay."

"Cheers." Jo raised her glass and clinked Sam's, their eyes barely meeting as she turned to toast with Anna. "To Mollie, the best pal in the world."

"Cheers to Mollie and cheers to Sam." Her mother clinked everyone's glass then took a sip. "It's been nice having you around, Sam, especially for Jo. I noticed an ad in the paper yesterday that one of our local law firms is looking for a criminal lawyer."

"Oh, Mom." Jo took a swig of wine. "Sam would never give up her job in Toronto for one here."

"Why not?" Anna asked, breaking off a piece of garlic bread.

"Because she loves the city life." Jo stared at her plate, wondering how she was going to eat anything the way her stomach was in knots.

"I'd much rather live in Timmins than Toronto." Her mother dished up some salad. "Life's too complicated in a big city. We have so much to offer up north that I don't know why anyone would want to live anywhere else."

"Big cities are better for lesbians. There's a lot more choice."

"Josephine, I'm sure Sam's not like that." Jo escaped to the kitchen sink, her mother's stern tone a warning to behave as she scraped her plate into the garbage bin beneath.

Anna's chair dragged against the floor. "Why don't we have dessert now? I brought some chocolate brownies I baked this morning."

"Chocolate brownies are my favorite," Sam said, her voice totally steady.

Anna unwrapped her brownies and Jo helped put them on a plate before they both returned to the table. She let on all was normal, hoping the awkward moment had passed.

"I was just looking at Mollie." Her mother spoke as Jo passed the plate of brownies to Sam, avoiding her eyes. "I think her nails could use a clipping."

"I know. I've been meaning to do it for a while now."

"Well you'd better do it soon before she scratches all of your floors," her mother said.

"I don't know why you want to change that nice bamboo flooring in your living room." Anna passed the brownies to their mother. "It's not like she put it in anyway. You did all the work."

Jo rolled her eyes toward Sam. "She's referring to my ex."

"I think Jo's reclaimed oak will be a lot nicer," Sam said. "Reclaiming is a good thing, especially when it means getting rid of baggage from an old life." She bit into her brownie. "Mmmm, these are so good, Anna. Aren't you going to have one?"

"Nope, I'm on a diet." She folded her napkin.

Jo fumed at Sam's insinuation about her having baggage. "Then why did you bring them?"

"Because I want to fatten up my little sister." Anna stood and began to clear plates. "Well, Mom, we should get going soon and let these two get on with their evening."

"We'll help with the dishes first." Her mother stood.

"I'll clean up the dishes," Sam said. "This family has been great to me and I'm really going to miss everyone."

"Are you leaving this week?" Jo's mother asked.

"I'm still finalizing plans," Sam said, as though it was nothing.

"It was great the two of you dropped by." Jo got up and ushered them to the door, her legs barely working. It was taking all her strength to maintain her composure. She exaggerated a yawn to fight back her tears. She couldn't get them gone soon enough.

"I didn't mean to spring my leaving this week on you like that." Sam stood near the kitchen sink, loading the dishwasher.

"I see." Jo felt numb. "I think I spent too much time in the cold today. I'm coming down with something. Do you mind cleaning up on your own?"

Sam approached Jo. "One of the senior partners in my law firm asked me to come back this week." She sighed. "I told him I'd be back for Thursday."

"So you're leaving tomorrow, then?" Jo swallowed, pushing back a sob.

"Wednesday, if that's okay." Sam reached out to give a hug.

"Don't touch me." Jo backed away, struggling to keep her composure. "You know I can't do this."

"Wait, Jo." Sam grabbed Jo's hands and squeezed. "There's something here between us. I know. Just because I'm leaving doesn't mean this has to end. We can talk every day and visit on weekends."

"Sam, no." Jo twisted her hands free. "It's better this way. I need to be by myself." She rushed to her bedroom, slamming the door shut behind her.

CHAPTER TWENTY-THREE

Sam diligently loaded the dishwasher, pondering her next move. The clanging of dishes and ticking of the kitchen wall clock were the only sounds in the silent house. Mollie was with Jo, the two of them sequestered in the master bedroom and already sleeping for all Sam knew. The end of dinner had been a disaster.

Leaving on Wednesday morning meant a new reality without Jo was soon approaching. Sam had to do something and fast, because the alternative of having a new pen pal instead of a long-distance lover was distressing.

Her phone pinged, and she picked it up to see a new message from Trish. The subject line was, *I can't wait until you get home.* Sam tossed her phone on the counter and resumed cleaning up the dishes. She knew Trish wanted her back, was willing to forgive her eviction notice and sudden departure, but Sam had realized the futility of this relationship months before ending it. She didn't love Trish and never had. The sex had been great, but passion soon sizzled out as Sam wished for something more.

She wanted her heart to palpitate for her lover, longed to melt in her eyes, and needed to see a long-term future together. They had discussed it a few times, but Trish was content to exist in a relationship with no future and undefined boundaries. Perhaps it was the age difference. Trish was only twenty-five to her thirty-seven, but Sam suspected it was more than that. She needed to feel completed by her partner in life. The way she felt with Jo.

The clock struck eight as Sam wiped the kitchen counter for the last time, every crumb and streak cleared up. She threw her cloth into the sink and resolved to approach Jo after a quick bathroom break.

Jo heard the bathroom door close and knew it was her chance to sneak out for Mollie's last trip into the cold before bed. She'd been lying in her room, feeling sorry for herself and fighting back tears. Sam had stirred something in her and, she had to admit, Jo liked having her around. The abrupt confirmation of the impending return to Toronto during dinner was like a kick in the stomach.

The night was cold and clear. Stars were abundant, and a hint of northern lights shimmered in the dark sky. Jo held onto Mollie's leash as the two walked along snowmobile tracks in her backyard. She normally would have let Mollie run around in the dark, but she was through taking chances. She was going to need Mollie's company more than ever.

Her heart thumped with each crunch along the hard-packed snow. Why did she have to meet Sam, and why did Sam have to leave so soon? If she really wanted to stay, she could have refused an early return to work. Or she could have asked to work remotely, like Jo often did.

Jo had wanted to believe they'd met for a reason and that Sam was somehow destined to stay in Timmins. The proclamation of a Wednesday departure put an end to that hope. How ironic for Sam to suggest kindling for her heart when Jo felt like she'd started a raging fire in the pit of her stomach.

"The night sky is so beautiful right now." Sam suddenly appeared, startling Jo. She was bundled up in her red parka and carrying on as though all was normal. "I've never really seen the northern lights before. This is such a special place. I can see why you love it."

"I'm sure you have lots of remarkable spaces in your big city." Jo leapt forward as Mollie tugged on the leash.

"Not like this." Sam followed, trotting to keep up. "Being here with you is better than any place I've ever been."

"Oh, give me a break." Jo yanked on Mollie's leash. "Let's go back inside, Mollie. We'll give Sam some space to enjoy our night sky."

"Jo, please don't be like this. Can we at least talk about things?"

"What things? How you really want to screw me before leaving?"

"I never want to screw you." Sam ran a mitt over Mollie's back. "I won't deny I want to make love with you."

"You must have a screw loose if you think I'm going to fall for that." Jo turned around to face Sam. "Making love sounds so much nicer than screwing, doesn't it?"

Sam approached, their breaths melding in the cold night air. "I'm the one who's screwed. My life's in Toronto, yes, but you're here."

"You propositioned me the first day we met." Jo swung around and marched to the house, her steps wobbly through the snow. "Nothing's different."

"I said I wanted to have sex with you." Sam followed behind, her breathing uneven as she struggled to keep up. "It's not like that anymore. I can't stop thinking about you, Jo. Please, let's talk when we get inside."

"What good is talking going to do?" Jo pushed open the door and stepped into the warmth. "Hurry up and get inside, Mollie, before we lose too much heat."

"I want you to hear me out." Sam kicked off her boots. "I'll make us each a cup of tea. Will you at least join me for that? What kind do you want?"

Jo sighed. "All right. Chamomile. I'll get into my sweats and meet you in the living room. Just a cup of tea, then I'm going to bed. Alone."

Sam rushed around the kitchen that was starting to feel more like home than hers ever did. A touch of honey in each steaming mug, and Sam was ready for the closing argument of her life. The only problem was that she hadn't rehearsed it or even gotten all of her facts straight. But then again, she wasn't straight, and neither was Jo. She gave a nervous chuckle to herself.

Sam handed Jo her tea, then sat on the floor next to a reclining Mollie. She looked at Jo sitting upright on the couch, her mug firmly gripped between two hands and resting on her knees. God she was beautiful, her swollen lips inviting a kiss, and Sam could hardly breathe. She searched for words and was afraid she'd only croak if she tried to speak.

"Well?" Jo sipped her tea, long eyelashes fluttering over her mug as she waited for a response. "You added honey. Nice. Trying to sweeten me up?"

"No...I...you're sweet enough." Sam focused on Mollie. She was thankful her cup of tea was on the floor because her hands were trembling as they sifted through the golden fur. "I'm sorry. That's not what I meant to say."

"Spit it out Sam." Jo's patience was fading, her eyes beginning to roll. "Why don't you sit up on the couch, so I don't have to stare at that fucking bamboo flooring."

"No." Sam struggled to find words as Jo glared at the floor, frowning and nostrils flaring with each breath. Suddenly it made sense. "You made love with Jan on this bamboo, didn't you? Right before she broke your heart."

"So what if I did?" Jo shot to her feet, tea splashing on the floor. "Fuck." She slammed her mug down on the coffee table. "Jan wanted to christen the bamboo and then she left me three weeks later. Can you believe it? This flooring was supposed to be about our future together. Something we'd chosen because of its lack of toxins and smaller environmental footprint. Look at it now. It's full of toxic memories and left a footprint on my heart."

"You need to desecrate this flooring and move on." Sam stood; adrenaline kicked in with the fear Jo was about to rush back to her room.

"Don't tell me what I need to do." Jo moved toward Mollie, who was now looking around, panting at the raised voices. "I house trained her in this room, you know. No amount of piss or shit could degrade this flooring enough to make me feel better about it. I'm going to have one of the biggest bonfires ever when I rip it from my house."

"I hope you do." Sam kept her focus on Mollie and edged closer to Jo. "I'd like to be at that bonfire with you."

"I'm sure you'll be too busy back in the city. Come on, Mollie."

"I've fallen in love with you, Jo." Sam's voice shook. "Please don't shut me out because I can't imagine going back to my empty life without you."

"Sam, I…"

"I feel like I've been waiting all my life to meet you," Sam continued, tears breaching onto her cheeks as she lost her struggle to hold them back. "Please give me a chance."

Jo stopped, her hand gripping the doorframe and her breathing shallow. "A chance for what?" Her words offered hope, a willingness to consider the possibilities.

"To see where this will take us." Sam closed the distance between them and gently placed a kiss on Jo's lips.

CHAPTER TWENTY-FOUR

Sam struggled to stay standing as Jo fell into her arms, but they finally toppled to the floor, their bodies entwined. A sharp pain jabbed her left knee as she hit the unforgiving bamboo, but her gasp was more of an excited response to Jo's tongue slipping inside her mouth. Mollie danced around their heads, panting as though she somehow wanted to play.

"Oh, Jo." Sam reached under a baggy sweatshirt to discover hard nipples. "I want you so much."

"Go lie down, Mollie." Jo pointed to the sheepskin rug across the room and Mollie retreated. Jo's uneven breathing warmed Sam's nose and exploring hands cupped her breasts.

Sam began to remove Jo's shirt, their tongues swimming together and their lips surely to be bruised.

"You're going to take me right here, on the floor?" Jo struggled out of her sweatshirt.

"Fuck yes." Sam pulled her shirt off, pressing her naked chest against Jo's. "I want you to think of me, of this, from now on whenever you look at this bamboo flooring. We'll cleanse it right here and now."

Jo rubbed their breasts together, massaging with an urgency that disclosed her desire. Sam resisted her attempt to push them back against the floor, her hand reaching into Jo's sweats. She was wet, oh so wet, and Sam knew they'd be making love.

"You're going to get me off right now if you do that." Jo squirmed, her hips swaying and rising.

"That's the plan." Sam's fingertips fluttered in Jo's folds, the silky skin so welcoming. Belonging. Sam felt like she'd just come home.

Jo's back arched, her hips off the floor. "Oh my God, Sam." Her breathing stopped until the orgasm released, sending out a gasp that ended with a shrill moan. She dropped down, panting, and grasped at Sam.

Sam grabbed a cushion and placed it under Jo's head. "I want you to lie back and enjoy while we do the next treatment on this floor." Sam pulled off Jo's bottoms and removed the rest of her own clothes.

"I sure hope my mother doesn't come to the door." Jo reached up for Sam, her hand fondling a breast.

"I'll be on top of you if she does, so it'll be my butt she sees, if that's what you're worried about. Otherwise, I think she'd be happy for us." Sam grabbed a fleece throw from the couch and put it beside them. "We can use this as a security blanket. I want you to relax and forget about your mother."

"Forget about who?" Jo pulled Sam onto her and tried to roll them over.

"I'm not finished with you yet, young lady." Sam planted another lingering kiss on Jo's mouth then began to work her way down.

"I'm older than you." Jo giggled as she convulsed with pleasure, Sam's lips and tongue tasting her rounded breasts.

"I refuse to call you my old lady." Sam smiled against Jo. "You have a body that could rival most women half your age, especially these beautiful breasts. Mmmm. They taste so good."

"You're a real charmer." Jo clawed at the back of Sam's head. "A smooth talker. Is that how you speak in a courtroom? Get the jury to believe you?"

"Juries are hard to convince." Sam hovered just below Jo's belly button. "Like you. I'm going to show you just how smooth my tongue can be when there's no talking involved. I want to prove to you how much I want you."

"I want you to need me, Sam. Like I need you." Jo raised her head off the floor and looked at Sam. "Let me see it in your eyes."

"I need you so bad right now, I could take a bite." Sam nibbled at the skin just above Jo's pubic hair then looked up again, blue eyes full of love glistening back.

"Oh Sam, what are we going to do when you leave this week?"

"Oh baby, we'll figure it out." Sam kissed Jo's belly button.

"So now I'm your baby." Jo leaned back. "What does that mean?"

"That I want to take care of you." Sam's kisses trailed further down, tasting Jo's readiness.

"I can take care of myself." Jo's hips swayed against the floor.

"Not like this." Sam's tongue claimed its target, and nothing else mattered.

Jo cried after she came. Long, loud sobs that stirred Mollie. "It's okay, girl."

"It was just okay?" Sam crawled back up, pulling the blanket over the two of them as she wrapped her arms around Jo.

"Oh Sam." Jo buried her head in Sam's shoulder. "I've fallen in love with you. Three years protecting my heart and in less than two weeks it's gone to you. I'm scared."

Sam kissed away Jo's tears. "I promise to take good care of your heart, Jo. I trust you'll look after mine because it belongs to you now. No one has ever touched my heart the way you have. I love you so much, Ms. Josephine Lavigne."

"It's my turn to show you what you mean to me." Jo sat up. "Let's go to my bed. This floor has become a literal pain in the ass."

"We can't have that." Sam got to her feet and offered Jo a hand. "I hope you can stand on those wobbly legs of yours."

Jo led Sam into the master bedroom and pulled back the blankets on her bed. "I missed sleeping with you."

"I knew it." Sam jumped against Jo and the two toppled onto the sheets. "Ooh, fresh flannel."

"I did change them this morning, but only because they needed to be."

Sam grinned. "Oh, come on, I bet you knew the vibrations of sharing the snowmobile seat would turn me on and we'd end up in bed."

"You think so, eh?" Jo giggled as she climbed on top. "Let's see just how turned on you are right now." Sam felt Jo's arm reaching down, her fingers sending sparks as they reached her wet center.

Sam clutched the sheets, her breathing ragged. Jo began to stir uncontrollable passion until her orgasm rushed from the tip of her toes to the reaches of her scalp in one sudden tingling tsunami.

"Those fingers of yours Jo...they're magic." Sam could hardly speak, not after that.

"If you think my fingers are magic, wait until you feel my tongue." She began to lick Sam, her soft lips and warm tongue exploring every peak and valley on Sam's convulsing body. She traveled up and down each leg then settled near her target, forcing Sam's second orgasm as soon as her tongue made contact.

Sam's hips thrust into the air and her body shuddered in a sustained moan that ended with a howl. She dropped back to the mattress and pulled Jo to her, breathing as though she'd just sprinted home. "Holy shit, Jo. You brought out the animal in me."

"The animal in you showed up as soon as we met in the bush." Jo kissed Sam's nose. "Only an animal in rutting season would have been so blatantly horny like that. I should call you my big moose."

"Well then you'll be my little fox." Sam kissed her. "My sexy little fox or my foxy lady, if you prefer."

Jo laughed. "Maybe you should be afraid I'd outfox you some day."

"I think you already did." Sam grinned. "You ended up stealing my heart."

"Excuse me, but you're the one who weaseled her way into my bed."

"So now I'm a weasel." Sam sat up and scooted to the edge of the mattress. "Well this little weasel needs to go to the bathroom."

"Me too." Jo sat up and wrapped the sheet around her. "You can use the one in here. I'll wait."

"No, you go ahead," Sam said. "I'll use the one down the hall and meet you back here in a few minutes."

Sam went to the washroom then rushed to the living room to grab their clothes. Her phone had been left on the coffee table and she noticed it flashing. It was another message from Trish saying she'd cleaned up *their* room and was ready for Sam's return. Sam quickly typed her thanks, put the phone on the kitchen counter and hurried back to Jo.

CHAPTER TWENTY-FIVE

Sam snuggled up to Jo, longing to stay in bed and preserve this moment forever. Monday morning morphed into a new reality of exciting opportunities and depressing difficulties of merging two lives from different worlds.

Sam loved living in a big city, with all its trappings of disappearing into a crowd while enjoying an abundance of people, places, and things to study. Small-town living would be a challenge, but she knew Jo would never move to Toronto. Long-distance commutes and calls were now imminent.

"Hey." Jo caressed Sam's bare breast, her thumb rubbing the nipple.

"Good morning, little fox." Sam gave her a lingering kiss, igniting a renewed passion to make love again before facing the world.

"Mmmm. I wish we could stay in bed, but I have to work today." Jo clung to Sam, their bodies still interwoven from their night of lovemaking.

Sam nibbled Jo's neck. "You're the boss. Give yourself a day off, especially since you worked on Saturday."

"Maybe tomorrow, but today I have to clean up my things from the hall. It's being used by another group on Tuesday." Jo groaned as she pulled away and flung her legs over the side of the bed.

"I'll make you a coffee." Sam reached out and rubbed Jo's spine.

Jo pulled the sheet up to her neck and stretched her back as Sam's fingers continued their massage. "That feels so good."

"I want to hang out with you today. Can I come? Please?"

Jo eased around and smiled at Sam. "Oh, you'll be coming today. I have to let Mollie out, and then I'll be back for my shower. Care to warm it up for me?" Jo went out to the kitchen while Sam turned on the taps.

"Hey, Mollie. Outside?" Jo let Mollie out into the cold air, making certain to hook her to the leash-line this time, then slipped in the hall bathroom. Mollie was still sniffing around the yard when Jo returned to the kitchen. Sam's phone was on the counter and flashing.

"Come on back inside, Mollie." Jo unclipped her leash and closed the door. "I put some fresh food and water out for you." Jo held Mollie's head and looked into her eyes. "You're such a good girl, Mollie, and I'm glad you like Sam. I like her too. A lot."

Sam's phone pinged, and Jo released Mollie to reach for it. "I should let her know someone's trying to reach her, eh, Mollie? Even though I want to keep her all to myself today."

She was about to head back to Sam when the subject line of the message scrolled across the screen. It was from someone named Trish. *Hope you had fun last night.* Jo grabbed the phone and stared at it, head throbbing in confusion when another message from Trish came in. *Can't wait to see you.*

Jo was confused at first, and then realized Trish was probably Sam's ex. Her heart began to shatter. How would she have known about last night? What did Sam tell her? The woman was *anxious* to see Sam? Was she really an ex or was Sam playing some kind of game, seducing women? Laugh about it afterward, like Jo often imagined Jan doing.

Maybe Sam was just like Jan. Break her heart then take off for Toronto. Perhaps the two even knew each other, devised some scheme so that Jan could dig her knife in further.

Her ears pounded. How could she have let her guard down, think Sam's seduction was about love rather than some stupid game to break her heart? After endless, painful days and nights trying to mend her broken heart after Jan, how could she have so easily given it to Sam? After less than two weeks? *Fuck! Dammit! Shit!* Her body trembled with fury, self-loathing. She should have known better than to trust Sam when she was leaving tomorrow. It was all so stupid. Pathetic. And she would put an end to it right now.

Jo flung the phone onto the counter. She'd just been duped by Sam and wanted to die. Or kill. Or both. Jo buried her face in Mollie's fur and collapsed against the soothing animal to capture her tears.

Sam finally turned off the water. She wondered where Jo was. Maybe someone had unexpectedly dropped by. Sam threw on some clothes and hurried to the kitchen. It was empty. She looked out the window and saw Jo sitting in her truck, the engine running and Mollie in the backseat.

What the heck? Sam grabbed her jacket, jumped into her boots, and rushed outside. "What happened?" She tapped on Jo's window, but Jo refused to look at her.

Jo's window lowered slightly. "I want you to pack up your things right now and get the fuck out of here."

"Jo, what's going on?" Sam leaned against the truck, her fingers about to be squeezed by the closing window.

"Back off and get the hell out of here." Jo pounded on the steering wheel.

"Jo. Please tell me what's going on."

The woman loved her last night, even a few minutes ago, but now it was as though she hated her. Had she done something wrong? Surely they could fix it. Sam loved Jo. This didn't make sense. There had to be an explanation. Her head dropped against the window. "Please tell me what happened."

"You tell me." Jo shouted through the closed window. "Was I some kind of toy? Is that how you see me?"

"What are you talking about?" Sam tried the door, but it was locked. "Please open up."

"Fuck you." Jo laid on the horn. "Get out of my face. I'll give you ten minutes to pack and leave, and the clock starts now."

"Jo, please." Sam put her cheek against the frigid window. "Tell me what's going on."

"Go. Now!" Jo screamed, and Mollie growled.

Sam returned to the house, numb with shock and her legs barely able to carry her as she rushed around, gathering her belongings. She only packed her clothing, not caring about anything else in what felt like a drunken stupor. Nothing made sense, except Jo wanted her gone. Now.

She stuffed everything into her wheeled suitcase and shoved her phone into her jacket pocket before closing the door on her way out. The big black bag clunked down the stairs as she dragged it to her vehicle. She hoisted it into the backseat, and then got behind the cold wheel.

Sam drove down the driveway, holding her breath as she looked into her rearview mirror. Half expecting, hoping, Jo would come running after her, saying it was all a big mistake. Her mind was spinning, but she didn't know what else to do but leave. Tears flowed as she paused at the road then sped away.

Jo watched Sam's vehicle disappear and wondered how she was ever going to face the inside of her house again, let alone look at herself in the mirror. How could she have been so stupid to fall for a woman with no moral compass? Her body heaved with sobs as she shut off her engine and trudged back to her tainted house.

The first thing she did was rip the sheets off her bed and throw them into the laundry. Next she had a long shower, cleaning her bathroom and her body to rinse Sam down the drain. The rest would have to wait until she returned from work.

The remainder of the day was a blur as she went through the motions with clients and dismantled her displays, as though everything could be neatly packed away. By the time she returned to the house and walked Mollie, her tight jaw trembled with fury. She needed to release some of her anger. As soon as she walked into her living room and looked at the floor, she knew where to start. That fucking bamboo flooring needed to be banished from her house.

An hour later, crowbar in hand and bamboo planks almost completely dismantled, she noticed her mother and Anna in the hallway, mouths gaping.

"Josephine, calm down." Her mother approached and reached for the crowbar. "What's going on? Where's Sam?"

"She's gone." Jo collapsed to the floor, wishing she could disappear from her shame and pain.

"Oh, Jo." Anna bent down and put a hand on her sister's shoulder. "What happened?"

"I kicked her out." Jo sobbed, her words slurred. "I let myself down. I fell for her and thought she loved me too."

"Sam seemed like such a nice girl." Her mother squeezed her shoulder. "Something's not right."

"She had me fooled." Jo could hardly speak, furious at herself for being so stupid about the woman. To allow her heart to get broken again after three long years of putting it back together. Why hadn't she stuck to her plan? Kept up her boundaries? Fuck.

"Come on," her mother said. "Let's get you up off the floor and out of here. Poor Mollie's trembling in the kitchen. She needs to see that you're okay."

"I'm not okay."

Her mother grabbed under her arms and helped her up. "Have you eaten anything today?"

Jo struggled to her feet, trembling and shaking her head.

"I figured as much." Her mother led her to a chair at the kitchen table. "Anna, would you put a few slices of toast on for Jo? I'll make some herbal tea, something to help her relax."

"How about a bottle of rum, or strong liquor?" Jo held her head on her knees and sobbed, the pain so raw. "I just want to forget."

Mollie crept up to Jo, tail between her legs. She nuzzled her head into Jo's lap and began to lick her hands.

"Oh, Mollie." Jo kissed the top of Mollie's head then held it between her hands, staring into friendly brown eyes. "I'm so sorry if I scared you."

"Why don't you wash up and try to eat a piece of toast," her mother said. "Anna's put some peanut butter and jam on it for you and the tea's almost ready."

Jo shuffled to the hallway bathroom and locked herself inside. Sam's toothpaste lay forgotten on the sink and the unchanged towel was covered in her scent. Jo threw the toothpaste into the garbage, shoved the towel in the laundry hamper, and sat on the toilet lid. She had to pull herself together.

CHAPTER TWENTY-SIX

Sam got on the highway and headed south, hands clutching the wheel, pushing as hard on the gas pedal as she dared. She left the radio silent as her ears rang with Jo's angry words.

The sudden outburst filled Sam with a numbness and concern like she'd never felt before. She couldn't figure out what happened, find evidence that something had changed. She knew Jo could be moody, but her behavior had become outright volatile in a matter of moments. What could have set her off?

Sam played the morning through, from when they woke. It didn't make sense. Nothing could have happened while she was in the shower. They'd just shared the most intimate night ever, at least Sam thought so, and yet morning brought disaster. Was that it? Did Jo regret having sex...making love? Was she afraid that Sam was going to dump her, so decided to end things before it happened?

The road was icy, and a lot of transports bogged the single lane highway, but Sam made it to North Bay in less than four hours. Halfway to Toronto, or hell for that matter, as Sam pulled into a gas station and slowly released her grip on the wheel. Leaving Jo like that was more painful than anything she'd ever known.

The air was bitterly cold as Sam stepped outside her vehicle that was caked in slush and salt. She shivered at the pumps, longing to cuddle with Jo or even Mollie. She still felt pained at the memory of the dog's growl that may as well have been a bite.

A clear windshield and full tank of gas, Sam parked at the restaurant and went inside to decide on her afternoon direction. She eventually sat at a table then ordered a sandwich and salad she knew she wouldn't eat.

Her phone had been buried in her coat pocket and she dug it out, hoping for some message from Jo explaining her behavior. When she saw the slew of messages from Trish, she knew things were not going to be good whichever direction she took that afternoon. But Sam figured she had to head to Toronto and get Trish out of her house before anything could be fixed with Jo.

Trish's messages had started out polite enough, even saying she couldn't wait to see her, but when Sam left them unanswered, the tone changed. By ten o'clock that morning, the rants began as Trish used every demoralizing term she could think of. Sam's long hours at work, forgetting about their six-month anniversary, breaking up, forcing Trish to move out…

In all, there were fifteen emails, each one more disjointed than the next. She refused to read them all the way through. What would somebody think of her if they ever found her phone? She'd delete them all when she got home, but for now she just wanted to get going. Sam shoved her cell back into her coat pocket, paid her bill, and braced for the next four hours of her drive to Toronto.

Traffic was heavy, and her windshield wipers were on high as Sam merged onto the off-ramp toward her house. Trish's car was in the driveway and a light was on in the kitchen. She was home.

Sam wanted to turn away, but a full bladder made getting to the bathroom her number one priority. The front door readily opened. Trish never locked it, despite Sam's repeated insistence.

Sam dashed to her bedroom, closing and locking the door before Trish could react.

"Hey, Sammie Poo." Trish tapped on the bedroom door. "Welcome home."

Sam flushed the toilet and splashed water on her face. Sex with Trish was waiting for her as soon as she opened that door, experience could attest to that. Sam's stomach heaved, and she had to swallow bile back down her throat as she opened the bathroom door. The bed was neatly made; Trish's alarm clock and water glass were still on the night table. Sam flung the bedroom door open.

"Get your things out of my room. I want you out of here tonight." Sam clenched her fists at her side, her rage threatening tears.

"I've missed you, Sam." Trish reached out, her neatly manicured purple fingernails flashing in the hall light.

Sam backed away. Her body was aching from the long drive. "Don't touch me."

"Oh, come on." Trish stepped forward.

Sam crossed her arms. "I mean it, Trish. It's time to move on and out of my life. I've had enough of your emails. I just want to be left alone."

"Where am I going to go?" Trish's glossy purple lips puckered into a pout.

"I'll put you up in a hotel until you find a place."

"Please don't make me stay in a hotel like some whore you're paying to keep."

"Take it or leave it, but you're out of here tonight." Sam brushed past Trish and headed to the kitchen. The sink was full of dirty dishes and the floor crackled with crumbs, as though it hadn't been swept in ages. Sam grabbed the broom and began to sweep up the mess.

"I know my rights." Trish sniffed, tears glistening in her eyes. "You can't force me to leave if I don't want to."

"I know when I've had enough." Sam shoved the dustpan toward the mound of crumbs, pushed them on with one fast motion, and then tossed the dirt into the full garbage bin beneath the sink. "This place is a disaster. The front door was left unlocked again."

"Oh, Sam, just chill for once." Trish took a step forward, her raised arm shaking as she pointed a finger at Sam. "You're the one who just up and left and was supposed to be gone for another two weeks. Then you show up and expect me to move out right now. Well, that's not happening. I still have to pack, and my new place isn't available until the first of February, so you're stuck with me until then."

Sam leaned against the sink, her shoulders drooping. "I can't take this anymore. Please get your stuff out of my room and leave me alone."

Trish tromped down the hall while Sam grabbed a bag of biscuits and jar of peanut butter she'd left in the cupboard. She shoved an unopened bottle of cranberry juice under her arm. Sam could spend the rest of the night in her room. She needed to think about the situation with Jo and try to make sense of it all. Maybe a phone call would be a good start, but her heart pounded with the thought. She knew she'd start blubbering the moment Jo answered.

"It's all yours," Trish shouted as Sam waited in the kitchen. "I'll take the guest room."

"Thank you." Sam hurried to her room, closed the door, and flopped on the bed. "Damn." She could smell Trish's perfume on the blankets. The bed would have to be stripped. Jo was the only woman she wanted to be reminded of—good or bad.

Fresh sheets and clean blankets on the bed, Sam looked at her phone and began to scroll through the messages. Trish had left many, starting with the polite ones the previous evening and ending with her rants. Sam threw her cell onto the blankets and cried.

Why did she have to bring out the worst in people? Is that why her mother really became a drunk? Was it that her daughter was such a disappointment?

No, Sam. Stop. She needed to get a hold of herself and calm down. Work would be starting in two days and she had to pull herself together before then. She dipped a cracker in the jar of peanut butter. A swig of cranberry juice was sour on her taste buds.

Memories of their lovemaking the night before tormented her, and she flopped back against her empty pillow. Eyes closed and breathing even, Sam meditated with pleasant memories of time spent alone with Jo and how complete she felt. It was as though she'd finally found where she belonged, a place to call home, a heart to meld with hers.

Two hours later, Sam woke scrunched and shivering. She pulled a blanket up and her phone banged on the floor. "Fuck." Sam tried to reach it without getting off the bed, straining her arm and dragging it closer with her fingertips, when it suddenly occurred to her that maybe Jo had seen her messages from Trish.

Her phone had been in the kitchen while she was in the shower. Trish had started sending them early this morning, her tone sweet and making it sound as if they were still together. There had to be a reason for Jo's rapid change in behavior, and it happened while she was in the shower.

Sam rolled off the bed and sat on the floor examining early morning messages on her phone. She read the ones Jo might have seen.

Jo's phone went to voice mail after the first ring. "Hey, it's Sam. Can we talk? I can explain. I love you, Jo." She ended the call and sent a text then an email, pleading with Jo to hear her out.

After three hours of repeated messages, there was no response. Sam knew what she had to do to get through to Jo. She got under the covers, turned out the light, and tried to get as much sleep as possible before morning.

CHAPTER TWENTY-SEVEN

Traffic picked up in the daybreak drive as Sam headed north for another long ride. She'd woken at four in the morning, showered, and was on the road before five. She planned to be back in Timmins by early afternoon and would head directly to Jo's to plead her case.

If she was guilty of anything, it was of falling in love. Something she never expected would happen with anyone. Now, she couldn't imagine her future without Jo.

Daylight brought gray clouds and mist as Sam motored on toward Timmins, determined to make things right. She'd have one night only to reignite the extinguished passion, and then the rest of their lives to sort out the future.

A promise to attend a meeting with the senior partner in her law firm on Thursday morning meant she'd be back on the road again tomorrow. She couldn't let the office down, too, especially since they'd accommodated her request for an extended leave when things were insanely busy. Her future career depended on keeping in good standing with the firm, and she always kept her word. Now was not the time to let them down, especially since her personal life was falling apart. She needed to at least preserve her professional self.

Sam stopped to refuel at the same gas station in North Bay she'd visited the day before. This time her only pit stop was a bathroom break before leaving with a take-out coffee and blueberry muffin. An urgency to get to Jo as soon as possible forced Sam to rely on setting her vehicle's cruise control, or risk getting a hefty speeding ticket. Most of the drive was a blur. Sam longed to turn back the clock to the previous morning when she was still cuddled in the sheets with Jo and their future was full of hope.

Sam stopped to refuel again just outside of Timmins, where the sun was starting to peek through the clouds. She wanted to arrive at Jo's with a full tank of gas and enough energy to do whatever necessary to fix things between them.

It was just after the lunchtime rush when Sam entered a restaurant and ordered herself something to eat. She fought the urge to leave before her bowl of carrot soup arrived. As much as she wanted to wolf something down and get on her way, Sam knew she needed to relax and a comforting bowl of soup would force her to recalibrate anxiety levels before meeting with Jo.

A south-facing window captured the midday sun and warmed the room as Jo worked in her home office. She'd spent the night at her mother's place, not wanting to be alone after her attack on the bamboo flooring, but insisted on returning home after breakfast to get some work done. Surprisingly, the morning had been productive, and Jo checked off another item on her to-do list. Mollie was sprawled in the middle of the room, right where the sun warmed the floor, and seemed content to have things back to normal.

Jo paused to look at her furry friend and shuddered at how close she'd come to losing her the other night. She could have lost her heart and her dog all in one weekend. Never again would she let her guard down. Wounded, but still intact, Jo knew she'd survive. A best friend in Mollie and undying family support from her sister and mother, she could get through this.

Mollie suddenly jumped to her feet, her tail wagging. She barked then rushed down the hall toward the kitchen door.

"What do you hear, Mollie?" Jo got up and followed, then gasped when she saw Sam's black SUV parked behind her truck. A knock at the door set Mollie into a fit of yelping and Jo's heart pounding.

"Jo, are you there?" She needed to calm down and show Sam she was going to be okay. "I need to talk to you Jo. Please? Can you just open up?"

"I'm busy working right now." Jo held onto Mollie's collar and unlocked the deadbolt, but kept the door closed. "What do you want?"

"To have a chance to explain." Sam's voice was muffled through the closed door.

"Explain what?" Jo inched the door ajar, but kept herself and Mollie wedged behind to prevent it from being pushed open. "How you were playing me and finally got what you wanted before going back to Toronto and Trish?"

"It's not like that, Jo."

"My ex lives in Toronto now." Jo was still so angry whenever she thought of Jan. And now she'd have Sam to think about too. "Maybe you should look her up. The two of you would make a good pair."

Sam stuck her fingers between the door and its frame. "I love you, Jo. We need to talk. Please let me inside. It's cold out here and I want to stop draining all the heat out of your house."

"You already did that." But Jo backed off and let the door swing open as Mollie jumped toward Sam. She just had to see her, look her in the eye and let her know any charm she ever had was gone. "You can step into the kitchen, but that's all."

"Hey, girl." Sam stepped inside and dropped to her knees to greet Mollie as Jo closed the door. "She still likes me."

"Of course." Jo leaned against the kitchen sink, wanting to keep Sam's focus away from the living room with its destroyed bamboo flooring. "She's a dog and very forgiving."

"Please tell me what happened yesterday morning." Sam's voice was soft, pleading.

Jo folded her arms and crossed her ankles, keeping herself together even though she was crumbling within. "You tell me. What kind of game were you playing? Did you think I'd be okay with your ex still in the picture?"

"You have it all wrong. I don't love Trish. I kicked her out of my room as soon as I got home yesterday."

"Yeah, right. Like I'm going to believe you drove all the way to Toronto yesterday and are back in my kitchen today. Where did you stay last night? No, forget it. I don't want to know."

"Jo, please." Sam started to take off her boots. "Let's sit down and talk."

"Oh no, you're not staying." Jo shook her head, looking away from Sam's sad eyes before her resolve really started to waver. "I want you out of here right now and you might as well head back to Toronto again, because the next time I won't open the door."

"I have to be at work on Thursday morning." Sam's voice shook. "We need to fix things before then."

Jo opened the door, gripping Mollie's collar for support. "There's nothing to fix. My life is fine the way it is and thankfully the fire in my heart has smoldered out." She forced a smile, holding back tears. "Meeting you was a good lesson for me. I wish you all the best. Have a safe drive home. Maybe we'll run into each other this summer if you come up to the cottage."

She practically shoved Sam out the door and clicked the deadbolt back into place.

CHAPTER TWENTY-EIGHT

On the long drive back to Toronto, Sam resolved to give Jo some space and find a way to fix things. Optimism was the only thing that kept her going, as it had so many times before when her choices could have been much different if pessimism prevailed. Such as going to university and getting a law degree when money was tight.

A haircut, two new business suits, and East Indian takeout for dinner on Wednesday, Sam set her alarm for six the next morning then climbed into bed. Trish had been out for the evening and the house was empty. Sam lay back on her pillow and stared at the glass light fixture in the middle of her bedroom ceiling. It was off, but the soft glow from her salt crystal lamp illuminated the outdated fixture in the 1960s house that didn't feel like a home. Not the way Jo's house had. Sam reached for her computer and pulled up the job ad seeking a criminal lawyer in Timmins.

Sam immersed herself in her work at Stanford and Associates over the next week. The firm regarded her expertise on legal analysis as invaluable. Her colleagues especially esteemed her ability to recite case law in the areas of criminal negligence and homicide.

A high-profile case involving an impaired driving conviction causing death and a possible life sentence was about to get underway. The senior partner defending the drunk driver was going through his own personal crisis of a divorce and a child custody battle. Sam's early return to work was much appreciated as she led preparations for defense during the upcoming trial.

Her first week was a blur of meetings, gathering information, studying case facts, conducting legal analysis, and building a defense for the trial that was scheduled to start the last week of January. She had support from the senior partner and his team, but Sam took the lead on pulling things together. It was how she was able to keep herself sane when all she could otherwise think about was how much she longed for Jo. Regular visits to the gym, sometimes twice a day, also helped her cope.

Contact with Trish was minimal. Sam left the house before sunrise each day and returned in time to crawl into bed for a short night of sleep to appease her exhaustion. They rarely saw each other and even then, their interactions were usually less than a minute as Sam dashed out the door or to her room. That is, until the second Saturday night when Trish was entertaining a date in Sam's living room.

The two women were entwined on the couch, kissing and half-dressed when Sam came home from the gym. Blond hair and fluffy curls flowed on the cushion as Trish planted kisses on the woman. She tried to sneak by unnoticed and rush directly to her room, but Trish called out.

"Hey, Sam. Sorry, but I didn't think you'd be home for a while. Come meet Jo."

"Jo?" Sam swung around.

"Hi." The young blonde pulled on a black T-shirt and sat up. "This is embarrassing." She looked at Trish. "I thought you lived by yourself."

"I might as well, because Sam's never here." Trish adjusted her sweater and got up. "Now that you're here, Sam, I'd like to introduce you to Jo." This wasn't Jo. Not the mature and refined Jo Sam knew, and loved.

"Hi." Sam turned to leave, just wanting to get to her bedroom.

"Wait, Sam," Trish said. "Why don't you join us for a glass of wine?"

"Thanks, but I'm tired and heading to bed." Sam closed herself in the bedroom and leaned against the door, her breathing uneven as tears welled up.

Jo. What was she doing? Sam looked for her phone then realized she'd left it in her coat pocket. It was hanging in the front closet. She needed to touch base with Jo. Her Jo. Hear her voice and talk long into the night. She swallowed back tears and found the courage to venture back out to get her cell.

"Great to see you changed your mind." Trish handed Sam a glass of wine when they almost bumped into each other in the hallway. "You look like you could use a good binge."

"I'm just getting my phone." Sam tried to push by.

"Forget your phone." Trish shoved another glass at Sam. "Here, take one for Jo and go talk to her while I get some for me."

"I don't want to talk to her." Sam whispered, but Trish bounced back into the kitchen. "I'll be right there. Go on in and sit down."

"This is for you." Sam handed a glass of white wine to the girl on the couch and sat in the recliner on the opposite side. She needed to keep calm, confident, and ready to chat even though her insides were falling apart. "What is Jo short for?"

"Joanne." She gulped her wine. Her blue eyes were nowhere near as deep as Jo's. "You looked surprised when you heard my name was Jo. Do you know anyone else called Joanne?"

Sam sipped the sweet wine that tasted more like juice than the dry chardonnay she was used to. "No. The only Jo I know is Josephine."

"Who's that?" Trish plunked onto the couch. "You never told me about a Josephine."

"No, I didn't." Sam played with the stem on her wineglass, struggling to keep it steady.

"Josephine sounds French," Trish said. "Did you meet her up north?"

"Tell me about yourself, Joanne. What do you do with your life?"

"I'm a university student, a third-year undergrad in political science. I'm thinking about law school after that." She flicked a curl off her face.

"I see," Sam said, cutting in just as Trish opened her mouth. "How long have the two of you been dating?"

"I don't know if I'd consider us dating," Joanne said, her cheeks reddening. "It's more like we're getting to know each other."

"How long have you been getting to know each other then?" They were so young.

"Sam, it sounds like you're cross-examining her." Trish straightened and took a swig of her wine. "This is our living room, for fuck's sake. Not a courtroom."

"She's a lawyer?" Joanne's eyes widened.

"You're right, Trish," Sam said. "It's none of my business and I don't care anyway."

"What's going on with you?" Trish leaned forward, her long brown hair hanging in front of her face. "Ever since you got back from up north, it's like there's nothing else in your life but work. What happened to you up there?"

Sam stood. She'd had enough. "It's time for bed. Nice meeting you, Joanne."

"It's Jo." Trish put a hand on the young woman's leg. "Get used to it, because I'm confident Jo's going to be around for a while."

"No, she won't." Sam headed to the hallway. "Not here, anyway, because you'll be moved out soon."

Sam retrieved her phone and dialed Jo as soon as she shut her bedroom door. Her heart pounded as she counted the rings. One, two, three, then silence. She expected it to go to voice mail, but heard breathing instead.

"Jo, are you there? Please say something."

"There's nothing to say." Jo's voice shook. "I should just hang up."

"Please don't. I want to fix things."

"There's nothing to fix."

Sam wanted to keep the conversation going, listen to Jo's voice all night long if she could. "Can we just talk then?"

"About what?"

"How's Mollie?" Sam sat on the edge of her bed, clutching the blankets with her free hand while trying to hang on to whatever conversation they had.

"She's fine."

"That's good. Is it still cold up there?"

"Yes, freezing." Her tone was softening. "And we got more snow, too."

"I really enjoyed snowmobiling with you. Have you been out again, making tracks in the fresh snow?"

"No." There was a long silence.

"Are you still there?"

"Sorry. I have a cold and had to blow my nose."

"I wish I was closer to make you some chicken noodle—I mean, vegetable soup."

"I imagine you've been eating lots of meat to catch up from being deprived at my place."

"I feel more deprived here. I'd give up meat for you anytime. I—"

"My battery's running low." Jo cut her off. "I should go."

"Plug it in. Please?" Sam leaned forward, wishing she could reach out and touch her. "I'm lonely and want to keep talking."

"Are you at home by yourself?"

"Sort of."

"At home or by yourself?"

"Both." Sam flopped back on her bed, so relieved she'd tried calling tonight. "I'm at home, locked in my room."

"Who else is there?"

"Trish and…"

"I should have figured." Jo ended the call.

"No." Sam redialed Jo's number and reached voice mail. "Please call me back, Jo. Please."

CHAPTER TWENTY-NINE

Jo sat on the floor, hunched over Mollie and ignoring her flashing phone. Why had she answered in the first place? She was curious, of course, and wanted to hear Sam's voice on this lonely Saturday night. Their conversation was promising until Sam mentioned her ex being there. Jo lost it and hung up, cutting off Sam before she'd had a chance to explain.

Thirty minutes later, she reached for her cell and dared to dial voice mail. Half expecting to hear a cocky Sam, Jo was astonished to hear her crying, words barely audible. The sobs sounded sincere, as though just maybe there was some truth to them. What if Sam really did love her? Was in an uncomfortable living situation with Trish, like she had with Jan?

Jo held her breath as she hit dial. It rang twice, and she was about to end the call when Sam answered.

"Jo? Is that you?" She sounded groggy.

"I hope I didn't wake you."

"I'm so glad you called back." Sam's tone livened.

"I see you've gotten over your tears."

"I've run out of tissues. I almost cried myself to sleep, but now there's a zebra standing in front of me and I want to reach out and touch it."

"What are you talking about?"

"It's on TV. I love watching nature shows." Sam sounded giddy now, as though thrilled they were talking.

"I do too." Jo tapped Mollie then stood up, needing to move around. "Especially when I'm exhausted. There's no plot to follow and they take me to a different world."

"But you live in the wild," Sam said. "Your place is beautiful. Being there is an escape in itself."

"Thanks, but I'd hardly consider Timmins to be the wild, and escapes are good with any place." Jo led Mollie to the back door. "Like escaping to the city to shop or a hot climate to lay on the beach instead of freezing my ass off up here."

"I hope you're nice and toasty right now." Sam chuckled, and Jo envisioned her dimples.

"I'll be chilly in a minute because I'm taking Mollie out for her last time before going to bed. I should let you go."

"I want to come outside with you. You can describe the night sky for me."

Jo smiled as she stepped outside with Mollie and looked at the night sky. The air was frigid, and her breath formed in front of her face, each puff renewing hope that this conversation would go well. "There are lots of stars tonight."

"What would you wish for if you saw one falling?" Was Sam playing her?

Jo kicked a frozen block of snow, trying to relax as it scraped along the ground. "If I tell you, it'll be jinxed. Wishes made under a falling star are supposed to be kept secret if they're to come true."

"I know what mine would be, but I'll keep it to myself because I want it to come true." Sam giggled.

Jo reached the dark road then turned back toward her house, Mollie following without tugging. "You have to do more than wish under a star if you long for something to happen."

"I'd do anything to make this one come true."

Jo surveyed the star-studded sky, wanting to share it, and wishing Sam was here with her. "The Big Dipper is out in full tonight. And I can see Orion and even Jupiter, because the moon is hidden. It's so spectacular Sam. I wish you could see it."

"I can hear it in your voice," Sam said. "I'm so glad you called back. I hope you have a full battery, because I could stay on all night."

"Come on, Mollie, let's get back inside." Jo needed to talk about more than just zebras and stars.

"I heard her bark. It's just like I'm there."

"How's your job going?" Jo locked her back door for the night, juggling the phone between her shoulder and ear.

"It's busy, but it's been good to take my mind off other things." Sam paused. "Like missing you."

"It's been hard, Sam." Jo suddenly felt exhausted as she headed to her bedroom and flopped backward on the bed. "This has really screwed up my life and taken a lot out of me."

"For me too.

Jo stared at the glass light fixture on her ceiling. "I wish we'd never met."

"Please don't say that." Sam paused again, her breathing soft. "The fact of the matter is, I'd be frozen in the ice on Button Lake until spring if we'd never met."

"If you put it that way, I suppose there is some good that's come out of this."

"We're talking now, tonight. This is better than good, and the best it's been since before my marathon drives between Timmins and Toronto."

"Did you actually drive all the way to Toronto that first night and then back to Timmins again the next day?"

"Yes." No hesitation in her response.

"Where did you stay when you got back to Timmins and I sent you away?"

"I drove home again."

"You what? Only an insane person would do that."

"Call me crazy if you want, but I like to think of it as determined. I needed to make things right."

"And what does that mean for you?"

"I want you in my life Jo. It's as simple as that."

"So we're talking now."

"Yes, we are, and I feel like I'm floating on a cloud."

"Maybe we could just be friends."

Sam paused. "I consider you my best friend right now, Jo. I know things got messed up, but you're the best lover I've ever had."

"Give me a break. We fucked twice and spent a night supposedly making love…"

"Jo, would you please stop this," Sam groaned. "I feel like you're unfairly judging me and if there's one thing I believe in, it's everyone's entitled to a fair trial."

"You're right." Jo sighed. "I'm sorry if I insulted you."

"I'm not offended, but I'd really like to move on." Sam's breathing picked up, as though she was pacing during a closing argument. "I know I was a sex-starved shit when we first met, but you changed me, Jo. I'm not like that anymore."

"So how are you now that you're no longer a horny poop?"

"I only have lust for you."

Jo laughed. "That sounds contrite, a funny way to profess your changed status. You expect me to fall for that?"

"Maybe." Sam snickered.

"Perhaps we should switch the subject and talk about more practical things, like your living situation with your ex. Are you still sleeping with her?"

"Of course not. Did you sleep with your ex when you were still living together?"

"Are you kidding?"

"There's nothing for you to worry about." Sam's voice softened. "Trish is moving out in another week, and I've locked myself in my bedroom for the time being."

"I hated being a prisoner in my house while waiting for Jan to leave after we broke up. It was awful. I'd never want to go through that again."

"I hope your bamboo flooring is at least more tolerable now and you think of me when you look at it."

"I ripped it out." Jo closed her eyes, wanting to forget that night. "It was impossible to keep the doubly-tainted wood in my house after you left."

"Oh Jo, I'm so sorry." There was pain in Sam's words as her voice softened. "I wish I could hug you right now."

"It's okay. The living room is ready for my reclaimed oak flooring. It'll be a good winter project for me."

"I want to help."

"Hey, Sammie poo." Jo heard someone calling out and banging on Sam's door. "Come and have another glass of wine."

"Shit, she's drunk." Sam moaned. "I'm sorry, Jo."

"Good night, Sam." Jo ended the call and kissed her phone before crawling under the covers for the night.

CHAPTER THIRTY

Jo had been intentionally ignoring her cell phone, leaving it off and charging for most of the morning so she could process the conversation with Sam. They were talking now, a big development, and she was starting to wonder if she'd been wrong about Sam. But still, Jo wanted to take things slow, and it was early afternoon before she finally checked the message on her phone.

"Hey." Sam's voice was soft, but confident. "I really enjoyed talking last night. I had the best sleep in a long time. Call me when you get this."

Jo held the phone to her chest to catch her breath. Sam's message was sweet, hypnotizing. Cocky. A redial reached Sam's voice mail.

"Hey to you too," Jo almost whispered. "I'm feeling good about talking too. I slept so well last night Mollie had to pull me out of bed this morning. I'm heading to my mother's for dinner, so maybe we can connect later. You call me."

Jo chuckled as she ended the call and buried her face in Mollie's fur. "Oh Mollie, what do you think? Should I give her another chance? Or maybe I'm the one who needs another chance. But she lives so far away. How are we going to deal with that?"

By the time Jo got to her mother's place for dinner, Anna had already set the table and her mother was taking a chicken out of the oven. The aroma reminded Jo of the chicken Sam had cooked at the cottage. Her reaction to remembering Jo was vegetarian and grabbing for some mozzarella cheese was definitely cute. Jo smiled as she heated up a soy *chicken* breast in the microwave for her protein.

"How can you eat that stuff when Mom's chicken smells so good?" Anna was preparing a lettuce salad at the island. "Oh, and by the way, Robert's on his way over."

"Is he able to join us for dinner?" Her mother stood at the stove, monitoring pots of cooking vegetables.

"I hope so," Anna said. "I forgot my bottle of wine and he's dropping it off."

"You girls don't have to bring wine for dinner." Her mother drained the potatoes, steaming the window above the sink.

"I'll put an extra setting on the table for him," Jo said.

"You look better this afternoon," her mother said. "I hope you got outside for some fresh air."

"Mom, I'm outside a lot with my job so it's nice to sometimes stay cuddled inside on the weekends." The microwave beeped, and Jo got her fake chicken.

"Hi." Robert pushed the door open, a gust of cold air coming into the kitchen. "It sure smells good in here."

"I hope you can join us for dinner," Anna said as he kicked off his boots and came inside. "Jo set a place for you."

"Of course Robbie will stay for dinner." Her mother gave Robert a hug. "Good to see you."

"Are you sure you have enough?" Robert looked at the table, his arms still wrapped around his grandmother.

Her mother patted his shoulder. "We have lots, especially since Jo brought her own chicken. Now go wash up and sit down."

Anna brought the salad and vegetables to the table then sat down. "I have vacation brochures with me. There are some good sales on right now. I think the three of us should escape for a week to get some sun."

"We have lots of sun," Jo said as she buttered a warm dinner roll. "It's so bright with all of the snow and can be blinding without sunglasses."

"Okay, then, I should have said warm sun because it's been so cold lately that being able to put on a bathing suit sounds enticing. All I can wear these days are long johns and wool socks."

Their mother put the platter of chicken in the center of the table then sat down. "Where did you have in mind?"

"I was thinking the Dominican Republic." Anna took a few pieces of breast meat and cut it up on her plate. "Punta Cana has some last-minute deals at one of their all-inclusive resorts, and I think it would be good for all of us to get away."

"Where are we going?" Robert came from the washroom and took his seat at the table.

"What about Mollie?" Jo asked. "I can't just leave her."

"I have that all figured out." Anna turned to her son. "Robert could stay at your place and take care of Mollie while we relax on the beach. Couldn't you?"

"I guess, sure. When are you leaving?"

"Next Saturday if all goes to plan," Anna said.

"Wait a minute. I can't just leave my work like that." Jo twitched when her cell vibrated. It was Sam, she just knew it, but sent it to voice mail without taking it from the front pocket of her navy hoodie.

Anna glared at her. "You need to take a break, Jo. Just look at you, your nerves are shot. You need a change of scenery."

"I'm sorry about Sam," Robert said. "Mom told me she jerked you around. I thought she seemed nice, but then I only met her for a few minutes."

"Let's not talk about Sam and enjoy our dinner," her mother said. "Anna, why don't you tell us more about what you had in mind? I've never been to the Dominican and would enjoy a winter holiday with my two girls. We all need to get away, especially you, Jo, and I know Robbie would love to spend a week with Mollie."

Jo couldn't wait for dinner to end so she could slip into the bathroom to check her message. She helped clear the table and load the dishwasher then saw her opportunity to flee to the washroom when her mother began to make tea.

"Sorry I missed your call." Sam's voice echoed against running water as Jo tried to conceal the reason for her visit to the bathroom from the rest of her family. "I was in a meeting and my phone was turned off. I'm turned on now, though, and ready for a call back. Hope to hear from you soon." Sam chuckled and blew a kiss into the phone to end the message.

Jo's hands shook as she typed a short text to let Sam know she was at her mother's and would touch base within the hour. She looked at herself in the mirror and smiled. Her cheeks were flushed. She longed to hit redial right then and there. She would wait, though, until she was alone and on her own turf where she could savor the conversation. Jo took a deep breath and headed to the after-dinner visit in the living room.

"Are you having hot flashes already?" Anna asked from the couch, sipping tea. "Your cheeks are all red."

"It must have been the wine." Jo sat in a matching chair across the room and nervously brushed at the front of her flannel shirt, as though removing crumbs from dinner. "It's too bad Robert had to leave right after eating."

"Have you heard from Sam?" Her mother's head tilted, voice softening.

"No, Mom." Jo shook her head, still shamed from the floor-wrecking episode and wanting her interactions with Sam kept private for the time being.

"That's too bad." Her mother's tongue clicked against the roof of her mouth. "I guess she had us all fooled. I thought for sure she'd be around for a while."

"Let's focus on the future," Anna said. "Like next Saturday when we could be on our way to an all-inclusive. I'd like to book something tomorrow."

"I have too much work to leave right now." Jo wanted to hang on to vacation time in hopes of spending it with Sam.

"You always have too much work." Her mother pointed to one of Anna's brochures. "This looks like a nice place. I think we should go ahead and book something."

"Are you okay with that Jo?" Anna asked.

"Feel free to book something for you and Mom." Jo stood, anxious to leave. "We just finished the open house and I have to review all of the comments on the draft forest management plan. It's a busy time for me."

"Think about it, Jo," Anna said. "You really should come with us to get a break."

"I agree." Her mother got up and hugged her. "You've been working so hard lately, and I won't enjoy myself as much if you aren't with us."

Jo put on her coat. "I'll let you know if I change my mind. I'd be staying in your room anyway, so it shouldn't really matter if I don't commit right now."

"But Jo, we'll be leaving next Saturday so there isn't much time to think about it." Anna came near the entryway as Jo pulled on her boots. "Sleep on it and I'll call you in the morning."

"Sure, whatever."

Sam sat in the middle of her bed, phone at the ready in her lap, willing Jo to call back.

Trish and Joanne were in the living room cuddled up on the couch and watching a movie when Sam got home from the gym. She'd spent the afternoon at the office, preparing for the next day of jury selection. She'd be there in the background only, but knew the arguments would be based on her work behind the scenes and she would be relied upon for support. Catherine, one of her senior colleagues in the firm, had commended her efforts just this afternoon, and insinuated she may be promoted from associate to partner. It had been a good day.

"Put it down!" Trish's voice screeched and was followed by a loud bang.

"What's going on?" Sam rushed to the living room to find Joanne putting on her coat and Trish crying.

"Look what she did." Trish pointed to a broken lamp on the floor near the TV. "That was my grandmother's."

"Forget the lamp, look at my television!" Sam was more concerned about the large crack across the screen.

"I told you I'd throw it if you didn't give me back my phone." Joanne clutched it in her hand as she pulled on her boots. "You have no fucking business reading my messages."

"I only wanted you to stop focusing on it and see who was interrupting our evening." Trish's voice shook.

"I should have known you were a stupid jealous bitch," Joanne said.

"Get out of here right now." Sam poked a stiff index finger toward Joanne.

"What do you think I'm doing?" Joanne grabbed the doorknob and yanked it open. "She wasn't even that great in bed, but then I guess you would know." The door slammed shut and Joanne was gone.

"Fuck." Sam looked at her destroyed TV. "That's it. No more guests here for you." Her finger turned on Trish, jabbing the air as she spoke. "And you owe me a television before you leave in six days from now. No extensions or exceptions or anything. You're getting out of my life."

"Please, Sam." Trish got off the couch and tried to approach as Sam backed away. "I want to fix things between us. I'll do anything you want."

"I want you out of here on the first of February. That was the deal. And clean up that mess." Sam turned to go back to her room.

"Can we just talk for a minute?" Trish sobbed. "Please?"

Sam groaned with aggravation. "There's nothing to talk about. I have a really busy week ahead and just want to relax for a bit tonight."

"You're always busy. I'm taking us breaking up hard, Sam. Can't you at least show me some compassion?"

"You weren't suffering last night while you were sucking face with Joanne on my couch." Sam knew Jo would be calling any minute now and resented the intrusion.

"I was trying to make you jealous." Trish plopped on the couch, put her head in her hands. "She's such a bitch and I'm glad you threw her out. I don't know what I'm going to do without you."

Sam closed her eyes and tugged at the back of her neck. "You'll be fine. We're at different points in our lives, Trish. I'm twelve years older than you. I need to get my shit together."

"You're a successful lawyer making lots of money, Sam. We had lots of fun times. What more do you want?"

"It's not fun for me anymore, Trish." Sam sat on the arm of the couch in an effort to calm Trish before her call with Jo was wrecked with another outburst. "I want something more out of life. Someone I can grow old with."

"Nobody wants to grow old." Trish wiped her nose. "Why think about that, especially when I can help keep you feeling young?"

"It's time for me to mature and start acting my age. For God's sake, I'm old enough to be Joanne's mother."

"You weren't the one sleeping with her, so that's irrelevant." Trish scooted closer to Sam. "She was obviously too young for me, especially since I prefer a more mature woman."

"I've met someone, Trish." Sam stood and began backing out of the room.

"I knew it. She's in Timmins, isn't she?"

"Yes."

"You want me out of here so she can move in, don't you?"

"No. That's not it at all." Sam crossed her arms in irritation and leaned on the wall near the hallway. "She's a forester. Her life is up north."

"Well how's that going to work?" Trish straightened. "I can't see you quitting your job and moving up into the boonies."

"It's complicated right now, but I'm hoping we'll find a way to make things work." Sam closed her eyes. This conversation was going nowhere. "Look, Trish, I'm exhausted and need to get some sleep." She turned away, rushing back to her room. Her flashing phone indicated a new message.

"Hey Sam. I was hoping we'd connect tonight. I'm heading to bed shortly so maybe we can try again tomorrow. Have a good night."

Sam fired off a text to see if Jo was still awake. No reply.

"Damn." Sam kissed her phone and retreated under the covers, not daring to call back and wake Jo, especially since she herself was exhausted. Sleep soon came and lasted all night long.

CHAPTER THIRTY-ONE

Wind whipped against Jo's back as she bent to fasten her snowshoe bindings. Her truck was nudged up against the snowbank and Mollie was already amongst the trees. They were back where it all started, just over three weeks before. Jo had a few more ground sampling tasks to finalize the data inventory report—at least, that's what she told herself was the reason for returning to the bush near Sam's cottage.

In truth, she wanted to see the cottage again, make sure everything was intact, and feel closer to Sam by being next to something that belonged to her. The wind died down once Jo got into the forest, and the walk was pleasant.

Her heart fluttered with thoughts of Sam making cedar kindling in her woodshed, Mollie by her side, and then what happened afterward. Jo had lost all control, consumed by a passion that took her by surprise and ignited a raging orgasm that still fanned glowing embers whenever she remembered. It was as though Sam had some kind of spell over her.

She played phone tag with Sam again this morning, both rushing off to work and promising to connect that evening. Jo could hardly wait.

Mollie remembered the trail and was out on Button Lake before Jo. The deep freeze of the last few weeks ensured the ice was thick, so Jo walked on it toward Sam's cottage. Her cell rang halfway across the lake.

"Have you reconsidered?" Anna said. "I'm just about to book and want to know if I should get two or three tickets."

Jo watched Mollie sniff in front of Sam's cottage, bounding in and out of snowdrifts as she explored near the empty cabin. "Just book for you and Mom."

Anna sighed. "Oh, come on, Jo. You'll be moping around here by yourself and Mom really wants you to come."

"I won't have time for any moping and besides, I probably have to go to Toronto tomorrow." Jo had been given the heads-up she might be asked to attend an ad hoc meeting with political officials regarding the forest management plan.

"Toronto? For how long?"

"Just the day, unless I can get Robert to look after Mollie." Jo's stomach twirled with excitement and anxiety at the prospect of seeing Sam.

"You never said anything about that last night."

Jo was anxious to tell Sam, but was going to wait until the trip was confirmed. "I just found out this morning. They'll tell me this afternoon whether or not the meeting is going ahead."

"I hope you're not planning to look up Sam while you're there." Anna's tone was crisp.

"If I go, it'll just be a whirlwind trip." Jo stepped onto Sam's dock and stared at the small log-sided cottage with its brightly painted yellow window frames. Her heart palpitated. She longed to see smoke coming out of the chimney, Sam inside with a pot of chili bubbling on the stove.

"I'm going to see if I can put a hold on a ticket for you," Anna said. "You can think about it while you're in Toronto and let me know by tomorrow night."

"It's not confirmed yet whether or not I'll be going to the city."

Anna snapped her tongue again. "Oh, if I know you, you'll be going to Toronto one way or another."

"What's that supposed to mean?" Jo hoped to keep things with Sam private until she felt confident about the possibility of maintaining a relationship.

"I saw the way you were acting last night at Mom's. You're still stuck on her, aren't you?"

"I have to go now, Anna. My hands are freezing and my battery's limited in this cold."

"Where are you right now?"

"In the bush." Anna would freak if she knew Jo was here, but it was none of her damn business. "I'll be heading home soon. Talk to you later."

Jo approached the woodshed door and propped it open. A small pile of cedar kindling lay on the chopping block, waiting to be brought inside and start a fire. Jo smiled as she fondled the little sticks of wood Sam had made, then shoved them into her pack. She'd bring the kindling to Toronto and maybe use them to start a fire at Sam's, if things worked out.

Sam sat in the courtroom and daydreamed about Jo as the jury was being picked. She knew her concentration was off, but also speculated the jury selected would be irrelevant if the charges against their client were stayed, which seemed likely because of improper record-keeping by the charging officer. The drunk driver would walk a free man, imprisoned in his own guilt of knowing a lapse in judgment had killed innocent people. Nobody would see it that way, though. The victims' family would condemn the culprit, as they had every right to do, and media attention would not be kind. Sam preferred to focus on the positive, like how good she felt with Jo and the possibility of making it more permanent.

Her application to the position at Maxwell and Associates in Timmins had been assessed and she was asked to attend an interview, but she'd yet to commit to a date. It was impossible for her to leave Toronto now that the trial had started, but the

Timmins firm would accommodate her schedule and wait until after the court proceedings to meet.

Moving so far north to a small place with just over forty thousand people was something Sam could never have imagined doing even three weeks before. Her stomach churned at the prospect of leaving behind her comfortable city life for a woman who could make her both miserable and euphoric in a matter of moments, depending on the mood of her scarred heart. Sam was determined to heal Jo's heart and harness her own wayward ways so they could have a happy ever after future together. If it had to be in Timmins, then so be it. Jo was worth it.

Jo received the call at six o'clock that evening informing her of the details of a fast trip to Toronto. Susan, her contact at the Ministry of Natural Resources and Forestry district office, explained that her attendance would be required at a senior management meeting in downtown Toronto the next day. It was set to start at one thirty on Tuesday afternoon and expected to last for at least three hours, maybe more. The forest management plan was only one item on a long agenda of matters to discuss. Jo would be attending by herself, on behalf of the forest management planning team, and her role was solely to be there as a subject matter expert to answer any questions.

A flight had been booked for her. It was to leave at eight thirty the next morning and she would be in Toronto by ten. Lunch with Sam would be out of the question because she'd have to make her way into the city, and Sam would be in court. Dinner, however, was a much more likely prospect. Her return flight was booked for eight that evening, but it could be changed for a small fee if she wished to spend the night.

She lined up Robert to look after Mollie, preparing him to stay until the next Monday morning, as she hoped to spend some time with Sam in Toronto. Jo knew Sam was extremely busy with the trial, but she was prepared to work remotely and keep herself occupied while Sam was in court. This would be like a mini trial on its own, helping Jo determine whether or not a long-distance relationship was feasible.

Jo needed to have a plan and feel comfortable with the targets. How often they'd see each other, objectives and strategies to make the relationship sustainable over time, a balanced approach to protecting their individual needs, and ground rules to ensure the successful fulfillment of their life together. As complicated as putting together a forest management plan was, Jo knew that the fundamental aspect of ensuring successful implementation was simple. All parties had to take it seriously.

Her hand trembled as she held the phone to her ear, Sam's number ringing and voice mail clicking in again. Disappointed at not reaching Sam, her voice clung to the nervous excitement of longing for the woman as she left a short message.

Sam finally got a moment alone after a long day held prisoner in court. At least that's how it felt, as she wanted to check her messages more often than possible. She knew there was a new voice mail, but the trip back to her office had been filled with discussions of the day's proceedings and no chance to listen to it. At seven thirty that evening, she shut her office door and flopped in a chair to give her full attention to the phone.

"Hey, Sam, I can't stop thinking about you." Jo's words sent shivers up Sam's spine as the voice mail played. "I hope you're free tomorrow night because I'm flying to Toronto in the morning for an afternoon meeting."

Sam almost dropped her phone.

"I know you're busy this week, but I'd really like to see you. It would be great if we could meet for dinner. Call me."

"Yes." Sam shot an arm toward the ceiling then hit redial.

"Oh my God, Jo, I'm so excited," she said to Jo's voice mail. "Let's do dinner for sure and you can stay at my place. How long are you in town? I can't wait to hear back."

Sam knew she'd skip to the gym, dinner too, and then all the way home as she thought about planning a date with the woman she loved.

CHAPTER THIRTY-TWO

"I'll meet you in front of the Eaton Centre and we can grab some takeout food before heading to my place." Sam sounded excited as they made plans over the phone.

Jo was sitting on her bedroom floor next to Mollie as the dog chewed on a rawhide bone. Her things were already packed. "I can't believe we're going to be together tomorrow night."

"Me neither. I'm so excited." Sam giggled. "I'll drive into the city tomorrow so we can share an intimate ride instead of taking public transit to my house."

"Sounds like a plan." Jo massaged Mollie's back. "We can keep in touch over the day. There's no pressure to rush to meet me by a certain time. I can always shop."

"And what are you shopping for?"

"Nothing in particular." Jo tossed a tissue toward her garbage bin, silently cheering as it went in. "It's just to kill time. I already know what I want. I'm not interested in picking up anything else."

"A woman who knows what she wants. I'm so turned on. I wish you were here with me right now."

"Me too." Jo's groin throbbed as she thought of touching Sam, and Sam touching her. "We both need to get some sleep tonight so we're well rested for our evening together."

"Evening? I'm thinking nights. I hope you can stay for the weekend."

"Have you already forgotten about Mollie?" Jo tapped the golden fur. "I can't just abandon her."

"I guess not. I hope you can at least organize to stay the night."

"I'll see what I can do." Jo stood up to look out the window. A fine snow was falling as headlights approached. "My nephew Robert just pulled into the driveway. I'm hoping to convince him to stay with Mollie until Monday morning. If that's okay with you."

"Are you kidding me?" Sam squealed. "I'm going to explode with excitement. It'll be so much fun. I'll be your personal tour guide and show you around the city on the weekend. Think about what you want to do, and we can go from there."

"I want to do you."

"Do me now, over the phone."

"Patience, Sam." Jo laughed. "I have to go. My nephew's at the door and it wouldn't be appropriate for us to continue this conversation. Get lots of sleep tonight and I'll let you know when I land in your city tomorrow morning."

"You rest up too," Sam said, "because when I'm finished with you, walking in those snowshoes of yours is going to be next to impossible for at least a week."

Jo ended the call just as she swung the door open to greet Robert and his cologne.

"Hey, come on in. Thanks for coming over on such short notice." Jo gave him a hug as he stepped inside, his black parka cold against her cheek.

He bent over to untie his boots. "Mom was hoping you'd change your mind about the Dominican. She made sure I'm available to stay here next week. Hey, Mollie, how's my girl?" Mollie's tail whacked against the wall as he rubbed her shoulders.

"I hope you can stay tomorrow night and through the weekend. I'm off to Toronto in the morning." Jo hummed inside as she hung up his jacket, the cedar scent in the closet reminding her of the kindling.

"She told me you might have to go to Toronto. Work stuff?"

"Sort of." Jo contemplated confiding in her nephew, knowing he could keep a secret. "What can I get you to drink?"

"Nothing for now, thanks." Robert looked in the living room. "Wow, you sure did a number on the floor. What happened?"

"Let's just say it was time to renovate." Jo pushed past him and plopped onto the couch. "I'll lay the reclaimed oak flooring once I get back."

"Back from Toronto or the Dominican?" Robert sat down beside her.

"Toronto."

"You're going to see Sam, aren't you?" Mollie's head landed in his lap and he massaged her ears.

"Yes." Jo sighed, resenting feeling like she'd just admitted to doing something wrong. "But I really do have to attend a meeting about the forest management plan. It's only for tomorrow afternoon, but I'm hoping to stay with Sam until Monday morning." She stared at a print of a peregrine falcon on her living room wall, nervous about what the next few days might bring. "I just have to follow this through, Robert, and see whether there's any hope for us."

He continued to rub Mollie, her collar clinking every now and then. "Mom and Grandma are so afraid you might move to Toronto."

"My life is here. Sam knows that." Jo figured they'd been talking about her. The sudden holiday south was a ploy to get her away to refresh and forget.

"And hers is in Toronto, isn't it? Big-city living with a fancy job and lots of money would be hard to give up. Long-distance relationships can be challenging, even in the best of times." Both of his hands were on Mollie, vigorously massaging her back. "I know all about that. It's why I'm single again."

Jo was shocked. She hadn't heard about him dating anyone before this. "Robert, I wasn't aware you were seeing someone. Did your mom even know?"

"No." His voice sounded a little sad.

Jo leaned forward. "Why didn't you tell us? What was her name?"

Robert shifted, his green eyes meeting Jo's with a slight grin. "John."

Jo sat back, a bit stunned. She brushed a hand across his smooth chin and smiled, a little embarrassed about the assumption. "Welcome to the club." She gave him a high-five, their palms slapping together. "You'd think I of all people in this family would be more careful before making assumptions like that."

"Not necessarily." Robert smiled. "Presuming someone is gay can be a lot more risky than letting on they're hetero. A few years ago, I would have died if anyone in the family insinuated I was gay."

"Well, I think it's great. I'm so happy you told me." Jo leaned over and gave him a heartfelt hug.

He ran a hand through his neatly coiffed light brown hair. "Please keep this to yourself for now. I'm just not ready for Mom to know yet. I think she'll be so disappointed."

"Robert, I know your mom just wants you to be happy." Jo squeezed his knee, pleased he trusted her enough to out himself at this point. "Of course I'll keep this to myself. It's your news to share and you'll know when it's the right time to tell your mom. Just like I know you'll keep my meeting with Sam secret. Deal?"

"Deal." He leaned back in the couch and let out a sigh. "Thanks, Aunt Jo. That felt good to tell you, and now I have a confidant in the family."

"Me too." Jo smiled, so happy to now have someone to talk to about Sam.

"Now tell me what's up with her. Are you in love?" Robert put his arms behind his head.

"Oh Rob, I have indeed fallen in love with her." Jo flopped her head back into a cushion and moaned with excitement. "What am I going to do?"

"Does she love you?"

Jo let out a sigh. "She says she does and I want to believe it, but our lives are just so different." She wrapped a curl of hair around one of her fingers. "Sam's had a long string of girlfriends, the most recent of which is only twenty-five years old. How can I compete with that?"

"Aunt Jo, you have a lot to offer a sophisticated lawyer like Sam that some baby dyke could never match."

"You're so sweet, Robert, but I see the sags in the mirror."

"Well, then I think you need to get a new mirror because you've got a great body that would put many young things to shame. And you've got your own wisdom and sophistication."

"And baggage too." Jo got off the couch and headed to the kitchen for a glass of water.

"Jan was a bitch to leave you like she did, and I never liked her anyway," Robert said, following her. "None of us did with the way she took advantage of you. If Sam is smart, and I have no doubt she is, she'll see the classy lady in you and hang on for life."

"I thought that's how it would be with Jan." Jo took a gulp of water.

"Forget about Jan," Robert said as they moved back to the couch. "She's ancient history. It's time to move on."

Jo put a leg underneath her as she sat back down. "I've been trying to. I thought I was finally settled with myself until Sam came along."

"What happened with Sam? Mom said the two of you looked so happy then next thing she's gone and you're tearing up this floor." Robert motioned with his glass.

"I know." Jo closed her eyes for a moment, ashamed of her behavior. "She's still living with her ex. It's complicated and I want to trust her, but she can be a sweet talker and I'm scared." She took another drink of water. "The only thing I know for sure is I miss her and want to see where this visit goes. Please tell me you can look after Mollie until Monday."

"Of course." Robert smiled. "You just have fun in Toronto, Aunt Jo."

CHAPTER THIRTY-THREE

Sam was in a deep sleep when a loud banging against the bedroom door startled her awake. Disoriented, she lunged for her phone and knocked over the glass of water by her bed.

"Fuck." She sat up and switched on the lamp.

"Sam, can I come in?" Trish's voice rang out. She gave another knock then pushed the door open.

"What's going on?" Sam registered the time, just after midnight.

Trish waltzed into the room and sat on the edge of the bed. "Can we talk? I don't know what I'm going to do and need your help." Her hair needed a brushing; her cheeks were pale, and she had big bags under her eyes. She started to cry, deep sobs and lots of tears. Her purple silk housecoat hung open and her black camisole began to blotch with tears, as though she were standing in the rain.

Sam sighed. "Please, Trish. I have a big day tomorrow and need my sleep. You know that and agreed to give me some space while my Jo's here."

"That's why I want to talk now." Her words were uneven. "While you're still by yourself. I don't have a place to move to anymore. Can I stay here a bit longer?"

"No, definitely not." Sam reached for a sweatshirt and pulled it over her waffle pajama top. "You promised to be out of here this weekend. I thought you had a place rented."

Trish's head drooped, hair covering her face. "I did, but it was with Jo." She whimpered. "Living with that bitch is out of the question now, especially since she broke your TV."

"Which you're going to replace." Sam swung her legs off the bed. The situation was so pathetic and worsening as she stepped in a puddle. "Shit, my water's all over the floor."

"At least your glass didn't break." Trish picked it up. "I'll get a towel and soak it up."

"The carpet's already done that." Sam stomped into the en suite and grabbed her bath sheet, then draped it over the wet patch.

"I'll pay you more rent." Trish dropped to her knees and began to knead the towel against the wet rug. "I'll even cook your meals, being that you're so busy all the time and not eating properly."

"My eating habits are just fine, and I don't need extra rent money." Sam sat on the edge of her bed, numb with exhaustion. "Look, Trish, I'm tired and need to get some sleep. You do too. Morning will come soon enough and we both have to work."

"I can't go into work when my life's in crisis." Trish sat on the floor and sobbed. "I'm such a screw up. I really miss you, Sam. Can't we try again?"

Sam sighed, cradling her head as fingers dug into her scalp in an effort to stop the dull throbbing. "Trish, we've been through all of this. It's over and you need to move on. Clinging to me isn't going to help. I want my house back. Now please let me get back to bed."

"Fine." Trish sprang to her feet. "But we need to talk about this."

"Not now and not while my Jo's here." Sam slid back under the sheets and turned out her lamp. "I want you out looking for another place to live, starting tomorrow. Close the door on your way out."

Lying in the dark, Sam mulled over her situation with Trish. How could she have ever lived in a relationship with someone like her? What would Jo think if she witnessed a pathetic outburst like that? She'd head right back to Timmins, that's what she'd do.

Three hours later, Sam was unable to fall back asleep. She was going to be exhausted for her evening with Jo and would have to skip her morning gym routine. Hopefully her commute into the office would be easy and the rest of the day would unfold without any extra stress to hinder her plans.

After tossing and turning for another hour and a half, Sam stepped into her shower at four thirty that morning. She planned to head to the office by five and beat rush hour traffic to enjoy a leisurely takeout breakfast of a coffee and toasted bagel at her desk. And she also wanted to avoid any morning interactions with Trish, hoping the problem would somehow go away.

By the time she was at her desk and had opened the morning paper, her coffee had cooled and her bagel hardened. She'd messaged Jo to say good morning and wish her a good flight. There was a short reply—Jo said she was excited to meet at the end of the day. They would both be busy and have little time for chatting, so she put her phone aside. That was okay, though, because Sam anticipated a fun-filled evening of re-connecting with Jo.

The office was bustling by eight thirty and Sam was rushing to head back to court when a text came into her phone. She grabbed the cell, multi-tasking as she also reached for files, and glanced at the message. *Can we meet and talk sometime today? Jo.*

Sam was confused because Jo knew she'd be tied up in court all day, but she was also in a hurry and quickly responded confirming she'd target five thirty at the Eaton Centre. She ran to catch the elevator, struggling to close her overflowing leather bag as she scooted inside as the doors were closing.

Jo reviewed her notes as she leaned against the airplane window, blue sky above and clouds below. The flight was only partially full, and she lucked out having two seats to herself. Visions of Sam sitting beside her made her stomach twirl almost as much as the pockets of turbulence that sent the plane bouncing.

Anna was anxiously awaiting Jo's response on the ticket to Punta Cana she'd put on hold. They had until nine that evening to either book or let it go. Jo wanted to release the ticket last night, but Anna insisted they hold on until the last minute. Jo suspected her sister knew she'd be meeting with Sam today and had her doubts about the outcome. Even Robert sent a text this morning wishing her good luck, as though a happy reunion with Sam was still not certain.

The plane began its descent, crossing through the clouds and opening up Jo's world to the mostly snowless ground below. Golden brown fallow fields bordered with paved roads gave way to housing blocks, busy streets, and then skyscrapers.

Sam was down there somewhere, and Jo could hardly wait to get through her day so they'd finally be together. She strained to study Toronto from her small window and began to wonder why Sam was so interested in her when the city world abounded with available women.

She'd visit Church Street, a ritualistic pilgrimage to the gay village each time she made it to the city. The first occasion had been more than twenty years ago while on an excursion to explore what was like a different planet to a very closeted lesbian. She'd felt like a kid in a candy store, popping in and out of all the rainbow shops that were still so foreign in smaller cities and towns.

This time she would be with Sam, holding hands as they walked through the gay village. She longed to find a women's bar with a dance floor so she could sway and smooch with Sam in a crowd. Jo's stomach churned as the miniature city grew larger and the reality of being in Toronto became imminent.

The wheels on the plane locked into place and the ground was fast approaching. Jo held her breath for the touchdown and let out a sigh as the wheels bounced on the tarmac then drove along the runway to the gate. It was raining out and everything looked so dreary, but Jo felt sunny inside.

She'd only brought a carry-on backpack with one change of clothes and extra underwear for an extended visit. The flight had been on time and there was no wait for luggage, so Jo headed directly to the taxi stand for her journey into downtown.

Her driver was a woman around her age and happy to chat as they drove toward the CN Tower for a central drop off. Jo's gaydar was on high alert; she felt pleased to have selected a likely lesbian chauffeur.

"Timmins," her driver said. "Wow. I've never been that far north. Isn't that where Shania's from?"

"It is indeed." Jo gawked at the tall buildings, awed at big-city life.

"Did you know her?" Twinkling brown eyes flashed from the rearview mirror.

"Nope, can't say I did." Jo thought of Sam's sparkling eyes and her stomach twirled.

"How long are you here for?" The driver merged onto Yonge Street.

"Until Monday morning," Jo said. "If all goes well."

"Sounds exciting." An attractive smile graced the rearview mirror.

"It is," Jo said. "I've never been in a long-distance relationship before. It's like we live in two different worlds. There isn't even any snow here. I'm glad I didn't wear my big boots and bulky mitts because I sure don't need them. I'm just so looking forward to spending time with Sam."

"What does Sam do in Toronto?"

"She's a lawyer." Jo held her breath, daring to out herself to the stranger.

"I pegged you for a sister." The driver grinned. "What do you do for a living?"

"I'm a forester."

"Gosh, there aren't many forests down here. Are you planning to move to the city?"

"Not really." Jo dug out her wallet. "You can let me off just up ahead at Yonge and Bloor."

"Sure, no problem." The driver pulled to the side and angled the meter toward Jo. "Do you need a receipt?"

"Yes, please." Jo handed over cash and a tip. "Thanks for the ride. It was nice chatting with you."

"Likewise." The driver turned around with the receipt and smiled. "I hope things work out with Sam. Maybe our paths will cross sometime."

"Thanks." Jo stepped out onto the sidewalk and shivered. She should've brought her heavier coat.

CHAPTER THIRTY-FOUR

When Sam realized she'd forgotten her phone at the office, she was already in the courtroom and looking to turn it off.

"Shit." She whispered to herself, fidgeting through her document bag in search of the cell. With a resigned shrug of her shoulders, Sam rose as the court started its session. She was at least thankful for Jo's unexpected message about wanting to talk and her confirmation to meet at the Eaton Centre at five thirty.

If nothing else, she'd scurry down there and meet up with Jo before retrieving her phone. It would be a good opportunity to show Jo her office, describe her work, and maybe even share a kiss behind her closed door while everyone else left for home.

The rest of her morning was filled with unobstructed concentration as the trial began. Sam was prepared, now more than ever, to have the charges against her client stayed and the trial over by the end of the day so she could spend the rest of the week with Jo. It took some of the bitterness out of helping a drunk driver walk a free man after killing innocent people. At least that's what she told herself as she witnessed the courtroom tragedy about to unfold for the victims' family.

Jo made it to her meeting in good time and sat in a chair along the wall of the packed room. She frequently checked her phone in hopes Sam would have answered her messages saying she'd arrived in the city. Nothing. Not even over lunch.

Jo sent another text saying she would head to the Eaton Centre after her meeting. Sam's lack of response was a bit disconcerting and Jo began to wonder what she'd do if she didn't hear anything by the end of the afternoon.

Her meeting went well, though she was asked only one question regarding the level of consultation for the forest management plan. Jo easily responded by citing high attendance numbers and valuable input at their recent open house. She then resumed her quiet position on the sidelines for the rest of the afternoon.

Jo was free by four o'clock and took her time popping in and out of shops on the way to her meeting place with Sam. She toured around inside the large shopping complex while clutching her phone in fear she might miss a call. At five fifteen, she decided to head back out to the street in front of the main entrance. The popular corner was busy with commuters, shoppers, panhandlers, and tourists like her. It would be hard to spot Sam with so many people around and she tried to keep herself visible by standing off to the side on her own.

She felt conspicuous and geeky in her hiking boots and backpack, hoping Sam would notice her against the hustle and bustle of the corner. There was a slight breeze and her teeth chattered while the wait became more uncertain as time passed.

Jo finally spotted Sam rushing down the street and her heart burst with joy. It was five forty and her feet were getting cold. Sam looked hurried and stressed as she maneuvered through the crowds toward her destination. The closer she got, the more Jo began to realize how different their lives were.

Sam sported a long navy wool coat, a red and blue patterned wool scarf loosely wrapped around her neck, black short-heeled leather boots, and dark gray leather gloves. Her right hand swung a document bag. Jo suddenly felt intimidated by the appearance of this sophisticated city lawyer rushing to meet with a casually dressed forester from the north.

Jo hesitated as she watched the approaching goddess, suddenly feeling insecure in her normal work attire and wondering what Sam saw in her. Heels clicking on pavement as elegantly dressed workers rushed by, Jo looked at her rubber-soled hiking boots and felt like she didn't stand a chance in this cosmopolitan world. Especially with a woman as suave as Sam looked in her work attire. Sam would set any courtroom on fire, or any heart for that matter, and the cedar kindling Jo remembered in her backpack seemed irrelevant now.

Jo saw Sam looking around as she approached and knew she hadn't yet been spotted. She raised a hand to wave when an attractive young woman stepped from the crowd and bolted toward Sam.

Sam had rushed all the way from the courthouse, so afraid she'd miss Jo and determined to embrace the woman she loved at one of the city's busiest intersections. Pedestrian traffic grew heavier and shoulders slammed into hers as she strained to look for Jo. Someone called out her name and she rushed toward the familiar voice, confused with the congestion. When she saw Trish pushing her way through other pedestrians, Sam stopped, her mouth dropping open with stunned surprise.

"How could you?" Trish shouted at Sam, shoving against her arm. "After what happened the other night, what were you thinking by agreeing to meet that bitch Jo here?"

"Trish, calm down!" Sam grabbed her flailing arms, wondering what the hell was happening. "What are you talking about?"

"You betrayed me! Jo's nothing to you and yet you're meeting her behind my back. What kind of game are you playing?"

"This has nothing to do with you." Sam was furious and losing her calm as Trish continued to swing her arms. "How did you know I'm meeting Jo here?"

"She told me." Trish's trembling hand brushed tears off her face.

"What? How did you get her number?" Sam glanced away from Trish, locking eyes with Jo, standing not ten feet away. *Fuck.* "Jo. There you are." She rushed toward Jo.

Jo backed up, pointing a shaking hand at Trish. "How could you do this to me, and to her? What kind of game are you playing?"

"Jo please, I can explain." Sam tried to get closer, but the busy intersection impeded her progress.

"Go ahead then, tell me what just happened?" Her voice started to shake.

Sam was confused and looked around for Trish to help explain, but she was gone. She shook her head. "I don't know."

"Fuck you!" Jo flung the bundle of cedar kindling at Sam and ran down the street toward a taxi.

"Jo, wait!" Sam tried to follow, but Jo got into the cab and they sped away before she could catch up. "Fuck."

Jo was hyperventilating as she got into the car. She managed to direct the driver to take her to the airport, and to hurry. She'd try to make the evening flight and get back to Timmins as soon as possible. The first thing she did, however, was send a text to Anna to book her ticket to the Dominican. The next message was to Sam, saying she never wanted to hear from her again and to not bother replying because all messages from her would be deleted, unread.

Unbelievable. Jo shook with shock from the scene with the pretty young woman named Trish, Sam's *supposed* ex. Sam must have fooled her too. The way she confronted Sam, crying and shouting because they were meeting. She must have somehow found out. Thank God. To think she'd been willing to consider this woman a soul mate and make a long-distance relationship feasible.

Her hands shook as she paid the taxi driver then hobbled into the airport, eyes wet while trying to cover sobs with coughs. She hurried to the ticket counter and managed to get on the evening flight to Timmins.

Getting through security and then finding a quiet spot to decompress was all she could think about to keep herself moving. It took her an hour before she calmed down enough to call Robert and let him know she'd be home later that night.

"Hi." She sniffed.

"Please tell me that's from a cold."

She choked back a sob. "I'm coming home tonight."

"What happened?"

Jo's jaw clenched, her emotions still so raw. "I should have known better. I let your mom know I'm going with them next week. I hope you're still okay to look after Mollie."

"Of course I am, but are you sure about this?" He paused. "I thought you and Sam had worked things out. Something doesn't seem right."

"That's because I was all wrong about Sam. I have to go. I'll see you when I get home."

Sam was in a daze when she got back to her office. Everyone had gone home for the day and she had the place to herself, but still closed her door before sitting behind the desk. Sobs followed tears as she dropped her head into her hands. What was supposed to have been one of the best nights of her life was now a nightmare and all she could think about was the look of horror on Jo's face.

Something wasn't right. How could Trish have known she was meeting Jo there? She remembered her phone and found it buried under some papers on her desk. The message indicator was flashing, and she had a slew of texts. She went right to the top, her eyes focusing on Jo's last message saying she never wanted to hear from her again.

As she scanned through the chain of messages, she saw that Jo had sent a number of texts over the course of the day, including the one asking to meet to talk. Jo let Sam know when she landed in Toronto, hoped she was having a good day in court, touched base when the forestry meeting was over, sent another text when she got to the Eaton Centre. Then Sam saw the message from Jo saying she couldn't meet that evening.

She looked at the number and realized it was different than the rest of Jo's texts. Sam scrolled to the second one of the morning and gasped. Shit. Fuck. The message was from Trish's Jo, not hers. It had to be. She must have gotten her number from Trish at some point. That's how Trish knew she'd be at the Eaton Centre and why she caused the scene.

Sam immediately dialed her Jo's number, but all she got was voice mail. "Jo, it was all a big misunderstanding. I can explain. Please talk to me. I love you."

Sam tried calling and sending texts, but all to no avail. Her evening with Jo was not going to happen. As tears fell, she clutched the bundle of cedar kindling Jo had thrown.

CHAPTER THIRTY-FIVE

Jo finally got back to Timmins after a painful flight of choking back sobs. She'd left her truck in the Timmins airport parking lot and was able to finally let her tears out during the drive home. Mollie was tied outside and scampered toward the vehicle, yelping as Jo stepped onto the driveway.

"Oh, Mollie." Jo fell to her knees and buried her wet face into cold fur. "What would I do without you?"

"Hey." Robert came outside, his coat open and boots unlaced. He pulled her up into his arms and stroked the back of her head. "I'm so sorry, Aunt Jo. I'm glad you made it home okay. Let's get you in the house where it's nice and warm."

"I need my pack."

"I'll get your bag." Robert ushered her toward the house. "Go ahead inside with Mollie."

"Thanks." Jo forced a smile as she stumbled into the warmth, Mollie tight against her legs. At least she had this to come home to. Her house was like a quiet refuge where she could hibernate and rebuild her life with Mollie and her family.

Jo managed to calm down and wipe away the tears after she'd had a numbing hot shower then threw on a pair of sweats. They sat in the living room, Jo self-medicating with rye and ginger ale.

Robert shook his head. "I never would have taken Sam for a crazy bitch like that. To think she could trick you into believing you were the only one for her when she couldn't even fool her baby dyke. Or supposed ex."

"No wonder she was hiding up in the bush when I found her. She's fucked up." Jo took a swig of her second drink. "She obviously slept with Trish the other night, saying I meant nothing to her while she's telling me I'm everything."

"She must have some heavy-duty mental problems," Robert said. "Count yourself lucky you got away when you did."

"Love and relationships are so overrated. Here's to being single." Jo held up her glass then took another gulp, ice cubes caressing her lips instead of the kisses she'd longed for.

"Cheers." Robert joined the toast. "Let's have a singles' celebration on Valentine's Day. It's coming up soon and all this talk of sweethearts is making me sick."

"Me too." Jo patted her knee to summon Mollie. "From now on, I'm rejecting Valentine's Day. No more talk of love or relationships."

"It's not so bad being single." Robert stared into his glass then looked up at Jo and grinned. "I'm free to do whatever I want and only have to answer to myself."

"And the best part about being single is no one else controls your heart. You and I are going to have a big bonfire this Valentine's Day to celebrate our freedom." She motioned to the floor, glass in hand almost spilling. "Those bamboo boards are getting in the way and will be perfect for a big blaze."

"Count me in." Robert stood. "But for now, I have an early morning meeting and need to get some sleep. You should go to bed too. It's been a long day for you."

"I will. Thanks for being here." She stood and they hugged good night.

Jo feared lying alone in the dark, visions of Sam still stifling her thoughts. She sat on the edge of her bed and stared at her blinking phone. There were messages from Sam, she was sure. The temptation to hear her out was strong, but Jo was determined to not give Sam the satisfaction of having her say. She began to delete everything. She would get a new phone and number first thing in the morning.

The sun barely made an appearance the next day and Jo was content to stay indoors with the lights on, redoing her living room floor. Concentrating on work was out of the question and hammering hardwood flooring helped ease the pain. She'd stored the boards behind the couch and was manically measuring for her planned installation when Mollie began barking out the window. Someone had arrived.

She instantly thought of Sam and jumped to her feet to see who was there. Her breathing almost matched Mollie's then suddenly slowed as her mother approached the door.

"How was Toronto?" The scent of her mother's lavender lotion was soothing as they hugged.

"It was fine." Jo stepped back. "Come on in and take your coat off. I'll make us tea."

"Are you sure? You look busy."

"I have been, but it's time for a break." Jo stood at her kitchen sink, avoiding her mother's eyes. "I've started to install my oak hardwood in the living room."

"Oh, let me see." Her mother headed in to have a look.

"There's not much to see yet because I'm still measuring and planning things out." Jo closed her eyes against the tears she would not allow in front of her mother.

"That looks like a big job. I thought you would have waited until after our holiday." Her mother focused on Mollie as the dog begged for attention. "By the way, I'm so happy you're joining us. Anna was thrilled when she got your message last night. What made you change your mind?"

"It was being at the airport in Toronto yesterday." Jo plopped into a chair. "I knew I had to get away and an all-inclusive where I can just veg on the beach sounded perfect."

Her mother sat at the table with her and reached over. "Are you okay? You look a bit pale."

"I'm fine." Jo jumped up. "I'm just tired from yesterday. The tea should be ready by now."

"You need to take care of yourself, Jo. This is not the time to get sick because we're leaving in three days."

"Don't worry about me." Jo brought steaming mugs to the table. "I'll be okay and on that plane Saturday morning no matter what."

Her mother stayed long enough to drink her tea then left Jo to continue with the installation of her flooring. Jo struggled to block out all thoughts of Sam, but ended up wishing she hadn't changed her phone and number so soon. She wanted to know Sam was trying to reach her and suffering from humiliation at being caught in a lie, if nothing else.

By the time Anna called at noon, Jo had laid three rows of flooring.

"Did you get a new phone?" Anna asked. "I didn't think you had to change your number for that."

"It was time for an upgrade so why not?" Jo had emailed her new number to a few close family members and work colleagues as soon as she got back from the store that morning. "I'm laying my oak flooring right now. It's starting to take shape and looks much nicer than what was there before."

"Have you started packing yet? I've been checking out the weather in Punta Cana and it's looking so nice. I can't wait. It's a good thing you changed your mind and are coming with us. It'll be fun."

"I'm sure it will."

"So why did you change your number?"

"It was time for a new one."

"You saw Sam yesterday in Toronto, didn't you?"

"Not really." Jo closed her eyes, wishing her sister would just drop it. "It was a short, fast trip and I'm happy I didn't get sucked into anything."

"With her? Has Sam been trying to contact you?" Anna paused. "Of course she has, that's why you changed your number. Has she been harassing you?"

"No, but I need to move on." If anyone was harassing Jo, it was herself for believing Sam could be trusted. "I'm glad Robert will be staying with Mollie next week." Time to change the focus.

Anna bit. "I worry about him sometimes. I wish he'd find someone to settle down with."

"It's not bad being single. And he's still young."

"I know, but still. I hope to one day become a grandmother and it would be nice to have grandkids here because I know Sarah will never move back north."

"Things don't always turn out the way you want." Jo's voice caught as she fought back tears. "I've got to go. Talk to you later." She ended the call just in time to release her sob. Moving on from Sam was going to be hard.

CHAPTER THIRTY-SIX

Sam slammed into a corner of her dresser then stubbed a big toe on the foot of the bed as she rushed to answer her phone. She'd just gotten out of the shower and was still dripping wet when the ringing began.

"Ouch. Fuck. Hello."

A telemarketer's robocall imitating the foghorn of a cruise ship blasted into her ear.

"Oh for fuck's sake!" She threw the cell onto her bed and plunked down beside it. She'd been hoping it was Jo, even though none of her calls, texts, or emails had been returned. It was now two days since Jo's number had been put out of service and Sam clung to a faint hope for a call back each time her cell rang. She clutched her bath towel over her shoulders and tried to find solace in the fact she'd be going to Timmins on Monday morning.

It was going to be a stressful weekend of waiting and wondering as she strategized for two meetings. The first one was an interview for the criminal lawyer position she'd applied for in the Timmins law firm. The second, more important rendezvous involved facing Jo.

How could she ever convince Jo of her love now? It's not like she'd bring Trish along to corroborate her story of the confusion over Joanne. She desperately wanted to get that job in Timmins to prove to Jo that she was serious about building a relationship.

She'd avoided the gym that morning to get a head start on preparing for her meetings. Sam had always been on top of her game, in both the job and women departments, but now felt insecure as she struggled to come to terms with what was at stake. Her life depended on making things right with Jo because there was no turning back now. She was in love.

Sam reached for the small bundle she kept on her bedside table. She recognized the kindling as ones she'd cut at her cottage. For Jo to have brought it all the way here must have meant she really believed Sam could start a fire in her heart. Already had. It was an insult to have it thrown at her, to be discarded on the street like garbage when she knew Jo must have treasured the cedar sticks. There had been such hopeful plans before that encounter. Sam had to get them back on track. The rest of her life depended on it.

Day turned into night faster than Sam would have liked. She'd been busy at the office, working like crazy to clear her neglected inbox and gather case files that could be useful for interview preparation. Lunch flew by without even an apple and she was starving by the time the garlic aroma of Trish's pasta hit her nostrils at the front door to her house.

It had taken her two days before she could even look at the woman she blamed for driving Jo away. Trish had been hurting, too, and Sam finally stopped condemning her for traumatizing Jo. She accepted her own responsibility in the mess and just wanted to move on to a more collegial cohabitation until either she or Trish moved out. Sam avoided talking about what happened with Jo, opting instead to keep things amicable while she plotted her next move to win back the woman in her heart.

"Hey Sam, I picked up some lasagna for dinner. Would you like some?" Trish was on her best behavior and even seemed to have matured while Sam shut her out.

"It sure smells good." Sam stopped by the kitchen, her arms weighted down with files.

"I'll get you a plate," Trish said. "I have a salad in a bag to go with it if you'd like some of that too."

"Thanks. That would be nice. I'll drop these off in my room then be right back."

Sam trudged down the hall, trying to ignore the fact she should have been sharing dinner with Jo instead of an all-too-pleasing ex that would be back in her bed with the slightest encouragement. Sex for the sake of sex was no longer an option. She could only think of touching Jo. Even having dinner with Trish felt like a betrayal of sorts, but she was starving and in a hurry to study because she had to get that job.

Things often happened for a reason and Sam allowed herself the luxury of optimism as she planned her next few days. The weekend would be spent studying and researching in preparation for her Monday afternoon interview in Timmins. After that, she would head to Jo's, and if all went well, spend the night making up. It had to go well. She could never go back to the way things were.

"How was your day?" Trish put a plate full of pasta and salad in front of Sam.

"It just zipped by." Sam took a bite, realizing how famished she was at the first taste of the cheesy lasagna. "This is good. Thanks for sharing."

"I've come to terms with things, Sam." Trish moved a lasagna noodle around her plate then looked up. "I know you've fallen in love with someone else. I want to be here as a friend for you. That's the least I can do, after all. I still feel so bad about the mix-up."

"So do I. I'm sure Jo feels like shit right now." Sam couldn't look at Trish. "Anyway, I'm not giving up and plan to speak with her on Monday when I'm back in Timmins."

"Have you heard from her? Does she know you're coming?"

"No."

"What if she refuses to talk to you? What are you going to do then?"

Sam sipped her water. "I already know she won't talk to me. My plan is to tell her about my intention to move to Timmins for her, job offer or not."

"I still can't believe you'd consider moving way up north for a woman." Trish dropped her head. "You never would have done that for me."

"I couldn't see you moving up there for me, either, especially after refusing to even go up to my cottage last summer."

"It was during bug season and you know how I hate mosquitoes. Besides, I'm a proud city lesbian and would shrivel up and die if I had to live in the middle of the bush."

Sam stood, her empty plate in hand. "Timmins is hardly the middle of the bush."

"Well, whatever, but you're going to be freezing your ass off up there at this time of year."

"Not at all. It can be snuggly and cozy, especially with the right conditions." She put her plate on the counter and looked for the bag for the leftover garlic bread. "Thanks for the dinner. I'll clean up, then I've got to lock myself away to study."

"Joanne wants to get you a new TV." Trish stuck close to Sam as they cleared the table. "She's offered to go shopping with me this weekend and buy a replacement. She feels like a shit. That's why she wanted to talk to you the other day."

Sam rinsed the dishcloth and wiped the table, her jaw tight. "I don't need a new TV and would rather not have her anywhere near here."

"The other day was my fault," Trish said. "I freaked when I heard she planned to see you. Can you blame me?"

"What were you doing talking with her anyway?"

"She's the one who contacted me." Trish crossed her arms and leaned against the doorway into the hallway. "She said she wanted to apologize. Then told me she was meeting you and...I lost it. I thought for sure she was betraying me and trying to move in on you."

"She's way too young for me." Sam tried to squeeze by, but Trish grabbed her arm.

"She's only four years younger than me. She wants to be a lawyer. I'm only an administrative assistant, so how can I compete with that? That's why you left me, isn't it?"

"Trish, our breaking up had nothing to do with our jobs." Sam sighed, pulling her arm away. "I was the one who screwed up, thinking great sex was enough when I really needed to grow up and find myself."

"We did have lots of fun, didn't we? I'm glad we're still talking, Sam. I hope we stay friends."

"We will if it's meant to be." Sam headed down the hall to her room.

"Good luck with Jo." Trish called out. "I really mean it."

"Thanks." Sam poked her head around her bedroom door before closing herself in for the night. "I really need to study and get my head into this potential job. Dinner was great. Thanks again."

Sam checked the Timmins weather as soon as she settled back into her bedroom. The city was heading into a deep freeze and it would be unbearably cold for her trip on Monday. She fondled the kindling, thinking of the green cedar hedge outside Jo's kitchen window.

Her flight was booked to leave early Monday morning and return later in the evening, but with a flexible ticket that could be changed up to an hour before departure. Sam smiled as she imagined knocking on Jo's door then falling into each other's arms for a night of hot passion fitting for frigid weather.

It had to be like that because there were no other options. By next week at this time, Sam planned to be well on her way to the rest of her life.

CHAPTER THIRTY-SEVEN

Friday evening at Jo's place was a bustle of getting ready for an early morning flight to Toronto then on to Punta Cana. Anna and her mother were already packed, but Jo was far from ready. She was still finishing up her living room floor, and brooding over the disaster in Toronto. How could she have let herself fall for Sam's lies a second time, especially after the heartbreak she went through with Jan? It was just so stupid. She needed to put it behind her.

Her mother and sister had dropped by to help get her suitcase filled with summer clothes and beachwear. They were in Jo's bedroom, going through her wardrobe and selecting appropriate attire. Anna flung a pair of sports sandals toward Jo's luggage. "You're not wearing hiking boots on the beach."

"Bring both of your bathing suits." Her mother tossed them into the open case. "You can wear the two-piece on the beach and have the other one available for your workout swims in the pool."

"Whatever." Jo let them have control of her packing. She was still numb with hurt, struggling to forget about Sam. At least she'd only be in Toronto for two hours the next morning before their flight south. She would stay in security and try not to think of being in the same city as Sam.

"This is going to be so much fun." Anna held up a navy golf shirt. "What do you think? It's looking a bit ragged."

"Put it in," Jo said. "It's one of my favorite tops and I want to be comfortable."

Her mother sifted through the bed full of clothes. "Let's pack some nice blouses so you'll have something to wear when we go out for dinner." She held up Jo's beige top. "This is cute. I like the fern leaves in the pattern. It'll be perfect."

"Here's another one with some pine needles on the fabric." Anna threw it onto the pile. "I can see a theme in your clothes. The bush. I sure hope you shave your legs."

"Anna, the hair on my legs is blond and hardly has to be shaved." Jo raised her pant leg and flaunted the peach fuzz. "You should be happy I'm not dark like you because my legs are always hairy."

"Ugh," Anna said. "I hope you at least cut your toenails so you look presentable in sandals."

Her mother held out her hands, jiggling fingers. "I had my nails painted a nice blue teal that reminds me of the ocean."

"How nice." Anna examined them. "I'm hoping to get mine done at the resort because I haven't had time and they're a disaster."

Jo looked at her short nails. Whites were starting to show at the tips, so it was time for another trim. Forget about anything else, though.

By the time her suitcase was full, Jo realized she'd only picked out underwear while her mother and Anna had decided on the rest of her wardrobe for the trip. An all-inclusive holiday was just what she needed. Now that her living room flooring was done, she had no energy left.

"Robert's here," Anna said. "I'll let him in."

Mollie beat her to the door and nuzzled Robert as he stepped inside, overnight bag in hand.

"Hey, girl." He bent to greet the bustling dog. "It's going to be just the two of us. We'll have lots of fun while our moms and Grandma lie on the beach."

Anna hugged her son. "We can't just lie around all day. We'll be taking some nice long walks along the shoreline to burn off the extra calories from all the food we're going to eat."

"I'd like to get a pair of larimar earrings." Her mother hugged Robert next. "We can walk down to the shops at the far end of the beach. A nice larimar pendant would look good on you, Jo."

Jo greeted Robert, their hug tight and reaffirming after their conversation of a few nights before. "I'm not in the market for any souvenirs for myself."

"I can't believe you're not more excited about this trip," Anna said. "This will be the perfect opportunity for you to unwind and forget about everything. And to relax."

"It's great you can stay here tonight and take us to the airport in the morning," Jo said to Robert in an effort to take the focus off her. "Maybe I'll bring you back a souvenir."

"There's no need to do that," Robert said as he followed her into the kitchen. "But if you feel like it, a nice bottle of alcohol for Valentine's Day would be nice."

"Oh?" Anna looked at her son. "Do you have something special planned?"

"Yes, I do." Robert carried his bag toward the guest bedroom. "Aunt Jo and I are spending it together."

"Have a look at her new living room floor on your way by," her mother said. "She's been working like mad to get it finished."

Robert put his pack down and walked inside the room. "Hey, Aunt Jo, this looks great. The boards are in really good shape."

"What are you going to do with the bamboo?" Anna asked.

"Burn it." Jo closed her eyes, her jaw tightening.

"Oh Jo, don't do that," her mother said. "I'm sure someone could do something with it, just like you used this beautiful oak flooring."

"The bamboo is toxic, and I want it destroyed." Jo picked up Robert's bag, needing to escape. "I'll take this to your room for you."

Jo stormed down the hallway and placed his pack on the floor beside the bed Sam had slept in. She ran her hand across the duvet then squeezed the pillow in a futile attempt to harness feelings of loss.

The trip south was a godsend. There was little to associate with Sam in a land so far away. At least, that's what Jo hoped. She took a deep breath and returned to the kitchen, determined to make this winter escape work.

Her mother and sister were standing by the outside door, ready to leave.

"Have a good sleep, dear, and don't forget your passport." Her mother kissed her cheek and gave a heartfelt hug.

"I won't." Jo kissed her mother's cheek, comforted by her caring. "And thanks for your help with the packing."

"It was fun." Her mother turned to Robert and gave him a farewell hug. "It's so nice of you to get up early on your day off to drive us to the airport."

"More like the middle of the night," Robert said, "but I guess it's payback time."

"For sure." Anna tied her wool scarf into a knot over the front of her coat. "You owe me for all those early morning trips to the arena to play hockey. I'll see you at four thirty." She kissed his cheek and they left.

Jo made a cup of chamomile tea then sat in the living room with Robert and Mollie. "I'm glad you could stay over tonight. It'll make things a lot simpler in the morning."

"Poor Mollie, she's going to really miss you." Robert sipped on a rum and Coke.

"I'm going to miss her too, but I know the two of you'll have fun together." She was glad he was going to be here with Mollie. "And remember, you can use my truck all week if you like."

"Thanks. My vehicle needs to go in for some muffler work and I was hoping to drop it off at the dealer's on Monday."

"Perfect, then. I filled up the tank this afternoon and Mollie's blanket for the backseat is by the kitchen door. I removed it for our ride to the airport tomorrow morning."

"Sounds like everything's organized. Mom and Grandma made sure of that tonight with your packing, I hear." He chuckled.

"Yeah, it was sweet of them to do that. I'm so lucky to have you guys as my family."

He raised his glass to her. "We're fortunate, too. I know we'd all be so lost if you ever moved away." He took a drink.

"I'm not going anywhere." Jo tapped her lap. "Come here, girl." Mollie's head bobbed onto her knees, the soft fur soothing under Jo's fingers.

"I know you're packed and have your passport by the door, but what about you?" Robert tilted his head. "Are you ready for this?"

"Yes, I am. I need to do something to try to forget about Sam. I could continue replacing all of the flooring in this house or go lie on a beach somewhere. Who knows what's best, but I may as well do something that's at least making our mothers happy."

Robert's eyebrows furrowed as he leaned toward her. "I was thinking about things. I still can't believe Sam would have done that to you."

"You hardly even knew her." Jo felt her blood pressure rising, the anger against Sam still so strong.

"I know, but Grandma's a pretty good judge of character." Robert shifted, a crease still in his forehead. "She really liked Sam and is still reeling over what happened. She called me up last night and asked if I knew how you were doing."

"And what did you tell her?" Jo's hand stilled against Mollie.

"That I thought it was great the three of you are going away and a vacation like that would be good for everyone." He paused to sip his drink. "I also told her your heart was broken and healing would take time."

"Did she say anything about Sam?"

"Yes. She said she had a mind to contact Sam herself and ask what was going on."

Jo's heart hiccupped. "Oh God, no. I hope you told her not to."

"Of course I did. Grandma really thought Sam was taken with you and feels something's not right."

"Something isn't right. I fell in love with Sam. I need to move on and the timing of this trip is one of the best things right now. I'd better get to bed. See you in a few hours."

Jo knew she would hardly sleep at all that night, but at least got under her covers. Her mind was racing with fear of sleeping in and missing her flight, or worse yet, getting to their destination and falling apart on foreign soil. Then she'd really be in trouble.

CHAPTER THIRTY-EIGHT

Vehicle exhaust wafted around the headlights of the idling truck in the frigid night air. Jo had backed her pickup out of the garage to let it warm up before Robert chauffeured them to the airport.

Out of bed at three thirty, Jo showered, had her first coffee by four, and wanted to crawl back under the covers by four fifteen. She knew her travel companions would be excited and full of exuberant chitchat on the way to the airport. Jo would have no part of it as she pined over Sam. She just wanted to mull in private over the woman who had reached her heart and set it sparking again only to end in disaster.

She resented Sam more than ever. How dare someone mess with her emotions like that? Jo would never again let herself get sucked in by someone. Her heart was dismantled, bankrupt, out of business for good.

"I think we should head out soon." Jo knelt by her back door, giving soothing hugs to Mollie, cuddling the whimpering dog. "It's okay, girl. I'll be back in a week and you'll have lots of fun with Robert."

Robert rushed into the kitchen, pulling a sweater over his head. "Mom already texted me twice, asking where we are. Any coffee left?"

"That red insulated mug on the counter is yours. Sugar and cream included."

"Oh, you're such a sweetie, Aunt Jo."

"It's more like a bribe. We do need to get going." Jo stood, kissing the top of Mollie's head. She wiped away a tear.

Snow crunched under their boots on the trek to the truck and a trail of exhaust hung in the air as they pulled away. Robert was at the wheel and Jo watched her house disappear as they turned onto the road. She was happy for him to drive, shivering in the passenger seat and preparing to shut down for the week in a mindless state of recuperation. That was Jo's plan for renewing a life that felt like it had been clear-cut by Sam and left on its own to regenerate.

When they got to Anna's, the front porch light glared and she stood waiting just inside the storm door. The glass was completely frosted, except for the small peephole Anna's breath had formed. She stepped outside, struggling to get her suitcase through the door, and put her key in the lock as Robert hurried to take her luggage.

"Oh my God, it's cold out this morning." Anna slid into the backseat. She was only wearing an orange summer jacket. "Here, Robert, put my bag on the seat beside me then hurry up and close the door."

"I can't believe this is the same woman who used to nag at me for not dressing warm enough." Robert buckled back in and they left.

"This is different." Anna tapped Jo's shoulder. "I'm so glad you're coming with us. Our trip's going to be a lot of fun."

"I'm looking forward to some downtime," Jo said. "I hope you and Mom will be okay with me staying back at the resort if you decide to book any day tours."

"We'll figure that out later," Anna said. "Oh look, Mom's already outside waiting for us. Doesn't she look like the little lost hobo standing there with her suitcase in tow?"

"Mom, Grandma looks just as excited as you." Robert stopped in front of his grandmother's driveway. "At least she's dressed for the weather and wearing her parka instead of a flimsy summer jacket."

"Good morning, everyone." Their mother was at the truck, her luggage waiting in the snow for her grandson to retrieve. "I hope my girls are ready to have some fun in the sun because I sure am."

When they got to the airport, passengers were already heading through security as the waiting plane warmed on the tarmac. Jo sat beside a stranger on the flight to Toronto, scrunched up against the window and trying to block out her trepidation at being back in the airport of misery.

The descent began. Jo's eyes closed, her teeth clenched in fury, and the pit of her stomach burned. She'd passed on a coffee or any type of snack during the flight, but still felt nauseous. A dip through turbulence sent her stomach reeling and her eyes opened to suburbia below.

Headlights beamed from tiny cars in the early morning Toronto traffic. Everything looked a dirty gray. There was no snow, and the trees were bare. Even the cloudy sky seemed to shroud the city with an aura of doom and gloom. At least that's how Jo felt as an overwhelming bitterness consumed her.

The plane circled over neighborhoods while waiting for its turn to land and Jo began to wonder if she was flying over anywhere near Sam's house. Was she comfortably cuddled up in bed beneath them with someone new? Or was she still reveling in her ability to fool two women who loved her? How many other broken hearts had she left behind?

Jo determined to mend hers, like she'd done before, and would take the week in Punta Cana to pull herself together. She put her unread forestry magazine away and braced for landing. In two hours they'd be back in the sky and on their way to paradise, so the vacation brochure said.

Sam sipped coffee as she scanned the Saturday morning paper. Trish was still in bed, so she took the luxury of sitting alone at her dining table and planning her trip to Timmins. The interview at Maxwell and Associates had been set up for Monday afternoon.

She would take a morning flight, pick up her rental car at the airport, attend the interview, then go to Jo's right afterward. She envisioned a surprised Jo answering the door. She'd have to know Sam was serious, going all the way back to Timmins to talk to her.

Returning to Toronto without talking to Jo was not an option. Sam would figure out some way to make it happen even if the door was slammed in her face. She needed to get the woman of her dreams to give her a break and listen. Surely Jo would realize the mistake and things would go back to where they were supposed to be.

Instead of snuggling in bed with Jo on this dreary Saturday morning, she was preparing for the interview. The newspaper folded back up and her coffee in hand, she hurried back to her room of study materials. Now was not the time to relax.

CHAPTER THIRTY-NINE

Whirring airplane motors droned against the quiet as awed passengers gazed at aqua-blue beaches below. Descent had begun toward the Punta Cana International Airport. Julia sat on the aisle and leaned over Jo in the middle seat to share the window view with Anna.

"It's so beautiful." Anna was giddy. "I can hardly wait to get in the water."

"We should be at the resort in time for a late lunch," her mother said. "We'll eat first before heading to the beach. Maybe some of the lounge chairs will have freed up by then as people start to get ready for dinner."

"I've been dieting and going to the gym all week so I can eat guilt-free while we're here," Anna said.

"It'll be so nice not to have to cook." Her mother leaned back in her seat. "It's time to wake up, Jo. We're almost there."

"Are we?" Jo feigned a yawn, fully aware of the imminent landing.

"Oh Jo, you have to see this." Anna tugged her sister's arm. "The color of the water is such a magnificent teal blue. It's just breath-taking, especially after all the snow we've had."

Jo rolled her head toward the window, a clear blue sky beaming back. She sighed with sadness. Her thoughts during the flight had been on Sam, replaying the disastrous meeting in Toronto. "I like the snow."

"Then you'll love the sandy white beaches," Anna said. "It'll be just like walking in snow, except in sandals or bare feet instead of big boots. Come on. Have a look before we land."

"Go on, Jo, admire the view." Her mother nudged Jo toward Anna. "You have to see it. The beaches are spectacular from up here."

Jo leaned into her sister, straining to see water and land out the small window. "It looks nice." The inviting aqua-blue beaches were indeed beautiful, and Jo's mood lightened. "It should be lots of fun. I'm looking forward to a change in scenery."

"Good." Anna kept her gaze on the beaches below. "I was starting to fear you'd mope the entire trip."

Jo settled back in her seat. "I'm sorry. I really do appreciate being here with the two of you. I promise to try to have fun this week. Let me know if I'm becoming a drag."

"It would be more of a drag if you weren't here with us." Anna tapped Jo's knee. "I'm so glad you changed your mind and decided to come."

"Me too." Her mother patted her hand. "We're going to have a great vacation together."

The three women held hands as the plane prepared to land. Jo began to focus on the positive. Things often happened for a reason. If things had worked out with Sam, she would be near the end of her stay in Toronto and missing out on this holiday with her mother and sister.

Passengers clapped after touchdown and Jo smiled as she joined in. For the first time in five days, her heart warmed with contentment as their vacation began.

By the time they got through customs and found their shuttle to the resort, Jo had replaced her hiking boots with sports sandals. The legs from her zip-off pants got tucked away in her suitcase and a new sense of freedom ensued as she swung her bare arms at her sides. She hopped onto the bus, determined to have an enjoyable week and let her guard down because Sam was now so far away.

Anna plopped into the aisle seat beside Jo. "Mom wanted me to sit with you. She managed to snag a front seat."

"More like the woman already there was okay to let Mom sit beside her." Jo chuckled as her mother chatted away, her elbow flailing around the high seat back in an animated conversation. "Look at her. She's just loving it."

"I knew getting away would be good for you," Anna said. "You're already looking so much better and starting to relax."

Jo tapped Anna's hand. "Thanks for organizing this trip. I'm sure it's what I need right now."

"Of course it is. We all need a bit of warm sun at this time of year to get our vitamin D levels back up to normal. I'm sure it'll help improve your mood."

"Have I been that bad?"

"Yes, almost worse than when you broke up with Jan." The bus started to move, pulling out from a long line of other tourist coaches. "What did Sam do to you, anyway?"

Jo squirmed. "She lied to me. We're done for good."

"Well, your oak flooring looks beautiful." Anna adjusted in her seat and glanced out her big tinted window. They were leaving the airport. "At least you got that finished."

"I must have looked like an insane animal when you and Mom caught me ripping out the bamboo." How could she have lost it like that? She felt so ashamed.

"What really happened with you and Sam?" Anna leaned closer. "You can tell me."

Jo sighed as she stared ahead at the navy seatback, her cheeks burning in shame. "She broke my heart, and left me feeling like an idiot. I should have known better."

"About what?" Anna nudged her shoulder. "Never fall in love with someone again after Jan? You're too hard on yourself."

"Maybe, but I'd rather just have peace of mind. Look at me. I'm a mess because I let my guard down and fell in love with Sam."

"So you took a risk and it failed." Anna rubbed Jo's arm. "If everyone quit because of that, where would we be? They were talking about it last week at work. Investing in a potential gold mine is risky because you never know how big the vein is. You have to look at the pros and cons then make a rational decision. And if I know you, Jo, you would have certainly rationalized letting yourself fall for Sam."

"That's the thing." Jo faced her sister's sympathetic frown, tears welling up. "My attraction to Sam lacked all rational thought. I was sure her feelings ran deeper than any risky mine venture. We're both professionals with good careers so it's not like she seemed after anything other than my heart."

Anna squeezed her hand. "It does sound strange. I'm just glad you're here with us now and hope you can put this behind. I want this to be a fun week for everyone."

"It will be fun." Jo smiled at her sister. "Now let's look out the window and focus on the landscape before we get to the resort."

After they checked into their bright ground-level room with its own patio, they ate lunch then headed for a look at the beach area.

"We should walk down and put our feet in the ocean before doing anything else," Anna said as she surveyed the crowded beach in front of their hotel.

"I'll race you." Jo started to run toward the water, dodging sunbathers as her feet slid in the soft sand until a small wave hit against her shins.

"That's not fair." Anna followed and splashed in up to her knees. "Ooh, the water's not bad."

"Here Mom, can you hold my sunglasses and wallet?" Jo tossed them to the shore and dove into a salty wave. The water was warm and there was lots of free space. She kept her eyes closed until resurfacing with a splash. "Whew. This feels great!"

"Poor Mom," Anna said. "I think she'd like to be in the water as well, but is too busy holding our stuff. Just like when we were kids."

"The two of you will always be my little girls." Their mother laughed from where she waited on the beach, both hands clutching their things. "I think it's time we look for some lounge chairs to park ourselves for a while."

"Sure." Jo shook her head, flinging droplets through the air as she got out of the water. She pulled off her wet T-shirt, thankful for her black sports bra that could pass as a bathing suit top, and felt herself starting to relax.

By the time dinner hour came around, Jo was ready to get out of the sun. The dining room was large with lots of white-clothed tables and a buffet of food choices galore. Anna plopped a heaping plate on the table and sat down.

"I can't believe I took a piece of chicken and a chunk of roast beef to go with all these vegetables and salads." She studied her choices.

"And a big bun too." Jo picked at some grapes and a few pieces of cheese, unable to stomach much more. "Where are you going to put all that food? A huge dinner roll can be filling on its own."

"I know, isn't it crazy?" Anna took a mouthful of pickled beets.

"Have you ever seen so much food?" Their mother joined them, her plate full, but with less variety than Anna's. "I can see that Jo's saving room for dessert."

"This is my dessert." Jo held up her grapes.

"That's hardly dessert," Anna said. "Didn't you see all of the cakes and cookies over there?"

"I'm not that hungry," Jo said.

"Oh Josephine, you have to eat." Her mother put her fork down and looked at her.

"We're worried about you, Jo. We want this week to help pull you back together."

"I am together. Just because I'm not eating like the two of you doesn't mean there's something wrong with me. Now if you'll excuse me, I've finished my dinner and think I'll head down to the beach."

Jo longed for some time on her own as she meandered through the resort on her way to a quiet place to relax. It was after seven in the evening and daylight had disappeared. She reached the empty beach. All the chairs had been put away, so she stood staring at the starry sky over the waves.

The salty air felt fresh against her skin and a slight breeze played with her hair.

Jo took off her sandals and sat on the edge of the cement walkway, digging her toes into the sand. It was really her head she wanted to bury in the sand on this deserted beach near the swishing ocean.

Sam hijacked her thoughts again. No matter how hard she tried, Jo just couldn't stop thinking about Sam. The way Sam had touched her, ran fingers and tongue over places aching to be caressed, and then brought her to orgasm with such force. She still lost her breath just thinking about it.

Jo decided her decadence for the week was going to be replaying sex with Sam instead of gorging on food. Maybe she could even learn to compartmentalize the pleasant bodily sensations from the hurtful feelings. If nothing else, Sam had given her a good time and she was going to make the best of it.

Sam needed to relax, studying for the day almost complete and her mind jumbled with case management scenarios. After a refreshing shower, she leaned back on her bed and stared at the muted TV. A tropical beach graced the screen and her mind drifted to Jo. Two more sleeps and she'd be in Timmins holding the woman she longed for, or so she hoped.

She'd checked the weather a number of times to make sure it still looked good for an early Monday morning flight. Leaving tomorrow had been a consideration, but Sam preferred to deal with the job interview first and then do whatever she had to do to convince Jo of her love, including spending the rest of the week in Timmins.

The bundle of kindling lay on the floor by her suitcase. She'd tied a red ribbon around the sticks and planned to return them to Jo to start a cozy fire in Timmins. Maybe they'd even snowshoe out to her cottage one day and spend the night. Mollie would love it, and it would be like a second chance from where it all started.

"Sam, are you home?" Trish called out from the front entry.

"Yes, I'm here."

"Oh." Trish paused. "Is it okay if Jo spends the night?" They had gotten back together, much to Sam's annoyance, but she no longer cared much.

"Whatever." Sam longed for her Jo, like it was supposed to have been. "Make sure you lock the front door."

It was just as well, though, that her Jo was probably already tucked away in bed in Timmins, getting rested for Sam's surprise visit. Although lonely without her, there had been no distractions, either, giving Sam the opportunity to be well prepared for her interview. So she told herself.

Maxwell and Associates had made it clear they were interested in meeting Sam and willing to accommodate her schedule to make it possible. Had things worked out with Jo's visit to Toronto, there would have been no time for studying anything other than that beautiful body. Sam liked to be prepared; she was confident the interview would go well.

Lights and television turned off, Sam slid into bed and pulled the covers up over her shoulders. She dared to allow herself the luxury of imagining Jo beside her, naked, ready to make love. A solitary tear dropped to her pillow as she readied for sleep.

CHAPTER FORTY

Anna scurried toward three free loungers in the shade and draped her towel over them to secure a place on the beach for the day. They hadn't yet eaten breakfast, as their priority of the morning was to reserve chairs before heading to the dining room.

"It's going to be a beautiful day." Anna clapped her hands together as she surveyed the open beach and ocean horizon. "There isn't a cloud in the sky and the temperature is just perfect."

"And there are no bugs." Their mother used a hand to shade her eyes. "It's so nice to enjoy warm weather without those miserable pests buzzing around."

Jo was eager to keep moving and stretch her legs. "Let's go for a stroll along the beach while the sand is still smooth from the tide. Our footprints can be some of the first for today."

"Oh, I can't go for a walk now," her mother said. "I'd have to rush back to the bathroom after a short bit because…"

"Okay, Mom," Anna said. "We get the picture. I'm ready for breakfast now, anyway. Especially since there's all this food calling out to us."

"You two go ahead then and I'll join you in a bit." Jo removed her sandals. "What better way to get a good start on the day than to walk in bare feet on pristine sand?"

"You'll miss out on all the appetizing choices," Anna said. "The best dishes always get snapped up first."

"I'll be fine." Jo waved them on as she headed to the water's edge, her sandals swaying at her side.

It had been a long, painful night as she tried to sleep to no avail. By morning, her mind needed a flushing in the soft sea breeze to rid it of leftover frustrations from hours of torment over her disaster with Sam. She longed for a few minutes alone to sulk in private and get it together.

It was early Sunday morning. Sam was probably still asleep. Jo hoped that she at least felt some pain at being caught.

The fresh air felt good against Jo's sticky skin and the salty-sweet taste of the ocean mist coated her lips as she sauntered along the shore. By the time she made it to her target of the bright yellow kayak down the beach, Jo felt relaxed and looked forward to the day ahead in paradise. She trotted back to the restaurant, arriving just in time to get some food while her sister and mother sipped their final cup of coffee.

Anna rubbed her belly. "The omelets are to die for. You get to choose whatever you want then they cook it up as you wait."

"I'll just stick with my pancakes this morning." Jo sipped her coffee, remembering how good Sam's pancakes were that first morning at the cottage.

"It looks dry," Anna said. "Where's the syrup?"

"I'm not going to have any. It's only some sugared water instead of real maple syrup."

"That doesn't look very appetizing," her mother said, "especially when there's so much else to choose from."

"I have some yogurt and strawberries to dress it up." Jo motioned to her side bowl. "Besides, if it's too good I'll eat more than I should, and I don't like feeling stuffed."

"Oh for God's sake," Anna said. "Let loose and enjoy yourself a bit. You can take a good laxative when you get home to clean yourself out."

"Speaking of which," their mother said, "I have to head back to the room now for the bathroom. I'll see the two of you in a bit." She hurried off.

"Yep, this is definitely a family vacation and not some romantic getaway." Jo chuckled as she adorned her pancakes. "Our only dirty talking is about the bathroom and not sex on the beach."

"Please don't tell me that's what you were looking for last night and again this morning."

Jo burst out laughing. "Of course not. This orgasmic spread of food doesn't do it for me, either, but I love the roaring of the ocean. It whispers sweet nothings into my ears."

"Seriously, Jo, how are you really doing?" Anna leaned into the table. "I hope you're managing to forget about Sam. I'm worried for you."

"Well don't, because I'm doing fine." Jo jabbed a fork at her pancake.

"You were moving around all night in bed and then the need to be by yourself before breakfast. You brought her here with you, didn't you?"

Jo's fork clanged against her plate. "What are you talking about? Sam's definitely not here."

"Figuratively speaking, she is. She's always on your mind. I can tell by the way you stare off into the distance. Do you want to talk about it?"

"No." Jo bit into a big chunk of pancake. How dare Anna speculate about her private thoughts?

"Well, I'm here for you if you change your mind. I hate seeing you hurting like this. I wish there was something I could do."

"Thanks." She forced a swollen cheek smile then swallowed. "I'm going to be okay. Just being here with you and Mom is helpful. I appreciate it, even if it doesn't look like I do sometimes."

"Good." Anna tapped Jo's arm. "Now let's hurry up so we can get going. I wouldn't want someone to steal our chairs."

When they reached their loungers on the beach, people were starting to fill the chairs. Anna and Julia both wore two-piece suits under beach dresses and big-brimmed hats, while Jo had on a one-piece suit under shorts and a white ball cap.

"I'm glad we got our chairs when we did because there'd be none left now." Anna fidgeted with her towel to cover her lounger.

"Maybe we should have taken the ones over there." Julia pointed to a group of chairs more fully in the shade.

"We're fine here." Jo just wanted to sit back and relax with her book. She'd chosen a lesbian romance and was looking forward to reading it in peace.

"*The Secret Pond.*" Anna studied the cover as she lowered onto her towel. "I've never heard of that novel before. Where did you get it?"

"I ordered it online." Jo opened the book and sniffed the pages. "Mmmm. This is going to be a good one, judging by the fresh-ink smell."

"Well mine is odor-free, but I know it's good." Anna illuminated her tablet.

"I didn't bring any books," their mother said, closing her eyes. "I brought my two daughters for entertainment."

"Look over there." Anna pointed toward the water. "Someone's scouring the beach with a metal detector. How exciting. I wonder if he's found anything?"

"Why don't you go ask him?" Jo poked her sister. "You never know what he might dig up. Or what you might find by going over there."

"No, it's okay." Anna leaned back. "I think I'll read my book now, if you don't mind."

"He's just found something and put it in his pocket." Their mother's neck stretched. "I wonder what it was?"

"Probably just some trinket or coin." Jo opened her book, looking forward to escaping into someone else's life. "Maybe you should go find out."

"Why not?" She swung her legs off the chair and was gone before Jo or Anna could respond.

"She loves this kind of stuff, doesn't she?" Anna held the brim of her hat. "I wish I was more of an extrovert like her."

"Me too," Jo said, turning a page.

"I couldn't believe how many people she knew at the open house a few weeks ago. I had a chat with Sam there, you know." Jo cringed as Anna put her tablet down. "I told her she'd better not hurt you."

"And what did she say to that?" Jo held her breath.

"That meeting you was one of the best things to happen to her in a long time."

"I bet."

"Her eyes really did light up whenever she looked at you, and I thought for sure she was going to get you to move to Toronto."

"Anna." Jo touched her sister's hand. "I would never leave you guys and move to Toronto."

"You were right, Jo." Their mother reclaimed her chair. "The American with the metal detector found a few peso coins and a silver earring this morning. He said the true fun is in the thrill of the hunt rather than the catch at the end of the day."

"Funny how that turns some people on." Jo pictured Sam armed with dimples and sparkling eyes for her lesbian detector that found lost hearts only to be dug up and discarded. Like the kindling retrieved from the cottage, only to be thrown away on the streets of Toronto.

So much for Sam's kindling for the heart having a lasting effect. It may have brought on a few sparks and small flames, but there were no smoldering embers to keep the fire going.

CHAPTER FORTY-ONE

Sam modeled her interview clothes in the mirror and approved of the confidence-building attire she'd chosen. Black wool pants, a matching blazer, and a dark purple, knit turtleneck made up her outfit. Gold studs in her ears and a sporty black watch were her only adornments other than the silver buckle on her black leather belt. She would wear low-heeled black leather dress boots and have on her long navy overcoat with a red woolen scarf for her entrance.

Sam's brown hair was spiky and neatly styled in a short cut that brought out the lesbian in her, so she hoped. Working in a discrimination-free environment was paramount to her accepting a position with Maxwell and Associates. If not offered the job, she would explore opening her own office to practice law in Timmins instead.

Packing and studying complete, Sam needed to burn off energy before settling in for the short night then flight to Timmins. She carefully removed her clothes and placed them on hangers, ready for the morning.

Her gym bag beckoned so she pulled out her running gear. An end-of-day jog around the neighborhood would help her relax. Sam was excited, adrenaline pumped for a good interview, and she would be with Jo by tomorrow at this time. She had to be.

Streetlights lit up her way along sidewalks in the quiet neighborhood of brick bungalows and outdated two-stories that housed many of Toronto's young professionals and their families. Sam longed for a family of her own, one with a dog and a woman to love.

No stars shone down as Sam glanced above at a passing plane. The day had been gray and there was no snow to brighten it up. A cool breeze sent chills through her jacket, but it was nothing compared to the frigid temperature she anticipated when stepping off the plane in Timmins the next morning. Snow would most likely crunch under her boots and the short walk to the terminal would have a biting wind. Her rental car would be waiting and so would Jo, but unbeknownst to her as she cozily worked in her home office.

Sam slowed to a cool-down trot and began to rehearse her meeting with Jo. She'd drive out to her house right after the interview and Mollie would bark to announce her arrival. Jo would come to the door to see who was there and Sam would be kneeling on the step. She'd hold up the bouquet of kindling with its red ribbon, roses to be added in Timmins.

Mollie would rush out and Sam would give her a big hug before beginning her opening argument to the one-woman jury. She'd start by begging Jo to listen, telling her about the mix-up with the names and that she wanted to move to Timmins so they could be together. She imagined Jo stammering at the door then rushing into her arms.

Thoughts of that first kiss made Sam gasp. She'd give Jo the bouquet and they'd head inside to make love with ferocity, shedding clothes and devouring each other with every moan. They'd both cry—at least, Sam knew she would because her emotions were so raw they brought tears just thinking about it.

She sat in the cold wicker chair on her front porch to fantasize before going inside. Trish's car was in the driveway and Sam wanted to be alone with her thoughts a bit longer. She leaned back and looked up at the bright sky of city lights and airport traffic.

Jo was probably out back with Mollie, looking at the same sky but with stars shining through the solitude. Each breath would blow out clouds of vapor and her eyelashes would be coated in ice crystals. Sam closed her eyes and grinned.

By the time she stepped inside, Trish was comfortably watching the new TV, lying on the couch under a gold fleece blanket. She muted the volume and smiled at Sam.

"Are you ready for your big day tomorrow?"

"Yes, I am." Sam kicked off her runners. "I'll be up early since I have to be at the airport by seven."

"You must be so nervous. If there's anything I can do to help sort things out with your Jo, let me know."

"Thanks, but I don't think so. Where's Joanne tonight?"

"She had to study for an exam tomorrow. Kind of like you, I guess. How ironic that we both end up with someone named Jo and mine wants to be a lawyer too."

"Their names are different." Sam headed to the kitchen. "Besides, they're not at all alike."

"I sure hope your Timmins Jo forgives you."

"For what?" Sam reached for a glass. "You're the one who made a mess of things."

Trish came into the kitchen. "I'm sorry. What I meant to say is I hope she can get past her anger at you."

"She got hurt here the other day and I need to fix things." Sam filled her glass with water.

"What are you going to do? I mean, what if she's not home and you don't get to see her?"

Sam backed away and took a swig. "She'll be there." She wiped her mouth with the back of her hand. "She has to be, and I'm not planning on coming back here until next week."

"Good for you." Trish playfully punched Sam's arm. "That's one of the things I like about you, Sam. Your confidence has always been admirable. I can't wait to hear how it goes. Will you text me to let me know how things turn out?"

"Only if Jo's with me when I send the message because I'm not risking anymore screw-ups. Now I have to get to bed."

"Good luck." Trish gave her a hug. "I know you'll do well in Timmins tomorrow."

"Thanks." Sam barely reciprocated then marched back to her room.

She sat on the edge of her bed and felt like she was going to be sick. She acted confident, but Trish had created some doubt in her mind. What if she couldn't reach Jo? What if she was back here on her own by tomorrow night at this time? That would be a nightmare. How could she ever survive?

No, it was not going to happen. Worst-case scenario, she would take a hotel room for the night and try again to see Jo the next day. If all else failed, she would visit Julia then Anna to plead her case. Surely she'd be able to reach someone.

CHAPTER FORTY-TWO

Jo lay sprawled on the brown-checkered couch in her shed, naked and about to explode. Her hips lifted off the fabric, arching toward the ceiling as exploring fingers teased out an orgasm on the brink of release.

"Oh yes." Jo's breathing was uneven, her full bladder preventing her from letting go.

"This is our shed now." Sam's words were muffled by kisses all over Jo's breasts. "I want to stay here forever."

"What the fuck is going on in here?" The door to the shed flung open and Jan's scowling silhouette glowed through the sunlight.

"What...what are you doing here?" Jo said.

"This is supposed to be your place. Not Sam's." Jan stomped into the shed and began to shove Jo.

"Wake up. Calm down."

"Anna?" Jo flinched out of the dream and sprang up. She was in bed with her sister, the room dark and their mother snoring. Her heart thumped. "Oh shit, I'm sorry if I woke you."

"It's okay." Anna clicked on her bedside lamp. "I need to go to the bathroom anyway."

"Me too." Jo's bladder was about to burst. "What time is it?"

"Just after five thirty." Anna got up. "I'll go first, if that's okay."

"Yes." Jo's heart pounded. She focused on the closed drapes, light shimmering through the cracks, and remembered she was in a resort with her mother and sister.

Sam's presence had seemed so real and the longing painfully strong. She fought back a sob and crawled out from under the covers, sitting on the edge of the bed in wait for the bathroom.

Why did she have to dream about sex with Sam when she was finally starting to get herself back together? And to be so aroused once again was like a kick back to the starting line. Getting over Sam was going to be a lot harder than she thought. By the time Anna returned to bed, Jo had resolved to go for a sunrise jog along the beach. Maybe that would clear her head.

Sam sat at her boarding gate, dressed for success and her adrenaline pumped for the day she hoped would define her future. Jo would probably still be in bed, as it was just past six in the morning. Excitement brought on an arousal that Sam needed to put aside until after the interview. Her focus had to be on getting the job. Nothing could happen without that.

She decided to go for a walk around the airport to clear her head and try to relax. Families and business travelers bustled through the terminal and browsed the shops. Sam headed to a coffee shop to treat herself with some caffeine and a muffin to get through the early morning jitters.

Two women stood in line in front of her. A lesbian couple, she was sure of it by the way they shared looks, touches, and smiles. Dressed in matching zip-off travel pants, hiking shoes, and waterproof jackets, they were probably off to some vacation destination with a sunny beach and warm weather. Sam envisioned walking along a sandy shoreline with Jo, planning their future together and making up for lost time on that ill-fated Toronto rendezvous. Perhaps they could head south for a romantic getaway near the end of February. If all went as planned with her day. It had to.

Jo was the true planner, but Sam found herself piecing their lives together. An addition to the cottage would be necessary because she'd want it to be a family place where Jo's relatives could visit. Her house in Toronto would be sold and some of the proceeds could go toward Jo's mortgage, allowing Sam to own an equal share of their home. She'd help Jo switch her living room flooring and they'd christen it on some starry night after returning from walking Mollie. Life would be so good.

She carried her coffee and muffin back to her boarding gate, glancing at the screen above the entrance to see a red alert. Her heart skipped a beat. The plane was delayed.

Sam rushed to the counter where other passengers gathered to hear about the status of their flight. Panic set in as she learned that the plane had mechanical issues and an unknown departure time. Staring at the clock, Sam eased into a seat to control her breathing. Jaw tightening and teeth grinding, she put her muffin aside and focused on reciting case facts to calm her nerves. There was an hour to spare for her to make the interview on time and after that, there were no guarantees it would happen today. Things just had to go as planned.

Jo broke into a sprint, with sand sliding like fresh snow under her shoes. A few other joggers were scattered along the shoreline, immersed in their own need for a morning run. The harder she pushed herself, the more Jo felt like her body was going to explode. Heart rate increasing and lungs about to burst, she screamed against the thrust of a large wave pounding the beach.

A release of emotions, a mixed sentiment of longing for lost love and yearning to find happiness, brought on an adrenaline rush to satiate the unfulfilled orgasm of her dream. Why was Jan in the dream, berating her for making out in the shed with Sam? Jo shook her head. Had she really let go of Jan or was she still feeling guilty about loving someone else?

It was her shed, dammit, and she could do whatever she wanted in it. Dreaming or not. It was time to finally let go of Jan. And Sam. When Jo got back to the room, she was ready for a cleansing shower and Anna was anxious to head for breakfast.

"Hurry up or all the good tables will be full." Anna flung a towel at her sister. "Just give your face a quick wipe and we can head to the dining hall."

"Where's Mom?"

"She's taking a picture of the gardens out front." Anna went to the patio door window. "Didn't you see her?"

"Why don't the two of you go ahead and I'll catch up?" Jo sifted through her clothes.

"She's not there anymore." Anna slid one panel open. "Mom?"

"Maybe she's already on her way to the restaurant."

"No she isn't because we were waiting for you." Anna stuck her head outside. "Mother, where are you?"

"I'm right here." Their mother stepped into the room from the hallway and noticed Jo. "Oh good, you're back. Let's go, I'm hungry."

"I just need five minutes to rinse off." Jo headed to the bathroom. "You can either wait or I'll meet you there."

"We'll wait." Anna groaned as she sat on the edge of the bed. "We're in a strange country and should be sticking together. And that includes getting up and going out for a run on your own in the middle of the night. Do you know how dangerous that is?"

"It was early morning and I felt safe."

"Anna's right," Her mother sat in the corner chair, all but wagging a finger. "This isn't the bush around Timmins and you don't have Mollie with you. If it was safe, the guards wouldn't have to carry around machine guns."

"I'll be out in a minute." Jo closed the bathroom door and sighed. The last thing she needed was to have her sister and mother gang up on her. The only security she worried about was keeping her heart protected from the likes of Samantha

White. Jo stepped in the shower and willed Sam to wash down the drain with the soapsuds.

Fifty minutes later, the plane was finally ready to depart. Boarding was rushed and Sam realized she should have visited the washroom one last time before leaving the terminal. Her uneaten carrot muffin fell on the floor as she lifted her carry-on luggage into the compartment above her seat. At least she'd had her coffee, but now her bladder was full and stomach empty.

Sam always preferred a window seat. She liked to hunker down and watch the ground disappear during takeoff, ignoring the passenger in the seat beside her. This time it was an obese man smelling of stale cigarette smoke. It was going to be a long flight for the one and a half-hour estimated arrival time, especially since she couldn't wait for the seat belt sign to be turned off and rush to the tiny bathroom.

She watched as the plane climbed through the clouds and left the dreary Toronto weather for a sunny blue horizon high up in the sky. A dip of turbulence sent her stomach reeling more than it already was with her anticipation at seeing Jo. She had to forget about Jo and focus on interview questions. She'd save those feelings for later. They'd fall into each other's arms and make love later that afternoon. Sam was sure of it.

CHAPTER FORTY-THREE

The plane circled over Timmins. Sam thought she saw Jo's house in amongst the trees, but her sense of direction on the lay of the land around the city was still lacking. The sun shone and there was fresh snow on the ground. Everything looked pristine from so high up. It was going to be a good day. Sam just knew it as she hunched in front of the small window and smiled at her Timmins prospects.

A new job where she could grow and expand her experience, maybe even open her own office one day, was exciting. Sam needed to ace that interview and claim the opening at Maxwell and Associates as hers. Confidence would be key, and she had to exude the ability to face any person or situation under duress. She would also need to demonstrate a keen interest in the firm and moving to Timmins.

Sam was prepared to answer why she wanted to leave her large firm in Toronto for a small one in northern Ontario. She would focus on the cottage rather than risk revealing her real reason before things were settled with Jo. A family inheritance of a childhood vacation property near the city and a desire to experience life in the north would be her rationale.

The wheels touched down with a jolt and Sam leaned back in her seat for one last moment of meditation. She closed her eyes and imagined petting Mollie. A smile hinted on her lips and her breathing was even. It was going to be an exhilarating day.

Her rental car was ready and the drive into town was quick, leaving her an hour to spare before the interview. She had a strong urge to drive past Jo's place but parked at a city meter then headed to a local restaurant for a bite to eat. A vegetarian wrap and glass of water graced her table. She was determined to give up eating meat for Jo.

For the first time in her life, Sam realized that someone else's desires had become more important than hers. She wanted to cradle Jo, soothe her pain, and begin the healing. And see her smile again, her barriers crumbling as she realized how much Sam loved her. Sam could hardly wait. She bit into her wrap, bringing her focus back to the fast-approaching interview time and reviewed her notes for one last time.

"I really enjoyed that breakfast." Anna rubbed sunscreen on her legs.

Jo spread her towel on the chair. They were back at the beach, preparing for another leisurely day in the heat. "Is that all you're thinking about here? What's on the menu and how much you can eat?"

"Of course not," Anna said, "but the food is such a big part of an all-inclusive vacation like this. I've been dieting all year and want to let loose for a week. You should do the same. Even Mom said so."

Jo threw her book on the chair. "Here we go again. I'm going for a walk and the two of you can continue to join forces on me while I'm not here."

"Jo, it's not like that." Anna grabbed her sister's arm. "A walk along the beach sounds like a good idea. Let's meet Mom before she heads back up from the shore. We can go for a stroll now before the sun gets too hot."

Midmorning mist from the ocean gave a salty sheen to their skin as the three women walked at the water's edge. Jo's feet were submerged while her mother and sister jumped back and forth to avoid getting their sandals wet. Their mother focused on the shops further down the beach, Anna studied her freshly painted toenails, and Jo pictured Mollie running alongside them.

"Mollie would love it here," Jo said.

"Don't you think she'd find it too hot?" Their mother held her floppy hat on her head against the wind.

"I guess you're right." Jo lowered the peak on her ball cap to avoid having it blow off. "It feels strange to be going for a walk without her. I hope she's doing okay."

"I'm sure she is," Anna said. "I forgot to tell you, Robert sent an email this morning reminding us he's off today and will be using your truck while his vehicle's at the shop. He told me he likes driving your truck and taking Mollie everywhere with him. Considering her uncle is spoiling her, I bet Mollie's having the time of her life. Just like you should be."

"Robert's not her uncle and I'm still in mourning, remember?"

"You need to move on and stop feeling sorry for yourself," Anna said. "It's not like Mom or I have someone in our lives, and it's not the end of the world or anything. Besides, there could be someone waiting to meet you right now."

"Not in Timmins, that's for sure." Jo resolved to live the rest of her life single.

"How do you know?" her mother said. "I'm sure there's a woman out there who would give the world to share her life with yours."

"Well, that would be too bad because I'm not available to have a relationship with anyone. Not now and not ever."

Her mother shook her head. "I wish Sam had never come around. I'd like to give her a piece of my mind. She had us all fooled."

"Can we talk about something else?" Jo said.

"It isn't so bad being single." Anna held on to her hat as the wind tugged at its large brim.

"Here, here." Jo raised a fist. "Life is so much easier that way."

"You girls are too young to stay single," their mother said.

"It's more that we're old enough to know what we want," Anna said. "I like my life the way it is, especially this week vacationing in paradise with my mother and little sister. Who needs anything more than that?"

"Maybe not if you're a nun." Their mother clicked her tongue.

"Mother, what do you mean by that?"

"Do I have to spell it out?" She turned to Anna. "At your age, your father and I still had a very active sex life."

"La. La. La." Anna put fingers in her ears. "Too much information."

"Parents don't have sex." Jo laughed. "Come on, let's head back to the resort and get a piña colada."

Sam walked out of the interview in tears. It had gone better than great, and they'd all but offered her the job. The experience she'd be bringing to Maxwell and Associates was a good fit with the Criminal Defense Lawyer position they were looking to fill. All those hours of reviewing litigation files and studying case law helped her to shine as she easily responded to each question.

Her synergy with the lawyers stimulated conversation and allowed for some frank discussion at the end of the evaluation period. Sam outed herself and was overjoyed to find out that one of the junior male partners on the panel was also gay. Things were falling into place. Now she just needed to talk to Jo.

It was slightly after three as she pulled away from her parking meter that charged only a fraction of the fees she was used to in Toronto. Traffic was light and the drive to Jo's would take less than fifteen minutes. Life seemed so much simpler in the smaller city where the love of her life lived. All she had to do was fix the mess from Toronto so they could be together.

Jo would surely be home by now, or almost. Sam spotted a flower shop and pulled over to get a bouquet for her sweetheart. She had her small bundle of kindling to give as a peace offering, but the flowers would be presented as a celebration of her love. And then she'd have to find a pet store or someplace to buy a treat for Mollie.

She bought a simple bouquet of a dozen red roses mixed with eucalyptus that would smell and look nice on Jo's dining table. Mollie would get a rawhide bone. Sam also picked up a pizza and six-pack of cold beer. She was confident they'd have dinner together, famished after ravenous sex.

Jo's truck was in the driveway when Sam turned in. The tracks were fresh, and the truck still looked warm. She must have just gotten home. Sam swallowed, her hand shaking as she turned off the engine. She was finally here, about to see Jo again and just wanting to collapse in her arms.

Mollie was inside, but Sam heard her bark when she shut her car door. Flowers in hand, she walked what felt like a plank to Jo's entryway. Her long wool coat with scarf was no match against the cold wind that bit right to the bone. She couldn't wait to get inside.

The door opened and Mollie burst out, almost knocking Sam over in her excitement.

"Mollie." Sam bent over and buried her face in the dog. "I've missed you so much." She was afraid to look up, waiting for Jo to say something, and held out the roses. "These are for you. Please, Jo, give me another chance."

"Jo's not here," Robert said.

CHAPTER FORTY-FOUR

Sam's heart sank as she gaped up at Jo's nephew. "Oh. Sorry, I thought you were Jo. Where is she?"

"I don't think that's any of your business." Robert hovered at the half-open door, squinting at Sam.

"Of course not." Sam's gaze drifted back to a squiggling Mollie, suddenly sick with worry. "What time will she be back?"

"Not until the weekend."

No. "Please don't tell me that."

Jo was gone. How could this have happened? She needed to talk to her, convince her how much she loved her, and make things right. All seemed lost now. She started to cry, the bouquet of roses falling from her hand. "I have to see Jo today and tell her how much I love her and want to spend the rest of my life with her."

"I'm sorry." Robert sighed. "It's cold standing here. Why don't you come inside for a minute?"

"Are you sure it's okay?" Sam spoke into Mollie's fur, struggling to contain herself and pressing her cheek against the welcoming dog for comfort.

"Yes." Robert opened the door and the sweet smell of Jo's house wafted outside.

"Please come in."

"Thank you." Sam reached for the flowers, and stepped through the doorway.

She felt like she'd just come home, the soothing warmth and familiar aroma of Jo's cedar closet beckoning her to stay forever. She felt the urge to rush into Jo's bed and bury herself there until the weekend, when Jo would be back. Instead, Sam stood on the entry mat and held out the bouquet to Robert. "You might as well have these."

He put his hands in his pockets. "I couldn't. They're so beautiful."

"Please take them." Sam's voice trembled as she shoved them at him. "I can't take them back to Toronto with me."

Robert finally took the flowers, raising them to his nose for a sniff. "They smell wonderful. Thank you. I'll put them in some water and they should survive until after Aunt Jo comes home." He moved toward the sink, speaking over his shoulder. "I think she'll love them. Can you stay for a while? Have a cup of tea at least?"

"That would be nice." Sam felt sick at the thought of leaving so soon, without seeing Jo. Her careful planning, right down to what she was going to say, all lost now as the reality of her failure to reconnect with Jo taking hold. She struggled to keep her voice calm. "I have something for Mollie too." Her hand trembled as she took the rawhide bone out of her coat pocket, giving it to the wriggling dog. "Here you go, girl."

"Come on in and grab a seat at the table." Robert found a crystal vase in one of the cupboards and began to unwrap the roses. He worked at the kitchen counter. "These are certainly meant for someone special, I'd say."

"They are." Sam kicked off her boots and hung her coat in the closet, the familiarity of it a small solace against her pain. "She's the love of my life." Her voice caught, and she fought back more tears.

Robert focused on the flowers, carefully arranging them in the vase next to the kitchen sink. "You broke her heart."

"I know." Sam sat at the table and pulled a tissue out of her pocket. "It was all a terrible misunderstanding." She paused to wipe her nose, her hands cold, but feet warm on the cork floor. "Today was supposed to be the day when I wanted to make things right with Jo."

"Long distance relationships are hard."

"I plan to move to Timmins for Jo." Sam could see the top of the cedar hedge in the distance outside Jo's kitchen window. The branches were covered in fresh snow and she longed to get up and look out the window.

"You're going to give up your job and lifestyle in the big city?" Robert paused to look at her, his hands on one of the eucalyptus twigs.

"Yes." Sam took a deep breath, seeing a resemblance to Jo in the way his forehead creased. The look was so familiar. "My life in Toronto is empty without her."

"That's not my understanding." Robert shook his head and resumed arranging the bouquet. "I hear you're still hanging out with your ex?"

"It's not like that. There was a big misunderstanding when your aunt saw me in Toronto. If only I could talk to her today and set things right."

"She's out of the country," Robert said as he poured hot water into the teapot.

"I see." Sam hunched back into her chair, feeling like a boulder had just been dropped into her stomach.

"Beautiful." Robert placed the flowers on the table then went back for the teapot. "Aunt Jo would love them."

Sam trembled with sadness as she watched Robert bring the pot of tea, two mugs, and some milk to the table. She would have been the one serving the tea while she stayed with Jo, but now felt like a visitor where she'd felt at home. An unwelcome one at that, because nothing had been resolved between them. "I want her to love me."

"Oh, she loves you." Robert pulled up a chair, his black wool socks covered in Mollie's fur. "Very much so and that's why she's terribly hurt and pissed at you."

"Please, then, put me in touch with her today. There must be a way. Can you send her an email to let her know I'm here and want to talk to her?"

Robert poured them each a cup of tea, taking his time to respond. "Do you think that's a good idea, considering how she feels at the moment?"

"What about your mother or grandmother?" Surely Julia or Anna would help her. "Are they around so I could talk to them?"

"Nope. They're out of the country too on some nice warm beach to cheer up Aunt Jo." He shifted one of the roses. "She was a real mess because of you. They wanted her to have a change of scenery to help get you out of her system."

"Shit. I really need to fix things, Robert." Sam's hands were wrapped around her mug, the heat soothing as they trembled. "Please help me."

Robert took his phone out of his pocket. "I'll send Mom an email. Aunt Jo's not looking at hers."

Fifteen minutes later and after Sam filled Robert in on the fateful day in Toronto, a negative response came in from Anna. She refused to let Jo know Sam was at her place in Timmins, desperate to talk with her.

"Mom can be stubborn sometimes." Robert shrugged his shoulders then put his phone back down on the light oak table.

"Would she at least talk to me then?" Sam grabbed onto his arm, feeling warmth under his sweater sleeve as he stayed still, even after she let go. "Please?"

He sighed. "She's written you off and says Aunt Jo is finally starting to move on. It seems the trip has been good for her mental health."

"Can we call your Mom's phone? I'll pay any bills on both ends." Sam reached for her cell, urging him on. "Here, I'll transfer you a hundred dollars right now in good faith."

"It's okay, I'm starting to believe I can trust you. Let me try calling Mom first and see if she answers."

"Please let her pick up." Sam held her breath while Robert dialed, watching Mollie gnaw at the rawhide as she lay on the rug by the back door.

"Hey, Mom. I'm here with Sam." Her heart began to race, preparing to speak with Anna and tell her how much she loved Jo. "Is it okay if I put you on speaker phone?" He nodded then put his cell in the middle of the table.

"Thanks for answering, Anna." Sam struggled to keep her voice steady.

"What the hell are you doing there?" Anna's tone was harsh, her anger loud and clear. "Haven't you screwed up Jo's life enough?"

"It's not what you think, Anna." Sam stared at Robert's white-cased phone on the table, her shoulders rigid with fear of Anna hanging up and breaking the only lifeline she had to reaching Jo right now. She had to convince the woman. "I love her."

"You almost ruined her life. I'm not going to let that happen again. She's finally relaxing and enjoying the beach. If you really love her, you'll leave her alone."

"Please, Anna…"

"Don't call back again." She ended the call.

Sam started to cry with the realization things were going to stay a mess. "I'm sorry." She sniffed, shaking her head in defeat. "I'm usually not this sappy."

Robert got up to get the box of tissues Jo kept on the counter. "Why did you come today of all days?"

"I flew in this morning for a job interview at Maxwell and Associates."

"No shit." Robert straightened, the table jerking as his knee hit a leg. "You're really serious about Aunt Jo, aren't you?"

"I want to spend the rest of my life with her. Will you help me, Robert? Please?"

Robert's face lit up. "Come back next week for Valentine's Day. Aunt Jo and I are going to have a big bonfire. It'll be perfect and you can surprise her, like you wanted to today."

"Do you think so?"

"I know so." Robert grinned. "I'll make sure it happens this time."

Sam's return to Toronto that night no longer felt like the disaster she was bracing for. She squeezed Robert's hand. "I'm so glad you were here today and let me in."

"Me too."

CHAPTER FORTY-FIVE

Sam hung up the phone and danced around her bedroom. "Yes!" She'd just been officially offered the position at Maxwell and Associates. It was Saturday morning and she'd been counting down the days for Jo's return. The fact that Jo would be going through the Toronto airport later in the day on her journey back to Timmins drove Sam crazy with anticipation.

She'd shared her beer and pizza with Robert then caught a flight back to Toronto Monday evening. Although disappointed at not seeing Jo on this visit, Sam was full of hope they'd soon be living together in Timmins. She dialed Robert, reaching his familiar voice mail and knowing he'd call back soon.

"They just offered me the job!" she shouted into the phone. "Give me a call when you get a chance."

Sam sat on the edge of her bed and clutched the bundle of cedar kindling close to her chest. All they needed now was a spark, and Sam was determined to make it catch this time.

Meeting Jo had certainly started a burning desire in her heart, an inferno like no other, and she could hardly wait until Valentine's Day to give the kindling back to the love of her life.

"Hey, Sam." Trish tapped then eased open her bedroom door. "Do you have a minute to chat?"

"Sure." Sam put the kindling in her suitcase, wanting it away from Trish. "What's up?"

"Jo's asked me to move in with her."

Sam sighed. "Could you please refer to her as Joanne when you're talking to me. I have another Jo on my mind right now."

"Sorry." Trish almost sang the word. "I'll start moving out this weekend and be gone by the end of next week."

"Perfect timing." Sam smiled. Things were falling into place. "I just got offered the job in Timmins, so I'll be putting the house up for sale."

"Are you serious? Congratulations, Sam!" Trish pulled her into a hug. "Does Jo know?"

"Not yet. I'll be heading to Timmins on Tuesday morning to tell her."

"Valentine's Day. How nice. I hope she'll be there this time."

"She will." Sam started toward the kitchen, wanting Trish out of her room. "Her nephew's going to make sure."

"Joanne and I are going to indulge in some stay-at-home naked chef recipes for our Valentine's Day dinner." Trish giggled. "At our new place, of course. I wouldn't dream of doing that here."

"Good." Sam's phone started to ring with the callback she'd been expecting. "I have to get this." She buried her head in the fridge, searching for something to eat. "Hey, Robert."

"Congratulations!" His voice rang out as she pictured him doing a little happy dance in Jo's kitchen. "I'm so happy for you and for Aunt Jo. When do they want you to start?"

Sam grabbed a bag of baby carrots, some cheese, and a bottle of juice. "As soon as possible. I'm so excited, Robert, but this waiting is painfully stressful."

"I'll be picking them up at the airport tonight and it'll be hard to not say anything."

"Are you going to tell her I was at her place?" Sam returned to her room and sat on the bed with her snack.

"Of course not." She heard the clinking of Mollie's collar in the background. How she wished she were there now. "My mother warned me against it because she doesn't want Aunt Jo upset again. You'll have to tell her yourself when you're here on Tuesday."

"What if she refuses to see me?"

"You're a smart woman and I'm sure you'll figure something out."

"Actually, I already have a plan." Sam eyed the kindling, hoping it would work. "I'll just have to sneak into her yard without being noticed. Maybe you can help with that."

"Sure." Mollie's squeaky toy sounded in the background. "I'm meeting Aunt Jo at her place right after work around four thirty. I can distract her if you want."

"That'd be great." Sam thrust her fist up in the air. "Wahoo! I'll leave here around five in the morning so I should get there in good time. Let's keep in touch."

Sam finished the call and got ready to head into her office. She had some files on her desk to clear up then wanted to get things prepared to work remotely while in Timmins. She also needed to draft her letter of resignation. Not that it would be a surprise to her firm, but she'd been with them for ten years and it had almost become like home to her. Yes, it was definitely time to move on. Her idea of a home now meant so much more than a job or a house. It meant being with Jo, and her heart fluttered at what this year's Valentine's Day would bring.

Jo sat in the Toronto airport after a long flight from Punta Cana. She was tired, anxious to see Mollie, and once again brooding over Sam. The trip had helped with the pain, but being back in Toronto brought it all crashing back.

Anna had seemed agitated ever since Monday and was certainly anxious to get out of Toronto. She paced near the gate and studied the crowd, as though expecting to see a familiar face. Her constant frown and the fact that she kept to herself gave Jo concern that something had happened. She approached Anna.

"Is everything okay with Mollie?"

Anna swung around to face Jo. "Of course it is. Why ask?"

"I don't know. You seem uptight and had me scared that maybe something happened to Mollie."

"It's been a long day and I just want to leave Toronto and get home." Anna sighed. "Besides, being here is like bad karma."

"What do you mean?" Jo frowned at her sister, taken aback by the comment.

"You even have to ask? Sam had us all fooled, you know. This is her city and I just want to get the hell out of it."

"What's going on?"

"Nothing, but it just makes me so mad to think of her weaseling her way around all of us. I was conned by her, and I don't like it."

Jo sensed there was more to Anna's anger. "Did she try to contact you?"

"No." Anna led the way back to their seats. "They're just about to board and I want to visit the bathroom one last time. I'll leave my bag with you and Mom if that's okay."

"Give it to me." Their mother took Anna's carry-on. "I'll go when you get back."

Jo sat beside her mother. "What's wrong with Anna?"

Her mother drank the last of her coffee. "I was hoping you'd find out. I thought maybe she was mad at me for something."

"That's not it." Jo put her mother's empty cup in the garbage bin next to her seat. "Did she say anything to you about Sam?"

"No. Why? Did she talk to her?"

"She says no." Jo paused, unsure of what to think. "Something must have happened to get her all worked up about Sam, especially since she's been desperately trying to get me to forget about the woman."

"Well, Sam hasn't contacted me." Her mother stood up. "Here comes Anna. They're starting to board, so I have to hurry in the washroom."

"Aren't you going to go, too?" Anna grabbed her bag.

"I'm good," Jo said. "Go ahead and get in line if you want. I'll wait here for Mom."

"Okay, I will." Anna headed to the queue at the gate.

Jo checked her phone, knowing there was nothing new. Had Sam sent an email to Anna? Was that why her sister was so agitated?

By the time Jo got to her seat on the plane, most everyone else had boarded. She was relieved to have the seat beside her empty and curled up against the window as the aircraft taxied for takeoff. She watched the city lights grow smaller then disappear as they ascended into the clouds of the night sky. A tear slid down her cheek as she said a silent goodbye to Sam.

It was dark and cold when they landed in Timmins. Robert had Jo's truck warmed up and waiting for them. He drove as they first dropped off her mother, then Anna. Everyone was tired and conversation was strained with the letdown of returning to reality from a vacation in paradise.

"I'm anxious for Tuesday," Robert said as he turned into her driveway. "The fire pit is ready, and I even got some red roses to decorate your table."

"Sounds nice." Jo forced a smile, happy to be home and anxious to be by herself. "I'm glad you're still game to spend Valentine's Day with me."

"Of course I am. It's going to be one to remember." Robert turned off the truck. "I know there's someone anxious to see you."

"I can't wait to see Mollie too." Jo rushed inside to greet her excited dog.

CHAPTER FORTY-SIX

Sam had been on the road for nine hours when she pulled into a restaurant parking lot in Timmins and let out a sigh of relief. The drive had been long, the roads icy, and her hands clenched the wheel for the last four hours. She was finally here, and her stomach danced with excitement as she rehearsed words for Jo.

It was two in the afternoon. Robert had agreed to meet with her before heading to Jo's. She sent a message to him then ordered a late lunch of a light salad and grilled cheese sandwich. By the time Robert got there, she was sipping on her second coffee.

"It's so good to see you." Sam jumped to her feet and squeezed Robert in a heartfelt hug. "Thank you so much for meeting me."

"Hey, no problem. I'd do anything for Aunt Jo and she's going to be thrilled by the end of today." Robert smiled as he sat and signaled for the waitress to bring him a coffee.

"You think so?" Sam's hands fidgeted with her coffee mug. The lunch hour rush was over and other customers were thinning out.

"I know so with the way she's been moping around the last few days." Robert stirred his coffee. There was a clatter of dishes in the background. "As much as she's trying to let on it's going to be a fun Valentine's Day with me, I know she'd rather be spending it with you. If things were different, of course."

"Which they are. I just have to prove it to her."

"Yes, you do, because she's still really pissed at you and so is my Mom." His smile warmed Sam. "I know you can do it."

"I'm glad you're here." Sam touched his hand in appreciation, her heart still so jittery. "Now let's talk about my plan."

Jo stood at the kitchen sink, peeling an orange and staring at the snow along her cedar hedge. She'd skipped lunch and decided to snack on fruit when she really felt like eating crap to console her heart on this Valentine's Day. What was Sam up to on the day for sweethearts? Was she charming someone else or lavishing her ex with sweet nothings? Not that it mattered to Jo, but still.

If ever there was any doubt about what really happened in front of the Eaton Centre that dreadful day in Toronto, Jo believed Sam would be longing for her on this day. No, she had to stop thinking like that. It really was time to move on. Spending this Valentine's Day with Robert was going to be her savior.

He'd called a few minutes ago to say her entertainment system in the basement was a bit flaky last week and he wanted to check it out with her before the fire. When he pulled up, Jo let Mollie scurry outside to greet him.

"Hey, Robert." Jo held the door open for him, the cold breeze not as bad as she expected with the shining sun. "Happy Valentine's Day."

"Happy Valentine's Day to you too, Aunt Jo." She fell into Robert's open arms, his coat still on and cool against her cheek. "Mmmm, it smells good in here."

Jo shivered as she got a whiff of Sam's peach shampoo from Robert's hug. Longing for the woman was really getting to her as she stumbled out of the embrace. "I've put a pot of chili on for dinner."

"You okay?" Robert pulled off his scarf.

"Yeah, why?"

"Nothing." Robert turned his focus to Mollie, grabbing onto her collar. "I miss you, girl. Come on downstairs with us."

Sam slowly steered into Jo's driveway and parked her vehicle behind Robert's truck. She carefully gathered the roses and small bundle of kindling. Knees buckling, she left the security of her SUV and trudged to the front of Jo's cedar hedge. She took a deep breath and held it while drawing a large heart in the snow. She lay the kindling in the center, put a single rose on top and began to complete her creation.

Peeling petals from a second red rose was like unraveling the layers she'd built around her heart through years of reckless relationships and unfulfilled love. She began to outline her valentine in the snow with the petals. Tears streamed down her cheeks as she rushed to finish her masterpiece that was sure to impress Jo. It had to.

"What the hell are you doing?" Anna's shout shattered the silence and Sam almost toppled onto the heart.

"Anna. Julia. Hi." She swung around, the stem of her unraveled rose dropping into the snow.

"Does Jo know you're here?" Anna glared at the almost complete heart.

"No, but Robert does." Hands trembling, Sam reached for the fallen rose and put the last petal in place.

"That's quite the valentine." Julia moved closer as she studied it, her voice soft. "And to come all the way back to Timmins to deliver it. It must be for someone special."

"Oh, Julia." Sam stood and fell into Julia's arms, clutching the soft puffy pink parka. "I love your daughter and will do anything to get her to understand that."

"Long-distance relationships are too hard," Anna said.

"I'm moving to Timmins." Sam spoke into Julia's shoulder, unable to let go quite yet. "I just got offered a position with Maxwell and Associates."

"So you applied after all." Julia gave a squeeze and patted her back. "Good for you. Congratulations."

"Thank you." Sam stepped away, tears wetting her cheeks as she looked at Anna. "I'm so sorry if I hurt your sister, but I never meant to, and she wouldn't give me a chance to explain."

"She can be stubborn sometimes."

"It's getting cold standing here," Julia said. "Let's go inside."

"You and Anna go on, but please don't tell Jo I'm here." Sam's breathing hastened, adrenaline taking over as she prepared for the argument of her life. "I want it to be a surprise and Robert's trying to help me." She tapped Anna's arm. "Thank God your son listened to me when I was here last week."

"I didn't know you were here last week," Julia said.

"Let's get inside Mom before Jo sees us." Anna nudged her mother toward the door. "We can fill each other in later."

"Our moms must be here," Jo said as Mollie started to bark. They were still in the basement, testing the sound system with loud music.

"I thought it was just going to be the two of us." Robert's head jerked toward the basement stairs.

"Me too, but when your mother found out we were having chili and a bonfire she insisted on coming over. She is, after all, single and somewhat of a Valentine's Day reject like us. And of course, I had to invite Grandma."

"Hello," her mother called out as she stomped snow off her feet at the door. "We're here."

Her mother and Anna were petting Mollie when Jo and Robert got upstairs. They were still by the entry and hadn't removed their coats.

"Let me take your jackets." Jo grabbed hangers. "I know it's cold outside, but there's something wrong if you need to keep these on in here."

"How is it out there anyway?" Robert looked through the kitchen window.

"All's good," Anna said as she pulled on a pair of gray ballet-type slippers she'd taken out of her purse. "Everything's ready."

"What do you think of the fire pit?" Jo asked as she took her mother's jacket.

"There should be a raging inferno tonight," her mother said as she pulled on a colorful pair of her knitted slippers. "Your chili sure smells good."

"If everyone's hungry," Jo said, "we could have an early dinner because the chili's ready."

"Are you sure?" Anna hugged her son. "Maybe you should check it."

"It's hot all right." Jo stirred the bubbling pot then turned to the sink for a glass of water. A flash of red against the fresh snow caught her eye. She leaned into the window for a better look. "What the heck?"

A large heart outlined with rose-petals adorned the snow at the base of her hedge. A small bundle of cedar kindling tied together with red ribbon lay in the center, and a single red rose draped across it.

"Happy Valentine's Day, Aunt Jo," Robert squeezed her shoulder, a big smile on his face.

"You did this?" Jo squinted at her nephew, confused.

"No." Robert gave a thumbs-up toward the window.

Jo gasped as Sam stepped out from behind the cedar hedge. Robert grabbed her arm as she almost lost her balance with shock. "Why is she here?"

"Go ask her," her mother said.

Jo's heart pounding and her breathing uneven, she slipped into her heavy boots then pulled on a parka. "Stay here, Mollie." She stepped outside, knees wobbling with uncertainty as she stayed by the house.

"Hey." Sam stood by the heart of rose petals in the snow, the image surreal as Jo tried to make sense of things. "I hear you're having a bonfire tonight and thought you could use some kindling to light it."

Jo let go of the doorknob and shuffled toward Sam, dragging her heels with each step as her legs barely moved. "What's this all about?"

"You." Sam's eyes locked with hers, pleading. "And me." Her voice cracked and she took a deep breath before continuing. "What happened in Toronto was one big misunderstanding. I love you, Jo, and want us to be together."

Jo's heart thumped. "What about your ex? How does she fit into this?"

"She doesn't." Sam took a step toward Jo. "I know it sounds crazy, but there's been one big screw-up after another with Trish. I can explain everything. I've never cheated on you, Jo. I can't even conceive of ever sleeping with someone else after you."

"I'm not moving to Toronto." Jo could hardly breathe, Sam's eyes glistening as she spoke.

"I'm moving to Timmins." Sam smiled, tears flowing over expanded dimples. "I've just been offered a position with Maxwell and Associates."

"Really?" Jo just stood there and gaped at Sam, numb with shock.

"I can start in a few weeks." Sam continued to approach her, small steps at first then one giant leap as Jo leaned forward.

CHAPTER FORTY-SEVEN

Sam's lips found Jo's and their tongues met with passionate urgency. The frigid winter air suddenly warmed and the bed of snow beckoned. It was as though nothing else mattered. Their lives were finally entwining.

"I think we're being watched." Sam spoke into Jo's lips, afraid to let go.

Jo leaned back; her blue eyes so warm, comforting, and full of sparkles as they locked onto Sam's. "I don't care. My mother and sister have been keeping an eye on me ever since you left. I missed you so much, Sam." She trembled, her words choppy with tears. "I can't believe this is happening."

"Let's go inside." Sam rubbed her nose against Jo's, overwhelmed with relief. "I want to go home."

Mollie was the first to greet Sam when she stepped into the familiar warmth of Jo's home, the savory aroma of chili cooking and reminding her of that first day at the cottage. The jumping golden retriever almost knocked her over with excitement. Sam toppled onto the dog, burying her face in the fur and shedding more tears of relief. "I've missed you so much." Mollie's tail flapped against the floor as she wriggled against Sam.

"I'm so happy for you, Aunt Jo!" Sam looked up to see Robert smiling as he gave Jo a big hug. She wanted to kiss him, her hero for helping make this happen, and would forever be indebted to him for listening when all seemed lost.

Sam felt Julia tapping her shoulder. "I'm so glad you're back."

"Oh, Julia." Sam stood and embraced her. "I love your daughter with all my heart."

"I know you do." Julia squeezed Sam, her warm embrace and familiar sweet lavender scent so comforting. "I can see how happy you make her. I'm so glad the two of you worked things out." She gave Sam a pat on the back as they stepped apart. "She needs someone to share this house with besides Mollie."

"Hey." Anna gave Sam a hug, her face relaxed with a warm smile. "It's nice to find out we were wrong about you. You and Jo both look so happy together. And just look at Mollie!"

Sam laughed as the dog danced around her feet, tags clinking as she looked up, teeth showing and jowls wagging as though smiling, too.

"I think it's my turn for a hug." Robert put his arms around Sam.

"Oh Robert." Sam buried her face in his shoulder and fought back more tears. "If it weren't for you, none of this would be happening right now. Thank you so much."

"He's a good guy, isn't he?" Jo wrapped her arms around the two of them and kissed both of their cheeks.

"We should let you two have some time on your own now," Julia said. "Come on, let's find a restaurant for dinner. I'm getting hungry after all this."

"It's Valentine's Day today, Mom," Jo said. "Most restaurants will be filled by now, and besides, you have to help us eat this chili and celebrate."

"I brought some wine," Sam said, so happy to be with Jo and her family. "I'll get it out of my vehicle."

"Did you drive all the way from Toronto today?" Jo asked as her head dipped toward Sam.

"Yes." Sam smiled as Jo gasped. She grabbed Jo's hands and pulled her closer. "And I'd do it again and again for you. I hope you'll be with me the next time I make the drive. Like next weekend. Maybe you can work remotely from Toronto while I wrap things up at the office."

"Sure, I guess so." Jo paused, her hands so warm and soft as their fingers entwined. "Will your ex be there?"

"No, of course not." Sam kissed Jo's hands, closing her eyes in relief. "Trish is moving out this weekend. I'll be putting the house up for sale because I don't need it anymore. My home is with you, here in Timmins." Sam felt Jo's lips on hers, the brief peck so validating.

"Enough already or we're leaving." Anna laughed as the three of them began setting the table.

"Let's get your stuff inside our home before it freezes." Jo smiled as she led Sam to the door.

Once her luggage was brought in the house, Sam was left on her own in Jo's bedroom to grab a quick shower. Following her long stressful day and drive, she was starting to fade and needed to be refreshed. Warm water washed over her skin as she rejoiced at her new life, luxuriated in the exciting moment, and hungered for later when she and Jo would make wild, passionate love.

When Sam got back to the kitchen, Jo was warming plates on the stove while the rest of her family chatted amongst themselves at the table. Mollie chewed on a rawhide bone, her tail flopping up and down against the kitchen floor. It was indeed a joyous day. Sam's heart throbbed with excitement over her new beginning.

"How's my sweetie?" Sam snuck up behind Jo, whispering into her ear.

"Horny." Jo's answer was barely audible as she turned and folded into Sam's arms. "Let's eat."

Sam and Jo followed everyone outside after dinner to bid their farewells. There would be no bonfire on this night as it was superseded by another burning blaze that was getting out of control. After everyone left, they took Mollie for a short walk in the moonlight. Before going back inside, Jo reached into Sam's heart of rose petals.

"This bunch of kindling is too precious to burn. I want to keep it as a souvenir." Jo rustled up the bundle of cedar sticks and red rose, her mitts clutching them in the dark.

Sam filled her lungs with the cold fresh air, and then breathed out a cloud of steam. "It's already done its job. It was kindling for the heart, not meant for setting a real fire."

"But it did." Jo clutched the kindling and rose against her chest. "The fire in my heart is more real than any fire I've ever felt before."

"Mine too." Sam hugged Jo under the stars until the cold chased them inside.

Sam followed Jo to her bedroom and closed the door to keep Mollie out. The ravishing began straightaway as they tore each other's clothes off, toppled onto the flannel sheets, and came together.

"I can't believe this is happening." Sam's voice caught as their naked bodies entangled. They fit together as though one. "I've missed you so much."

"Oh Sam, I'm so sorry for the way I've behaved with you." Jo's tears flowed, dripping onto Sam's chest. "I was sick to my stomach every time I thought about you. I felt so betrayed, but now I know that the real deception was my own heart. I was so sure you were going to tear it apart like Jan."

"Shhh." Sam wiped Jo's tears with the sheet, gently drying her eyes. "You had every right to be worried. It was my fault for being such a jerk in the beginning."

Jo swallowed, her breath soft against Sam's neck. "That first time at the cottage… My God, Sam, you made me feel something I'd never felt before. And I was scared."

Sam rubbed the back of Jo's head, fingers kneading her scalp. "You sparked my heart that night too. It was totally unexpected and began to change the way I saw things. I need you so much, Jo."

"And I you." Jo rolled on top and kissed Sam's lips, her tongue exploring. She began to caress Sam's breasts with her own, then reached into the center of Sam's arousal.

Sam's hips lifted off the mattress and her hands clung to Jo's arched shoulders as fingers slipped inside. "Yes. Oh yes."

"You're so wet. And soft." Jo's stroking hastened, circling and adding pressure. Sam held her breath, writhing as an orgasm began to crest. "Breathe."

"I love you, Jo." Sam gasped then wailed as her body convulsed and her hips dropped back to the bed in exhaustion. She gripped Jo, her overjoyed heart pounding with desire to please as she let out her breath.

"It's your turn now." Sam rolled onto Jo, fighting against exhaustion and mustering up energy to travel Jo's body. She crawled up and down, planting kisses everywhere in the desire to please. She brought Jo to orgasm with her tongue, lightly flicking and bringing release almost immediately.

"Oh Sam." Jo's gasp lasted the duration of her sustained climax and ended with a yelp. "This is the best Valentine's Day ever."

"For me too." Sam's eyes closed, her smile wide. "This has been such a special day. I wish I had the energy to prolong it for another round. I hope it's okay if I fall asleep now. I've been up since four thirty this morning."

Jo kissed Sam's forehead. "Of course it is. I'm looking forward to just holding you all night and listening to your breathing."

"And my heart beating for you." Sam felt herself fading, her words almost a whisper.

"We're going to have a wonderful life together." Jo squirmed against Sam. "I'm so excited to see your place in Toronto. We can take my truck, and I'll do most of the driving since I think you've done more than your fair share over the last little while."

"Sounds like a plan." Sam smiled as she drifted off to sleep, a crackling fire in her heart.

Bella Books, Inc.

Women. Books. Even Better Together.

P.O. Box 10543
Tallahassee, FL 32302

Phone: 800-729-4992
www.bellabooks.com